MW00466403

Polliwog

Steven Ing

"What happens...when a female can conceive only when she elects to as an act of volition...?"
Robert Heinlein (Stranger in a Strange Land, 1961)

And now imagine a world where a woman chooses to remain pregnant, also through an act of her own volition.

Polliwog

Copyright © Steven Ing, 2019
Registration Number:
TXu 2-144-649

The right of Steven Ing, MFT to be identified as the author of this work has been asserted by him and issued under the seal of the Copyright Office in accordance with title 17, United States Code, and has been made a part of the record of the Copyright Office records.

Published in the United States of America by 2023 by Ingenious Books

Library of Congress Control Number: 2023905495

ISBN 978-1-960621-01-6

Edited by Mikalee Byerman

Polliwog Art by Ryan Harris

Watercolor Art by Rafael Mariano

Graphic Design by Alison Cervelli

Book Layout by Mike Kitson

The characters and events in this book are fictitious. Any similarity to real persons, living or dead, is coincidental and not intended by the author.

If you would like permission to use material from the book, other than for purposes of review, please contact IngeniousBooks@gmail.com.

Land Acknowledgement Statement

This book was written on land taken from the Washoe People.

Today the State of Nevada is home to the Washoe, Paiute, and Shoshone Peoples. In Polliwog's narrative lie a number of characters based on the Awajún People in the area now known as Peru. Only by remembering these peoples with their own unique histories and colorful stories, are we able to see through the lens of indigenous wisdom – a lens desperately needed in our own troubled times.

Tentatively, Ankuash entered the small clearing just off the path of the nearest town. The townspeople were decidedly not his people. This is where the newcomers had chosen to settle. He had heard of them but had never come this close to any town where the invaders lived. The weight of his hatred for them was a near constant burden on him, but his tribe had never developed a way to deal with them. They were the ones who raped Mother Earth, Núgkui. He had pondered the question but had never understood how so few men could need so much timber. The living forest he so loved was less alive with each foray they made into it. He had heard that they lived in a large village, one so large that other travelers reported that they had never seen anything like it. He was equally sure that there, they were plotting their next invasion. He shuddered thinking of their perversion, bleeding the rubber trees, chopping down the ancient hardwood, fouling the rivers in their search for the yellow metal that also seemed so precious to them that the river spirits, the Tsúgki, had become sick with their greed and contamination.

The young shaman felt unsure of his proper role in this moment and place, but he was confident that he was exactly where he had been led by his visions. He knew he was to expect something beyond his imagining – what exactly, he didn't know, but something great for his people, the Awajún. He believed it would be something great for all the world. The quiet of his thoughts was broken when he heard an infant's cry from the largest of the three structures in the clearing. It was not the normal cry of a baby who wants attention or who merely wants to be held. This was a more desperate cry. Even a hysterical one. But the baby's voice, even as he listened, became noticeably weaker – and then stopped altogether. The young shaman's eyes narrowed as he opened his spirit vision and recognized the approaching figure of Death, slouched leisurely in the shadows just outside the building, waiting for the right time to claim the soul of the child. That was when he knew what to do. Squaring his shoulders, he strode confidently toward where he guessed the sound of the infant had emanated. Death noticed him and did not look happy about his intervention. Again, he heard the baby cry, and this time, he knew it for the keening of death. Somehow this...this baby knew death was near and was already mourning its own too-soon passing from the world. The shaman's stride quickened, and trying the latch, he opened the door and entered the small home. The keening stopped. The infant somehow knew he was there and perhaps might not have to die.

Peering into the wooden cradle, he saw the little face, red from exertion, become suddenly quiet with expectation. The little one's eyes tracked the brown hands of the shaman as he reached in to pick up what seemed a too-light weight. He gently pinched the skin on the baby's arm. Just as he thought – the skin puckered with his pinch but was slow to return to normal. "Ah...you need a drink," he thought to himself. Sensing he was finally being cared for, the baby quieted.

Looking around him at the unfamiliar objects of chairs and tables, paper and books, he sensed the utter wrongness of their placement and disarray. "There was a struggle here," he thought. "Something bad happened." He decided he needed to move fast to get away if he still could.

Hugging the baby, he began a song of protection. Gradually his voice swelled, and although he never looked directly into the face of Death, Ankuash felt the spirit world's protection come over him as he slipped past the grasping hands of the specter of Death.

Still holding the bundled child in his arms, he began to walk quickly. Fortunately, within minutes, he found what he was looking for and bent one of the fronds of a young tree until the water trapped at the base of the leaf poured out through the funnel shape he'd made of the broadleaf. The baby seemed surprised and then eagerly swallowed each drop. The shaman did this multiple times until he was sure the thirsty infant had adequately eased his dehydration.

"Next for you, little one, a rinse," he whispered as he headed to a stream the shaman had passed on his way from his own community. He stripped the wisp of a body naked, letting the soiled garments fall to the ground. After plunging the little one's lower body into the water, the young shaman took a moment to hold the naked boy at arm's length and look him over carefully. He noted the deformed foot, and he knew immediately why he had been led to the small hut. With his inner eye, trained by his own childhood shaman and his many personal journeys into the spirit world on the wings of the ayahuasca medicine, he knew that the clubfoot of the infant he held was a wound received from battle in the spirit world long before entering their emerald forest. His problem would be in convincing the rest of the tribe. The helpless baby's survival depended on it. But he knew that he would do this because this child was the one he had been waiting for. He was, in fact, the one the world had been waiting for.

Chapter 1

"This is going to hurt," Theo thought as he watched the couple settle in for their first marriage counseling session. A personal trainer, Blake's powerful build and shaved head gave Theo the idea that the wife Tammy was quite brave in facing up to him. He grimly considered how no one would ever suspect how Blake treated his wife when he thought no one was watching.

Even though he was tired from another full day at the office and knew he still had one last client in the waiting room, Theo focused all his attention, took a breath, and exhaled, making a smile, "Did you have any trouble finding the office?"

"No, not at all, " Blake said with that common liar's smile that began and ended with the corners of the mouth while his eyes remained empty.

Theo continued to smile, nodding, as he noted to himself, *OK, this is kind of early for the first lie of the session.* He couldn't help but wonder how the attractive pharmacist with the stunning violet eyes had ended up with someone who, even before starting his first session, was already three layers deep into a classic display of narcissism.

Theo didn't pursue a business-as-usual counseling approach with this couple. "Due to how late we are getting a start today, I have a question for the two of you: Do you prefer that I go slow or fast?"

Tammy worriedly asked, "What do you mean?"

"Well, some people appreciate therapy going quickly — when the therapist doesn't spend a lot of time getting to it. Other people prefer to go slow, because — well, because they're scared, and they don't want to feel pushed.

She looked at her husband and responded tentatively, "Well I suppose fast would be best." Her husband Blake nodded in agreement.

****

After they'd left, Theo made his notes on the session: "Husband malignant narcissist, incapable of love. Wife has irrational belief that her love is sufficient for them to have a successful relationship. Treatment should focus on her accepting Blake's limits and the reality that his limitations mean he will be forever incapable of the love she is looking for."

Theo sighed, closed their file and returned his pen to his pocket, and then pulled himself up out of his chair using his arms more than others would. Grabbing his cane, he gingerly made his way, limping, to the door Tammy and Blake had left open. Favoring his clubfoot, Theo thought ruefully, *I need to stop shooting hoops with Chris.* He thought of his son Chris, his *perfect* boy with his, thankfully, perfect feet. He thought, not for the first time, of the Bible phrase that so described his feelings about his son because Chris truly was "the apple of his eye."

His next appointment, another referral from the church, was sitting out in the waiting room. Before he opened his mouth to greet his new client, he noticed the direction of her gaze. He was used to this, and laughed gently, "Oh, don't worry about that, I don't counsel with that foot."

She quickly recovered enough to realize that she'd been staring and that it was time to stand up and make polite eye contact. Theo continued. "You must be Rachel, I'm Theo Van Prooyen," Theo smiled kindly. "C'mon in and let's get started."

Rachel continued to stand awkwardly for a moment, not knowing what to do with the clipboard holding the new patient paperwork. She'd never been in a counselor's office, and she was confused by Theo's need for a cane and then his attempt at humor. She froze.

"Oh, I can take that," Theo said, reaching for the clipboard. He gestured for her to take a seat as he made a couple of pained steps over to his chair. Going through Rachel's paperwork, Theo noted that she'd signed the "Consent to Treat" form but that she'd left a lot of empty blanks on her "New Client Information" form. Looking over them, he asked, "Is there some reason you've skipped so many of these, Rachel?"

Rachel took a quick breath before the words began to tumble out. "My youth pastor said I should come to see you, but I don't want to talk to my parents about any of this."

"OK, so...how old are you, ah...Rachel, is it OK if I call you Rachel?"

"Yeah, that's my name so...yeah. I turned 18 last week."

"But you're still in high school?"

"Yeah. Is that a problem?"

"Not for me, I was just asking. And you live at home with your parents?"

More uncomfortable now, Rachel nodded and asked, "Do we have to bring them into this?"

"Absolutely not, you're 18 and the law says you're legally entitled to get counseling by yourself. So...we're good, right?"

Rachel looked down, nodding her head again but this time much more slowly.

"Now, if I get to call you by your first name it's only fair that you call me Theo, OK?" Rachel quickly nodded yes, and he continued, "Did you have any other questions about confidentiality or treatment? I wouldn't be surprised if you did since this is your first appointment with a therapist, isn't it?"

"We can talk about anything? And you won't tell anyone what I said?"

"We're not talking about someone abusing a minor, are we?" Theo asked. The young girl's face relaxed at the thought that, after all, as bad as things were, they weren't complicated by *that* kind of problem. Theo's face relaxed in a reassuring smile, "Well, if you don't know about any minor who's getting abused, then I think we're good...unless you're planning to hurt yourself?" He paused, waiting for her to respond. His young patient shook her head negatively. "Planning to hurt anyone else?" She again shook her head.

There was a longer silence. Rachel decided to go with a "what if": "So, if someone wanted to talk about abortion, would you have to tell anyone?" Her posture on the edge of her armchair indicated she wasn't about to really settle in until she'd heard his answer.

Theo could feel something, some long deferred whisper of an idea, stirring in him. He smiled a small bit and his voice sounded, even to his own ear, more like himself, and there was a tone of reassuring authority in his answer, "No. That kind of conversation would be completely confidential." He waited for her to speak, holding his knowing within him, that his world was about to be altered forever.

Ankuash, the young shaman, carried the baby a great distance from Death's embrace until they came to Ankuash's home village. He was increasingly at ease from his earlier encounter with Death and the unknown source of violence that had resulted in the baby's abandonment. Ankuash walked the well-worn trail past the homes of The People and felt more confident as he first passed one prominent warrior's home and then another's, each with their display of the shrunken heads of invaders who'd gone too far for The People to tolerate. "Now you understand, don't you?" he asked aloud of one head hanging still in the heavy air.

Ankuash saw his young wife, Chipa, in her garden tending to her patch of sweet manioc. He slowed just a bit to enjoy the view of her beauty, and he took an instant as he did daily to savor his good fortune in having such a strong partner for his journey through this world. "I need your help," he called. Chipa looked up from her work and looked in surprise when she saw the baby in his arms.

"What is this?" she asked, as she noticed the weakened appearance of the infant. Quickly taking the underweight bundle from her husband, the young woman gave her husband a stare that said, "You. You have a lot of explaining to do." She slipped a breast out from her light work dress. Fortunately, she too had an infant, her first born son Kujak, who was still feeding at her breast but who dwarfed this little frog she now held. Once the starving baby had latched on and began sucking, Chipa placed her strongest gaze directly on her man's eyes. He was everyone else's shaman, but he was her partner.

Ankuash explained what had happened in the clearing and how Death had nearly claimed the child. He didn't need to remind Chipa of his visions, as they had spoken of little else in a long time. As they continued to speak of all that the visions had revealed, Ankuash watched Chipa's heart melt with love and adoration for the tiny miracle she nursed. As he watched her reaction to the child and his story of the day's events, Ankuash's anxiety about what The People would say about this child – who clearly looked like one of the invader's children – was replaced by a new confidence. They will know him as the fulfillment of all visions, he thought to himself.

Chapter 2

Rachel swallowed uncomfortably, and, in doing so, realized that there was no safe place inside herself, and no reassuring thought she could hold on to.

Sensing the growing stillness created in Rachel's musings, Theo began his work right away before she became so upset, she would get up and leave. Scooting forward in his own chair, Theo began more mindfully reflecting his client's body language. He used the pain from his own throbbing foot to help him to allow his face to fall into its own version of Rachel's pain. His posture, mirroring hers, became incrementally stiffer and more still. He allowed his own breathing to gradually but steadily mirror hers. As he did, each inhalation of his breath became shorter, heightening his body's distress with the loss of his normal easy consumption of oxygen. In a few moments he had so captured this young girl's manner that he had become her. He had become empathy. And still the seconds ticked by.

Rachel didn't know and couldn't have put words to any of her feelings, but she was already feeling less alone.

When Theo sensed that Rachel was already unconsciously responding to his initial attempt to join with her, he began to increase the sound and length of his breathing. He did this until the sound of his breathing and not her own became the dominant rhythm in the overture to what he hoped would become therapeutic for her.

Having taken the lead, Theo intentionally shifted the tempo of his breathing to something slower and more sustainable. In the many seconds of silence following their last exchange, everything had changed. Rachel wasn't yet comfortable, but she was much less uncomfortable. She wasn't relaxed either, but she wasn't as tense as she had been. As she allowed her shoulders to sag a bit and she sank into the cushions of her armchair, Theo began to suspect that his new client was a natural at trance work. His hope for this appointment, one he'd spent his career waiting for, once again began to kindle. With an effort, he set his thoughts aside, "So, Rachel, what's going on in your life that you thought talking to a counselor might help?"

Rachel had never talked about her problem and literally didn't have the words to begin. "I don't know how to talk about this," she admitted.

"I can see you're bothered by something. How long have you been feeling out of sorts?"

"A few weeks. You see I...," and her voice trailed off into the quiet of the office. She suddenly became aware of the gentle whisper of the air diffuser, pumping out a lavender scent. She allowed herself to be caught up in the sound for a few seconds of calming distraction.

Theo began with the gentlest of inductions as he intoned in a voice that was gentle but more directive. "You can be aware of the sounds in the office and around the office, and you can know that you don't need to attend to them."

More grounded in the moment, Rachel shook off her torpor, "A month ago I found out I was pregnant. Hmm...Pastor Skip, you know him, I mean Pastor Houton, Skip Houton, I mean, oh my God, he's not my boyfriend. She paused to again gather her words, "He doesn't know but he saw that I was depressed about something, and he said I should talk to you. He said you go to the same church?" Seeing Theo nod, she continued, "So you know how everybody would think about this if they knew I was pregnant and not married."

"We go to a pretty conservative church," Theo said, encouraging her to continue.

"And if they found out who the father is, I think it would be even worse because he's Pastor Barton's son, you know, Rob, the one who got the prophecy last week that he was going to be a great leader in the church and that as a man of God his love for God would never be compromised." Tears came to her eyes, "All that is ruined now." Theo nodded and breathed another calming breath for the both of them. "Tell me how Rob feels about this," Theo directed.

"He's feeling guilty...and shocked...we only had sex the one time and, well, I guess I have the worst luck. At first he said that we would have to get married right away."

"And that made you feel...?"

"Good for a second, and then I panicked. It seemed like it was all happening too quickly. I had plans to get married someday, sure, and maybe even to a pastor, but I thought I'd have a chance to go to school or something. Now I don't know what to do."

"You have a number of options."

"I know, I know," Rachel blurted out impatiently. She'd been through this drill a hundred times. "I could have the baby and give it up for adoption. I already know the Crisis Pregnancy Center would help me with that. Or the CPC would help me have the baby and keep it."

"Do you feel ready to be a mother?"

The 18-year-old looked at him dejectedly, "I don't even have a driver's license. I've never even had a real job." Rachel shook her head in quiet despair.

"What are your other options?"

"I guess I could marry Rob. Then this would all be OK I guess."

"Do you want to marry Rob?"

"I didn't want to marry anyone before, but lately it seems like it might work out."

"I'm wondering if you've considered any other options."

"Like what?"

"I'm not sure what other options you've thought about."

"Well, of course abortion crossed my mind as a possibility. But

I can't do that. That's murder. That would only make all this even worse, right?"

"Ever see *Pinocchio*, the old Disney movie? The one with the puppet who wanted to be a real boy?"

Rachel, distracted, nodded, "Oh yeah, when I was a kid at family movie night at the church."

"So, you remember Jiminy Cricket, the guy who would stand on Pinocchio's shoulder and whisper into his ear about right and wrong? Well," he smiled, "I'm a counselor, not a conscience." And here Theo stopped smiling abruptly, "It's my job to help you see your power and your choices so that you can see clearly what you want to do with your life and make decisions that work for you."

"Then I don't want to be pregnant!"

"And, like any intelligent person, you're aware of other options."

"Like abortion...?"

"Abortion is certainly one option like you said, logically speaking, but maybe you're not ready to consider it. Maybe that's unthinkable to you."

"It sort of is. Unthinkable, I mean. I've been told my whole life how wrong it is. It's killing a baby."

"There might be another option if you'd like to hear about it." Theo paused.

"I have no idea what you're talking about."

Theo smiled, "Not many would know what I'm talking about."

"Well, if it's not abortion and it's not adoption and it's not being a mom, I don't know what you're talking about."

"What if you could decide to not be pregnant and that was the end of the matter?"

"Yeah, right, 'the end of the matter,' just like that." Rachel's sarcasm was reflexive as she thought to herself, *This was dumb coming in here. He's just another man and kind of a jerk and no one from church would understand anyway and....* and then Theo interrupted her train of thought with a startling offer.

"If you were interested, I could teach you how to be in touch with your own body in such a way that you would stay pregnant only if you wanted to."

Rachel was flabbergasted into a long silence before blurting out, "What are you talking about? I don't understand. How?"

"You believe in the omnipresence of God, right? I mean that he's everywhere all at the same time?

"Sure, I guess."

"Well, we Christians don't talk about it much, but that means that the living presence of God is in everything at all times. It means our very existence is sacred and full of God. It means that there's a web of life such that every living thing is connected to every other living thing. For the person who can really see all these living connections, there is an awareness that even every living cell has its own awareness of itself. In fact, that every atom is connected to every other atom and that in each of them there lies a consciousness. To go even further, God consciousness has to even be in the space between the atoms. How could it be otherwise, if you think about it, if you believe as I do that God is all and in all?"

"I don't understand. I mean, no disrespect, but what does all of that have to do with me? I really don't need a theology lesson right now. Her voice became tight with repressed irritation. "Are you saying that if I don't want to be pregnant, all I have to do is tell the universe or...God that I don't want to be?"

"No, you don't have to tell the whole universe. You already are connected to that universe. You're already a part of the sacred web of life, the web of existence of all that is."

"OK...but you said you could teach me something so I wouldn't have to be pregnant."

"I can teach you a new way to be in touch with your own body so that your body remains pregnant only with your consent."

Rachel's mind was reeling, "Is that OK? I mean, first of all, is that even a thing? And if it is a thing, is it OK? 'Cause that sounds like abortion too, only I'm doing it...this is so confusing..."and her voice drifted off becoming smaller as she lost hope.

"You might be having some trouble with the whole 'beginning of life' thing?"

"Well...yeah! I was taught that from the time the egg and the sperm are joined, well, that's a human life."

"The church didn't always believe that. But we're not talking about abortion, remember? We're talking about a woman's God-given ability to consent to pregnancy or to withhold consent. About the whole human 'sanctity of life' teaching, I'd like you to consider something that will seem unrelated. You know what a frog is, right?"

"Yeah." Rachel could simply not resist using the sarcastic tone she so typically used with her parents as she felt her irritation grow.

"Well, frogs go through stages of life just like we do. And so, when does the frog become a frog? It starts off as an egg, just like we do, but is an egg, fertilized or not, a frog?"

Rachel snorted at the childish question, "No, of course not."

"I don't think it is either," Theo continued, smiling. "And what about a polliwog? Is a polliwog a frog?"

Rachel became distracted for a moment as she remembered better days, camping by the lake and her delight when she'd seen some polliwogs in the shallows where she was wading. "No, a polliwog is not a frog." Her words became more deliberate as she started to see where Theo was going with his ideas.

Theo warmed to his subject, "So, the eggs aren't frogs, the polliwog isn't a frog, and even the next stage isn't a frog. Only when this growing animal is a frog do we call it a frog."

"So, you're saying that a baby is not a human...that's horrible."

"No, I'm suggesting that an egg, even one that's fertilized, is not a human being. If an egg is not a human being, then maybe we consider that an embryo is not a human being, any more than a polliwog is a frog. I'm saying that at about the time the embryo becomes a fetus, at 2 to 3 months of development, it's still not a human being. It's human in the sense that the tissue is human tissue, but it is not a human being." He added gently, "I think even a child can see that a polliwog isn't a frog, and I think you can see that your pregnancy is like a polliwog in that it's headed into becoming a human being but it's not there yet."

"I don't know what to say." Rachel felt both scared and strangely excited.

"Well, there's no pressure on you to make a decision one way or the other. I will support your right to your choice about how to think no matter what you decide. But...it is a decision, and even avoiding a decision is to make a decision."

"If...if I was open to the idea of learning how to do this. Do I have to go through with anything? I mean, if I learn how to do this, would I have to, you know, check in with you or someone?"

Theo laughed his first relaxed laugh of the day. "No one would be in control of you but you. Your life is your own, and what you do with your life is your business. All I'm offering is a path toward your taking responsibility for your choice rather than letting others tell you what you should do with your life and your body and your future."

"I don't know what to think." She paused before continuing, "I think I need to think about this. Is that OK?" Seeing Theo's raised eyebrow and his smile grow bigger, she realized he had just taught her that she, not anyone else, was in charge of her body and her future. She added, "OK. I need to think. I can come back next week, right?"

"Certainly, if you like. Like everything in your life from now on, Rachel, that is your choice."

Theo stood up, cuing Rachel that she really was free to go. As the young woman left, she felt less afraid than when she'd first come in — but far more confused. She felt like she could dare to dream she wasn't really trapped.

As he watched his new client walk out of the clinic, Theo became possessed of a calm knowing. "She is the one," he thought.

Kujak, the older of Ankuash's two sons, had always been a gifted hunter. Strong and tall for his age, he walked the forest with stealth and cunning. Even without his having much knowledge of magic he was nearly always more successful than other hunters.. As a very young boy, he'd use his blowgun to quietly take animals out of the trees, including curassows – and once, even that treasured delicacy, a spider monkey, had fallen to the deadly accuracy of his poisoned darts. Both animals were succulent trophies any adult would have been proud to bring back to his home. Kujak's mother, Chipa, had praised his skill and devotion in helping the family. Even their neighbors were in some jealous awe of the young man. But this was not enough for Kujak, because it was not enough to capture his father's praise. His heart was jealous of the attention that his father seemed to lavish on Kujak's younger brother, who had been adopted into the family.

Even the younger brother's name was an irritation to the older boy. Why had his father named the younger boy Etsa? Everyone knew that was the name of the sun's human form. Why had his father wasted such a name on someone whose clubfoot so obviously demonstrated that he'd been born a victim of sorcery? Once, he had asked his father to explain this. A distant look had come over his father's eyes as he gazed far into the spirit world. Kujak hated it when his father did that. He seemed even more distant at such times, and the father-hunger that the older son felt so keenly went as unanswered as the question he'd asked. His father had only said somewhat cryptically, "You know I am an iwishín, a curing shaman. Trust me, Kujak, you will understand the good in this soon because you too will partake of the medicine that will take you into the spirit world. You know how to kill very well, and I love you and I am proud of the way you care for us. But soon, you will become educated beyond your imagining – civilized beyond all peoples of the earth. And then you will understand everything.

Finally, the day came when Kujak and other 10-year-old boys his age were to be included in an ayahuasca ceremony for the first time. He fasted for three days as his father had taught him. He wanted so much to be able to have this connection with his father. His father had made an especially strong brew for the ceremony, and the sacred medicine moved less like water and more like honey, thick and heavy in the mouth. Before he succumbed to the powerful hallucinogen, his father whispered into only his ear, "Join with the Queen of Tears. Let go of any thought to fight her or fear her." Kujak had no idea what this meant at the time. He had no idea who or what the Queen of Tears was. And then the medicine took hold of him, and he fell into the earth.

Many things were revealed to Kujak on his first journey into the spirit world, but nothing was as welcome to him as his encounter with the Queen of Tears. He had feared that she was so named because of great sorrow and was, for the first time in his young life, overjoyed to be wrong. He did not know that hearts could melt as his had upon seeing her and coming to know her. She was, he discovered, called the Queen of Tears simply and only because she was possessed of such radiant and transcendent joy that, when he entered into her, he became one with the entire real world, the magical one, and he could see how love was the foundation of all of this. Then he understood the Queen of Tears as an ajútap, a most powerful spirit of the old warriors. He came to see how her love was the ultimate in warfare.

After a full night of journeying, Kujak finally rose from the medicine's embrace at dawn. He was possessed of a calm he'd never known because he knew, even before his little brother did, how Etsa and the Queen of Tears were to come together in a way that would be greater than the sum of their parts.

Chapter 3

Rachel slumped into the seat of her ride. She sat there a moment wondering to herself, *What was that?* She had never heard anything like what Theo had said in her entire life. She remembered what her youth group had learned in Bible study, "God's Word is clear," she thought, quoting to herself Pastor Skip's last teaching about how abortion amounted to murder. But now she was somehow not finding that clarity so accessible. The reality of being pregnant herself changed how she felt about the issue. Before the whole subject was just another, well, subject, like something from a history class that could be memorized for a test. Now that she was actually in the test and her life was the test, the problem no longer seemed as it had been. She snorted aloud as she thought, *This is gettin' real now.*

She continued to think to herself, *He's not just someone else from church. Pastor Skip recommended him. I wonder if Pastor Skip knows what my counselor is telling me?*

As her ride made its first turn out of the parking lot, her phone rang. She was flooded with relief to see that it was her boyfriend, Rob. "Oh, I am so glad you called, I mean, I have a lot to talk to you about and...." Her boyfriend interrupted, "Ah...Rachel, I need to talk to you, too. I really don't know how to start this...um, look, I know it's been a few days since we talked, but I wanted you to know. I'm leaving town. I can't stay here anymore, and I can't be a preacher's kid anymore. It's sort of hard to explain, but I'm leaving for L.A. I'm going with John. We're going to stay in L.A. and find jobs and live together and...Rachel, we're a couple now, I mean John and me. I've been fighting this forever, and I really hoped and believed that my dad's exorcism to cast out the demon of homosexuality was working. You were my last hope. But I want to be OK with being gay. I want you to be OK with it too. I'm sorry Rachel." He paused for her to respond.

Rachel felt as though she had been punched in her belly. "Oh. I...I don't know what to say. I really don't know what to say," she repeated.

Rob finished, "I'm really sorry, Rachel. I hope you won't hate me. John's here now. I have to go. Bye, Rachel."

"Ah...bye," Rachel, too shocked to say more, spoke as if on automatic response mode.

On her way home, this new shock kept her preoccupied to the point that she didn't remember how she made it home — suddenly she was just there. If it had been a normal day, she would have gotten out of the car, but instead, she just sat there for a moment, forgetting about her driver. Not getting out meant that she chose to stay with her thoughts. Sitting there, reflecting on her first counseling experience made her realize that she no longer felt as overwhelmed about her pregnancy as she had. She realized that she felt more irritated than she did afraid. Getting mad felt better.

But her thoughts still troubled her even after she came back to the here and now, calmly getting out of the car and going inside her home. Distracted, she failed to give the usual shout out of "I'm home." Walking into the kitchen, she ran into her dad, who looked up expectantly. "Oh, hi baby. How's your day going?"

Rachel fell into her usual noncommittal family routine, "Fine," she said lifelessly, opening up the fridge.

"Hey, don't forget we have a date next weekend?"

"Huh?"

"Are you even listening to me? I was saying that we have a date next weekend. You didn't forget, did you?"

The memory returned like the weighted vest she was given before a dental x-ray. How could she have forgotten? "No, Dad, I remember. The dance."

"You sure don't sound too excited about it. Well, I'm excited and I can't wait. They're inducting new girls too, and so a lot of people will be there, pumpkin."

This was not the best day for Rachel to be thinking about Pure Love Waits, the church's virginity-pledge program. And this wasn't just about the local church either, as Rachel's father had told her that there were now millions of girls who'd promised to maintain their virginity until they were married. Rachel felt hypocritical, and she felt more irritation too, realizing for the first time that the abstinence-based program hadn't helped her at all when she really needed it. She thought to herself, *Maybe it would have helped if Pastor Rob had pushed his son Rob to take a pledge too.* For a moment she was lost in the "what ifs."

"Penny for your thoughts, sweetheart."

"Dad, I don't want to go." Her blunt words hung in the air of the room. As surprised as her dad looked, Rachel was even more surprised by her own courage. She'd never said she didn't want to be involved in Pure Love Waits, because to say no to that was like saying she was going to have sex.

Or at least, that I want to have sex, Rachel thought ruefully. *I might as well have said that I want to be a slut.*

Rachel's father's face darkened as if he'd read her thoughts. The chronic eczema on his cheek bloomed red while she watched him prepare to explode. "What are you talking about Rachel? Of course we're going to the dance. It's the last Father-Daughter Dance of high school!" His words came out like bullets from a machine gun. He continued, "Your example of living a chaste life is part of what motivates younger girls to do their part. And you. Are not. Going to let them down."

"I'm not going. I'm 18 and I don't even go to a regular high school, and I've never been to a dance with anyone but you. I'm not going. I'm sick of it."

True to form, every time his anger didn't work to control his family, Larry Carson changed his tone from intimidation to a sort of whiny mewling sound that sounded unendurably irritating to Rachel's ear. "C'mon sweetie, you know I've been looking forward to our date for a long time."

Rachel didn't want to go for so many reasons, but she also didn't want to talk more to her dad about why she didn't go. So she just stood there for a moment, shaking her head no as she stared at the floor. Something about the angry set of her jaw led her father to think that, if he pushed this now, he'd probably lose. He didn't care. There was too much riding on this for him to just let it go.

"Rachel, you know I'm being considered for the Eldership, so this isn't just about you anymore. This is for all of us." With his last comment he put his hand on her shoulder, then began massaging it as he had done in the past. This time, to Rachel, it felt suddenly very creepy. Yet he kept it there. The seconds ticked by, and then for the first time in her life, she shrugged her shoulder to push his hand away.

"That's why you want me to go with you. I get it, Dad. You want to be on the Board of Elders so you can feel important. But I don't want to go, and I'm not going to go. It's creepy and weird and sick, and I'm not doing it."

Larry stood back and didn't know what to say. It felt as though his daughter had played some kind of sexual deviance card, and Larry was utterly unprepared to go there. He'd never talked to his daughter about sex before — except to explain that it was wrong in general, that it was lust in particular, and that those who engaged in willful sin crucified Jesus again as He wept in heaven over the sin of young people who'd turned away from the path of righteousness. He wasn't ready to talk about sex with anyone, and he certainly wasn't going to start by trying to justify to his daughter that there was nothing creepy or incestuous about a father being his daughter's only date. He looked nervously at her ring finger to see if she was still wearing her purity ring. He could see it and some of the engraved words, "True Love Waits." Larry felt some relief as he absentmindedly scratched at his eczema, oblivious of his daughter's disgust as she turned away.

For Rachel, her revulsion at her father's skin condition cemented her resolve, but her revulsion came second to the power her anger had been giving her. She turned and strode purposefully out of the kitchen, her interest in getting a snack having evaporated.

Upstairs in her room, she threw herself on her bed and waited for her father to walk in so he could guilt trip ("Now, a promise is a promise, young lady."), or nag ("I've told you and I'm going to keep telling you, you're going to that dance."), or cajole ("Come on sweetheart, you know you'll break Daddy's heart if we can't go to the last dance of the season together.").

Right now, she felt absolutely angry enough for all of it to mean nothing to her.

But her father didn't come bursting into her room. Instead, she heard him go outside, start the car, and then drive away. Rachel fished her phone out of her pocket and stared at it. Normally, she'd have called Rob to talk about her dad and how she felt, but just thinking of him driving with John made that idea completely pathetic. This was on her and Rob was gay. "Rob is gay," she said to herself, trying this new idea. Truth was, his orientation wasn't significant any more. What mattered was getting real about her life and her pregnancy. Rob was never going to save her.

She stared at her phone, frozen, not knowing what to do. All of her options seemed to have closed down. *Could this get any weirder?* she wondered to herself. Her counselor had advised her to become a baby-killer, and her dad was creepier than ever and pressuring her to celebrate an abstinent purity that she no longer had — nor, truth be told, even wanted anymore. But now, she realized that she'd given up her virginity to a boy who wasn't ever going to marry her, which meant the possibility that if she carried this pregnancy to term, she might always be alone as a parent. Forget college. It was just too much to process right now.

She thought again and again about calling Rob before finally giving up and just lying there in silence. After all, even if she got Rob to pick up, what was there to say? "Hey Rob, I know you're gay, but I'm pregnant now and I really need someone to play house with me. You know, so the whole world doesn't think I'm a slut. I know you're gay, but can't you do this one thing for me?" She laughed at the absurdity of it all. Then she broke down and cried.

It was late fall, and the shadows were already lengthening across the city. As she listened to the rasp of the dead leaves blowing against one another, it felt to Rachel that her whole world was dead and empty. Rachel thought of how disconnected she felt from church now that she knew herself to be so on the outside. She was just a pregnant, stupid outsider who'd broken the rules and was now condemned to a wrecked life. Just a few weeks ago, maybe two months at most, she felt on top of her world. She was a leader in her church's youth group, she was about to graduate from high school, and the most important boy in her world, the pastor's son, had told her he really liked her a lot.

Rachel laughed at herself and then cried some more. Her thoughts drifted back to the calm she'd felt in her counseling session, and she thought, *I'm going back. I need to know more about my options. I need to talk to my counselor.*

By the age of 8, Etsa was able to supplement his family's food needs by faithfully seeking out the delicious palm grubs that so delighted them all. The thick wormy grubs were the size of his father's thumb, and it only took one lucky discovery to make the difference between his family's merely surviving and the elevation of that status to one of thriving. For Etsa, helping his family eat was an important offering for the weakness his foot brought him – and, by extension, them. He could never keep up with the other boys as they hunted and wrestled. Like most of the men, he already knew how to cure the severed heads of the tribe's enemies, but he knew he would never be a great warrior, although he dreamed.

He also had learned all the plant knowledge of his father and knew exactly how many of the vines and the leaves he had to collect to make the right amount at the right potency for each ceremony. He was excited to know that someday, he, too, would take the medicine that separated the civilized from the uncivilized, the educated from those who could not even begin to see the link between all things. Etsa knew about these things from overhearing his father, but he didn't know them the way his brother Kujak now knew them. Etsa was in awe of the transformation his brother had experienced. Formerly consumed with a hostility that Etsa had never understood, his big brother Kujak was now possessed of a knowing calm and a surprising tenderness toward his little brother.

So it was with great excitement that Etsa heard his father's announcement that he was ready to enter ceremony. He knew that only some were invited at such a young age. He felt proud.

Finally, the day arrived, and Etsa discovered that no other young people were to join in. Strangely, only he and the core of the tribe's wisest advisors were partaking. He had never seen this. After drinking a large draft of the thick liquor made from the cooked and steeped vines and leaves, Etsa waited to fall into the earth as his brother had told him he would. There, he became aware of the many ancient warriors, the ajútap, surrounding him and the tribal counselors. They were waiting together expectantly for what Etsa soon learned was a war council.

And then Núgkui, the earth mother appeared. Etsa's mother revered Núgkui because the feminine master of the undersoil made women's gardens the wonders that they were. Without her, the women's gardens would not grow the sweet manioc that sustained them. Without her, they couldn't grow the tobacco so necessary for teaching one another anen, the magical songs that allowed hunters to draw game and lovers to find their beloved. And behold, Núgkui began singing a powerful anen that gathered the thoughts of the wise together into one mind. The ajútap kept guard over them all to prevent any evil shaman from attacking their council before it could even get started. And Núgkui continued to sing from the one mind that was all of them until – off in the mists of his vision – Etsa saw who Núgkui was summoning. Her form was feminine, and Etsa as young as he was, could see that she was beautiful. As he looked closer, Etsa saw that the beauty ran through her and not merely over her.

Núgkui then spoke, reminding everyone of how her first daughter had been given to humanity to teach them how to achieve the superabundance made possible through gardening the earth. But even in the spirit world, men had failed to respect that which was feminine. In the end, even that daughter had been mistreated and abused until finally she left the people alone to themselves.

Then Núgkui spoke of her older daughter, the Queen of Tears, who had volunteered in the spirit world to conjoin with the master of the craft of war. Their enemy was those who attacked the forest, fouled the waters, and tortured the earth. So distressed had The People become that their women had begun committing suicide in frightening numbers. Everyone knew that this path was unsustainable, and its end was death. But one and all agreed that the tribe would have to become far shrewder, even more than they had in their defeat of the Incas centuries ago.

Everyone present agreed that the plan of joining the spiritual powers of the Queen of Tears with those of the consummate spirit warrior was the only way to slip an army into the bowels of the enemy's body, where ultimate victory might just be possible. All eyes turned on Etsa as the Queen of Tears first approached him, smiling. Then she asked for his permission to enter him. Etsa could see that there was nothing to fear, and so he too smiled as he reached out his arms wide to the universe – and the two became one.

When the medicine released Etsa from her embrace, he breathed more calmly than he'd known was possible. He thought to himself, "Ah! That is why I am here."

Chapter 4

Rachel dropped her weight into the armchair with a sigh. Theo had already greeted her in the waiting room, and he sat silently before gently smiling at Rachel. Gently leaning forward, he assumed an alert but relaxed posture. She didn't want to waste any of this session, and so without needing any further prompting, she brought Theo up to date with the events since her first session.

When she had finished, Theo began, "So...if I followed you, then your hope of not being alone with your pregnancy is over because your boyfriend, who was using you to prove he wasn't gay, is leaving town with his boyfriend. Does that pretty much sum it up?"

Rachel didn't even bother to make eye contact with Theo. Looking down, she murmured, "He never even loved me. I...I was just his proof that he wasn't gay."

"So, if you can forgive the cliché, how does that make you feel...?"

Rachel interrupted, blurting out, "Like a fool!"

"And, when you think you've acted like a fool, how does that make you feel?"

Rachel pondered this last question, and she realized she hadn't really shared a feeling and needed to go deeper. "I feel ashamed. And angry. I was so caught up in the romantic crap that I was stupid, and now I'm pregnant and my life is ruined." Her eyes filled with tears.

Theo sat comfortably but attentively. He needed to hear more if this session was to be all about processing Rachel's feelings. He also knew that, actually, what Rachel needed was power. He waited until a full minute passed. Then another passed as Rachel pulled it together enough to stop crying and ask the questions she'd been pondering since her last appointment.

Three tissues later, Rachel asked, "Did you mean what you said about your being able to teach me how I could not be pregnant? And...wouldn't that be murder? Isn't the Bible against abortion? How can you even talk like this?"

Theo gave a quiet laugh before saying, "So, a lot of questions... can we take them one by one?"

"Can you do what you said you could do?"

"*Yes.*" He paused before continuing, "You are more than your body. But you are, or at least, you *can be* in control of your body in this."

"I don't understand. And isn't the Bible against abortion? I mean, that's a serious, serious sin."

"Well, you're sneaking in two questions in there, but I'll try to explain. You remember last week I told you that every cell, even every atom of the universe knows the presence of God because *He is 'all and in all.'*" He paused to allow Rachel a moment to nod before continuing, "Well, the Bible also says in Jeremiah that, 'Before I fashioned you in the belly I knew you, and before you came out of the womb, I consecrated you.'"

"I know that verse. But doesn't that mean that abortion is murder then?"

"That's not the conclusion that some thinkers might draw. It's not really a political statement about a pro-life position, as it is a spiritual comment of great insight. For these people, these thinkers, it's a statement about the profound level of intimacy that can exist in our relationship with God. In fact, it's about how special we all are and how, for an eternal God, time is simply one moment. How else could it mean that he knew us before we were formed in the womb? Doesn't that mean before we were even conceived?"

"I...I never looked at it that way." Rachel fell silent for a moment of thought. "But it says that before we were born, he consecrated us — what's that about?"

Theo's eyes seemed to overflow with emotion, but his gaze sharpened as he said, "It simply means that you are not just another one of the herd. God knows you. God knows how special you are. He has fashioned you for a purpose. You have a destiny different from all others. You are...a unique wonder."

Rachel shivered. She had heard this sort of thing countless times at Bible study, at youth camp, and in sermons. But today seemed different. Theo seemed to know her personally, and these same old words became new to her. For the first time since she'd met Theo, she began to really feel some of the calm that he seemed to have in endless supply. Finally absorbing the concept, she continued, "So, it's not all about the baby...or the pregnancy or whatever. This is the first time in a while I can really feel me."

Theo nodded, "Yeah. That's got to feel better, right? So maybe we can approach your faith from a new perspective?"

"Like?"

"You know the story where Jesus and his disciples were walking through the field of wheat and picking grain as they walked, and how they ate because they were hungry? You have to know it — the one where the Pharisees criticized them because it was the Sabbath, and working on the Sabbath was a violation of God's law of keeping the Sabbath?"

Exasperated, Rachel snorted derisively, "Yeah, but what does that have to do with...?"

"Well, remember what Jesus said to them?" He paused before reminding her, "'The Sabbath was made for man, not man for the Sabbath.'"

"I don't see how that...."

Theo continued quickly, "Rachel, it means that just as the Sabbath was made for us and not the other way around, faith itself was made for us, to serve us. We weren't made to serve it. Our faith is designed to help and comfort us. It's supposed to give us direction and provide meaning to our lives. We are definitely not here to serve the faith. It's actually the other way around. God doesn't need our service. Humanity does."

Rachel's head was spinning. She could see that he was so right, and that she — and everyone who'd taught her — had been so wrong. She felt the vertigo of seeing her concept of faith turn upside down.

After giving Rachel a moment to absorb this, he continued, "And point of fact, the Bible has never been against abortion. There's nothing on that. Just the opposite, really. Not that I've ever even suggested abortion to you, but you did say you thought it was a sin."

"But...how can you say...?"

"OK. I can explain what I just said if you really want to hear. I..."

Immediately, Rachel interrupted, "I do."

"OK, but I don't want to go all Biblehead on you. You are what's important here, and I don't want to get lost in some nerd search for the right verses to prove my point."

"No, no. I need this. I feel like something big is about to happen, and I don't want any nagging doubts about my decisions."

"OK, so you know there's no specific verse forbidding abortion, right?" Seeing Rachel nod impatiently, he continued, "So all we have are stories through the Bible that illustrate the beliefs of the people of the time."

"Yeah, but none of those stories are about abortion, are they?"

"If abortion is the untimely termination of a pregnancy through human agency, then yeah, there are stories that are about abortion. But I warn you, they're not what you think."

"OK, OK, go on. I want to hear this."

"Alright, but I think one story is enough for today because really, they're all the same." He paused, waiting to see if this was acceptable to Rachel. "So, in *Genesis 38* we have the story of Tamar. In some ways she was your opposite. She was trying to get pregnant, she needed to get pregnant, but she wasn't allowed to by any means acceptable to her society. So, she sneaks her way into getting pregnant by having sex with her father-in-law, Judah. I mean she really tricks him by pretending, with some serious disguising, to be a prostitute so her family line can continue."

"That sounds so gross."

Theo continued, "So, when Judah finds out she's pregnant, yet he doesn't realize he's the father, he gives the order to, 'Take her out to be burned,' for violating God's law."

"What a hypocrite," Rachel said in disgust. "Yeah but, how does...?"

"You see, Rachel, even if Tamar were pregnant through some violation of God's law, then the question is what sense does it make to kill her unborn child in the name of God if abortion is unacceptable?"

"Oh. Crap." The vulgarity leapt out of Rachel's mouth, and she was too overwhelmed to even feel the smallest bit of self-consciousness. "Oh, crap, crap, crap," Rachel shook her head, feeling like she was watching her family Bible being ripped from its spine page by page. After some minutes, Rachel nodded numbly, but her eyes began to shine with a new light. "But that's just one story and...."

"There are so many more. In *Numbers 5*, the priests gave women potions to induce abortion if their husbands suspected that the child wasn't his, and this potion only worked with God's cooperation and the women's intention. And then there is how God's law dictates that injuries to women resulting in loss of a pregnancy weren't to be treated as manslaughter or murder."

"How are they treated?"

"Like property crimes. You get a fine. That's it." Seeing Rachel's skeptical eyebrow rising, he added definitively, "*Exodus 21*." He cocked his head and smiled as he gave a brief nod as if to say, "This is legit."

After a lingering silence during which Rachel was turning these thoughts over in her mind, she finally spoke in the calmest angry voice she'd ever heard come out of her mouth, "OK, I'm done. Everything I've ever been taught about this is just crap."

Theo sat with her, holding space for the new being she was becoming. Finally, he spoke, "Well, we are at the end of our session..."

"No, no, no. It can't end like this," Rachel erupted. "I don't want to stay pregnant one day longer than I already have. I get it, I understand that staying pregnant or not having this baby isn't what I thought it was. I'm ready to do something different. We can't stop now. Please."

Theo paused within himself while his head nodded, confirming that he was listening. He made a decision, and taking a breath and releasing it, he released his previous notions of agenda and relaxed himself into his thoughts. "Well, Rachel, our appointment is at the end of my day, and I don't have to get you out of here so that someone else can have their session, but I do have to let my wife know I'll be late. Why don't you take a break for a moment and use the bathroom if you need to." Seeing Rachel nod affirmatively and rise to take care of herself, he pulled out his phone and texted Jessa, "Have to work another hour. Home soon. Love you." Before putting his phone away, he thought to check whether Chris had anything going on tonight and glanced at his schedule to see if his 14-year-old had any school commitments. *Nope. The coast is clear. OK.*

And, with that confirmation of his flexibility, Theo put his phone away. As he began to prepare himself for the work of the induction, he recalled how Rachel, in her first appointment, had proven receptive to trance work. He knew what to do.

Rachel entered the counseling suite again and took her customary position in the comfortable armchair opposite Theo. The moment she had settled, he began, "You probably know what hypnosis is, but I'd like to take a moment to review some aspects of it that you may not be familiar with." He didn't wait for her to nod before continuing in a voice that Rachel associated with storytelling. He began, "The human race has been doing trance work for thousands of years. A trance state allows us to let go of all that blocks us from a higher level of focus, a state few can achieve outside of a trance. We can lose control of certain mental faculties, if you want to call them faculties, like distraction, preoccupation, and worry. We can lose control of our actions or even have a near miraculous level of speed and strength that we've never known before. In this state, a person can give themselves over to seeing visions, hearing voices, experiencing ecstasy, or falling into different altered states. The apostles Peter and Paul fell into trances and saw visions. So did the prophet Ezekiel. Samson experienced strength this way when 'the spirit of the Lord came upon him.' King Saul had a similar experience. I will be helping you give yourself up to such a state, but you can achieve this state only if you surrender of your own volition."

Rachel nodded and simply said, "OK."

Theo's voice slowed in pace, and he seemed to be speaking at a lower volume, "In this state, many people have demonstrated the ability to control body functions like their pulse, their blood pressure and even their body temperature. This can happen because your body belongs to you, and every cell of your body is interlinked with your mind. We can learn to make a cold hand warm simply by using this power and increasing our blood flow to one part of the body over another."

Rachel again simply nodded. She gradually became more focused. Theo continued, and his quiet voice seemed to fill the air around her. She grew more still, and her eyes became less focused even as her mind followed his every word.

"We can look on trance work as hypnosis or even enchantment because in all our folk tales dealing with this, there are words — incantations you might call them — that seem to warm us and to draw us in. Perhaps it's not so much the right words as saying them in the right tone and pace. This is your first induction into this state of enchantment. Because of this, we will carefully review how your trance work will prepare you for healing by changing the way your mind is filtering all information you take in so that your mind...becomes freer. Your mind...is working more efficiently. More effortlessly."

"And when your mind is free," Theo continued, "then it can attend to all the information you want. You are becoming awakened in a way you've never experienced before." Just then a noisy motorcycle went by. Theo used this to his advantage, "Yes, you *can* hear the motorcycle going by, and you find you can be aware of it without needing to attend to it. Within your trance, all anxiety and all distraction slip away. Everything slips away."

Theo realized that his first impressions of Rachel had been correct: She'd shown strong natural ability for trance work, even when he was using only subliminal breathing.

His voice continued in a sing-song cadence that Rachel found lulling, like rocking a baby. He continued, and as he did, Rachel found that each word seemed to match the slowing of her beating heart.

"Now Rachel, turn your mind's awareness to your small intestine, with its wrinkles gathering in the food from your stomach. Just below, where we feel full or hungry, that's where you'll sense your small intestine. This happy part of your body has only one goal, and that is to gather up the food from your stomach to feed you from the little fingers of tissue in it, the villi, that absorbs the nutrition you need. And just knowing your body is taking care of you is a happy thought." Rachel smiled. "Imagine the feeling your stomach has when you eat. Nod your head if you can locate your stomach." Rachel nodded within moments. "Now I want you to draw your mind's awareness to the space directly below your stomach, your small intestine. When you find that you can hold this place in your mind, please smile."

"Now we turn to your womb. I want you to mentally locate your womb. It is behind and a bit above the bladder. You know what you feel like when your bladder is full, right? OK, then, bring your consciousness up a bit and behind your bladder. This is the part of you that provides a home to the embryo. Nod when you sense where it is." Rachel nodded. "Now Rachel, you know and you love this part of your body, your womb and every other part of your body. Knowing this makes it easy for you to extend love to each individual bit of you. Please share your loving awareness with your womb and your small intestine."

"Now I want you to become aware of how much life you have yet to live. You have so much life to experience and so much experience to digest. You feel how your body helps you with this need to digest your life experience. Nod your head when you feel this." Seeing her nod, Theo continued the induction, "I want you to imagine how you can draw blood from your womb and send it to your small intestine. You can do this simply by thinking, because your thoughts and your body are one now. In your blood is a wonderful enzyme called trypsin. With less blood, there is less trypsin. And you can feel this drawing of blood from your womb. Your womb is sending a message to the new life within you that now is not the time. Now is not the time. Now is not the time. You need your trypsin for your small intestine to digest all that you are going through in this life. And you have so much life to live first that you need your trypsin. And when you see this flow of trypsin from your womb, you smile with your feelings of confidence and power." Minutes passed and then, just when Theo thought that they would need another session, Rachel smiled. "Please continue to draw your blood and your trypsin into the walls of your small intestine. Remember, you feel an enormous and insatiable need to digest your life, all of it. All of the good parts, the bad ones, the pleasant ones, and the unpleasant ones. You need them all because 'for those loving God, all things work together for good...'"

He continued, "Rachel, now that you know where your womb is and you know where your small intestine is, you can draw your blood's supply of trypsin from the one to send to the other anytime you wish. Today, Rachel, I'd like you to simply let your body know to continue this work whether you're awake or asleep, whether you're focused or distracted – until you are satisfied that you have done enough for now. Over time, this practice will result in your not being pregnant anymore. It may take one day or it may take more, but know inside yourself that this is your body, and that, of course, it is here to serve you. You alone can control your body. Smile if you still are maintaining the flow of blood and trypsin from your womb to your small intestine." Rachel's smile beamed.

"And now Rachel, we are coming to the close of your trance. When you come out of your trance, you will remember everything we have talked about, you will remember everything you have learned including how to enter a trance, you will find joy in knowing your body as you have never known it before, and you will cherish the gift of your body so long as you have need of it. I will count backward from three to one, and when I say 'one,' you will awaken refreshed and knowing and joyful. Rachel, you are aware of your trance and aware of your desire to return to your normal state, three. Now you are aware of the need to move from where you are to where you want to be, two. You are becoming truly present in the here and now, one."

Rachel's eyes opened. She smiled quietly with a new understanding. She sat quietly for a time before saying calmly and gently, "I don't think I'm going to have a baby just now. I have so much more to do first."

Theo smiled. "Please continue to practice until you are satisfied that your body and your mind are truly one. I'll see you next week."

Etsa sat patiently and waited for the forest to begin his lesson. Sometimes Nugkui brought him his lesson, but today, Etsa could see that the Queen of Tears herself was his teacher. There was just too much unrelenting joy in her for him to ever mistake her for another. And here was his lesson. The hummingbird with the shock of dainty red feathers as a crown zipped before him like a spirit animal, so fast he could barely follow even with his eyes. He watched as she gathered nectar from the flowers around her, hovering as she sipped from the purple blossoms.

Etsa watched the little bird, so beautiful that she too seemed like a flower (only one that could fly). Just as he was wondering where this lesson was headed, his bird saw another hummingbird who had entered her air space. Without pausing even a moment, she flew to the attack and, after stabbing him once with her sharp beak, the interloper fled, permanently driven off.

Etsa wondered at the lesson: Danger can be beautiful, and beauty can attack with deadly ferocity. Still years away from puberty, he had little understanding – but still, he carefully stored the lesson away.

Etsa watched the snakes of the forest. He had seen the anacondas and other big snakes in the river take on epic battles, and even sometimes lose to another predator – like the day he'd seen a jaguar sink his powerful jaws into a boa constrictor and then snap its spine before feasting on the serpent. But today, in a deep and shady ravine, he watched a much smaller bright yellow snake with its skin extending like eyelashes over the vertical pupils of her eyes. She is beautiful, Etsa thought, And so small, no longer than my two hands end to end. As he watched the viper work her prehensile tail to help her climb up the small foliage surrounding a tree, he wondered, What does she think she can hunt in the high treetops? She should be down here looking for a mouse. He stared, captivated, as he watched the assassin slither into the forest canopy. He lost sight of her for a moment but then discovered her approaching a small bird's nest. He was amazed to find her quite the actress, capable of wiggling her tail like a worm at a small and ultimately fatally curious bird. Moments later, the bird fell, poisoned by the fangs she hadn't noticed at the little worm's other end. Watching the snake feed, he carefully archived another lesson about the hunter becoming the hunted when feeling safest and most in control.

Chapter 5

"It was so good working with you two today. I'm really looking forward to our next session." Theo exchanged warm smiles with the young couple as they thanked him and moved toward the office exit. As he turned, he noticed his officemate Liz sitting in her office, typing away.

"Oh, hi, Theo. Do you have time to talk for a minute?"

"Sure, what's up?"

"Just a sec, I have to get this note finished on my last session before I forget." She typed a few more moments before, with a flourish, she closed her laptop, got up and said, "Ah, can we sit in my office or would yours be better? I only need a few minutes."

"No worries, this is my lunch break." Theo settled into one of the two overstuffed chairs in Liz's office. "What can I do for you?"

Liz sighed, "I don't really know if there's a comfortable way to start this conversation, Theo."

Theo smiled and waited. He'd been expecting something like this from his auburn-haired officemate.

"When I approached you to share this office space, I was excited because I knew we were both of one spiritual mind. Or at least, that's what I thought at the time. But, in the last couple of years here I've had some...mmm...concerns that have come up."

Theo ignored Liz's reliance on speaking to him in the diplomatic parlance of a therapy session and then smiled again before asking, "OK, Liz, what's bugging you? I know I must have done something wrong...again...so what is it?"

"That's just it," Liz said, "I'm always unsure where you stand on the issues that I thought we agreed on when we opened a Christian counseling office. We went to the same church then, and...we still do," she drifted off.

"Yes? We still go to the same church, and I'm still a Christian and I haven't wavered one bit in my faith. So, what's the problem?" Again with that maddening smile.

"That's just it. On the surface, you and I seem like we're on the same path, but I've been sensing for a long time that you're following a different...I don't even know what to call it, but I'm afraid you're following a different gospel. You seem wishy-washy, and I never see you taking a stand on the issues, and you know, God wants us to be hot or cold and not lukewarm."

Theo's heart softened, and he found himself admitting to what he already knew bothered her. "So, you're talking about the pro-life marches? That I don't attend them?"

"Yes, I am, but not just that. You don't go to anything political, and that's just wrong in my book because God's people need every vote to overcome this holocaust that is plaguing our country. Babies are dying, Theo, and you just don't seem to be bothered by that. And there's other stuff like that couple who just left. I know who they are. I was there at church when she asked for prayer for her husband's porn addiction, and I don't think you're calling out porn addiction for what it is. It's sick and it's sin, Theo. And there's no end to this with you. I don't hear you loud and clear with encouraging young people to embrace abstinence. I heard you last week when we were talking, and you said teens need sex ed, and you know how our church feels about that. You have to start taking a stand."

"OK, Liz, I'm still just listening, and I don't want to sound defensive. But what I did say was that we need to teach young people how to manage their sexuality intelligently. How can that possibly sound like a bad idea?"

"It sounds like a bad idea if what you mean is ignoring God's word in all this. The scriptures are pretty clear on fornication, Theo, and you know that. You know the church's position on masturbation too. What's to be intelligent about? It's a question of obedience to God's Word, not intelligence. Theo, I saw a boy I know is gay coming out of your office, and he was smiling. I don't think it's because he was healed of his gayness. I don't think you even believe in conversion therapy. I think you're going down some sort of secular path of self-acceptance and anything goes, and that bothers me. Sometimes, I'm not sure we should be sharing an office, because it seems that we're not equally yoked, that we're not pulling in the same direction." She paused, spent with the effort to get out what she'd been thinking for months. "What is up with you and sexuality Theo? God's word is so clear on all this."

Now it was Theo's turn to sigh. "Liz, I get it. You think I'm not exactly orthodox or obedient to the Word, right?" Liz opened her eyes broadly, cocked her head and spread her hands out as if to say, "You think?" Theo continued, "But isn't it true that we can be brother and sister in church and disagree on matters of conscience? And, before you answer, you have to know that there are some hardcore people in our church who believe that divorced people, like yourself – right? – shouldn't ever remarry. Because they're still married in God's eyes, considering divorce is a sin. Some of those same people believe that we shouldn't even be having sex with our spouses unless it's for the purpose of having children, and speaking of that, many of them view birth control as little more than 'slut pills.' You know who I'm talking about, right?"

Liz nodded. "I know, I know, Theo. And to them, I'm edgy, even radical. But Pastor Rob has my back on the divorce thing, and he thinks it's OK if I date and whether or not I use birth control is nobody's business but mine," she said indignantly.

"Whoa, hold up, I support you in your privacy and in your right to make your own de...."

Liz interrupted, "But Theo, that's the point, I'm not making my own decisions. I'm coloring within the lines. I'm living my life following the teachings I've received from my teachers in Christ." She paused, not certain she liked what she'd just said before continuing, "You just seem to have a focus on sexuality that I think is unhealthy for a Christian."

Theo's smile softened indulgently. "I know I can be hard to be around Liz. I know I have some thoughts that, if they're not heretical, at least they're really different from what a lot of people think. I'm just doing the best I can with what I see and what I know. I hope you don't hate me enough to break up our business partnership, but...I know I can be trying."

"Please don't put words in my mouth Theo. I never said that I hated you, I'm just upset. My kids are counting on me to provide for them, and I'm all they've got, and I feel, well, threatened by how you seem to be looking at things. Like abortion, isn't that just as clear as can be to you? How can anyone who's got a degree in theology not see that?"

Theo glanced at the clock and made a decision to go on. Lunch could wait for another day. "I guess I don't see it as clearly as you do. Maybe you can help me because you have so much clarity on this. You know how the Old Testament goes. In Hosea and Isaiah and other places too, the enemies of God's people get their babies 'ripped from the womb.' And who's doing the ripping? Sometimes it's the Israelites, sometimes someone else, but isn't it always God punishing the wicked?"

Liz nodded, "Well, yeah...duh. What's the problem?"

"Let me go on a bit because it seems a bit less clear than it's been presented sometimes. Even King David, 'a man after God's own heart,' had what we call imprecatory prayers in the Psalms." Seeing Liz's confusion at his use of the technical term, he added, "You know, the ones where he curses his enemies? These aren't angry outbursts either, these are God-inspired words based on serious meditation, right? These are said out of zeal for God and his standards, right?" Liz nodded, growing suspicious of where this was headed but also curious now.

Theo continued, "And David, that 'man after God's own heart,' says in Psalm 139 that 'Happy shall he be, that taketh and dasheth thy little ones against the stones.' And what about the prophet Hosea who says that 'Their pregnant women will be ripped open,' of those who will be punished by God?"

Liz tried being patient with his wrong thinking, "But Theo, that's not about abortion, and it's not that God wants that."

"Really? Isn't that the Bible saying that violently ripping the unborn from the womb is just a fair consequence if the parents were considered to have rebelled against God? It's not exactly a strong stand on the 'sanctity of life' is it? If the unborn are innocent babies, then how is that possibly right? Words like these make me think that there's a bigger picture because sometimes God seems to be OK with terminating pregnancy...for the sake of righteousness."

Liz decided to give up. "Look, I just don't agree, but can we at least talk about this later? I need to pick up my son at school and I have to go...but that doesn't mean I don't want to talk about this more. I want to help you, Theo."

Theo ignored the condescending remark because he knew exactly which battles he had come to this country to fight. It was easy for him to say, "Sure Liz. I look forward to it." And because he did look forward to it, he smiled a small and loving smile at her.

Liz smiled and said more warmly, "Thanks, Theo."

"Please know, Liz, I've never encouraged anyone to get an abortion. I don't think I ever will. I just don't think that it's the best solution."

Something about the way Theo phrased his last comment puzzled Liz, but she forced herself to let go for now. Smiling nervously, she said, "OK...then, till next time."

By the time he was 10, Etsa had been traveling into the spirit world for years. It had become as real or sometimes more real than the physical world. He had learned that the veil between the two was quite sheer and that the two realms interacted far more than most realized.

As the months passed, the pace of the training of the young war shaman was increasing. Much of his training was now no longer under the guidance of his father. Instead, the Queen of Tears taught him. Early on, she brought the lesson that his warfare was not against the horribly ignorant enemy to the north but against their way of thinking and their failure to see the sacred nature of the earth. Instead, she explained, the enemy was destroying humanity's home, because he saw that home simply as one oversized toilet that he could use for his own filth. As she explained the notion of greed for gold, logging, and land, the Queen of Tears became somber. And then, just as Etsa began to despair, he saw in her eyes the beauty of the earth's deliverance, rescued from the false spirituality that made such greed into a needed drug to cushion the blow of lovelessness. Etsa saw in her eyes the beauty of those spirit warriors whose fierce nature flowed from the desire to protect. He saw himself. He saw the endless ranks of his loving allies. Etsa knew he would feel alone, yes, but he knew that he would never be alone.

Chapter 6

Rachel got home shortly after 5 o'clock. That day, she and her father successfully managed to avoid one another. Her relief upon ending her pregnancy was as much a part of her as the hormones that lingered in her bloodstream.

That night she felt compelled to go to the Internet to understand more about her work with her therapist, smiling at her use of the term *my therapist*, an idea she'd never considered would be hers to experience. But then frowning, she reminded herself that she never thought she'd be pregnant either, and certainly not pregnant while unmarried. Shaking the thoughts out of her head, Rachel began her research. She needed to know more about the power she was feeling following her trance and that she knew was hers to use as she saw fit. She knew that she had wielded this power to end her pregnancy, and she wanted to understand it and the God who had given her such power. The power of her decision overshadowed the emotional fragility she felt. Each was as real as the other.

As the minutes passed, she fell into her own sort of trance going deeper and deeper down the rabbit hole of search terms, websites, and personal observations. After about an hour, Rachel heard her mother call up to say that dinner was ready, and it was time for her to come down. Rachel shouted, "Coming!" But she sat for a few more minutes, her mind riveted by a quote that had followed a search that had taken her from 'hypnosis' to 'trance' to 'flow state' and then to, of all things, an athlete's experience that surprised her because it expressed what she'd been trying to articulate since her appointment with Theo. The words sunk into her as she sat, staring at her computer's monitor. They were from Roger Bannister, the first man to break the four-minute mile and, surprisingly to Rachel, a man who'd gone from accomplished jock to distinguished neurologist. He was talking about his famous record-breaking race,

> 'No longer conscious of my movement, I discovered a new unity with nature. I had found a new source of power and beauty, a source I never dreamt existed.'

Rachel's mind absorbed these words. They perfectly expressed her experience from earlier in the day that up until then was simply indescribable. She said to herself, *I did lose my consciousness of sitting in the office, and I did feel closer to nature by being closer to my body. I did have a new source, not only of power, but it felt beautiful too. I felt beautiful.*

Her mom yelled about dinner again, and Rachel calmly closed her laptop, smiled, and quietly, without hurrying, made her way down the stairs. She noted her mother's irritation at having to call her twice and calmly apologized in a manner that seemed to her, that felt to her, more adult than her normal response as a nagged teen.

Startled a bit by her daughter's sense of calm, Stephanie Carson breathed in with relief. She'd noticed that her daughter had been uncharacteristically both agitated and close mouthed lately. *Things must be going better,* she thought to herself. Stephanie looked at her husband, Larry, and was made aware of how he now seemed to be the one with a repressed sense of subdued disquiet. Still to herself, she wondered, *Now what's his problem?* She frowned and finished placing the meatloaf on the table as they all bowed their heads to say grace. Waiting there, as the silent seconds ticked by, she squeezed Larry's hand and prompted him whispering, "Honey?"

Larry was jostled from his thoughts and pounded out some words of thanks with an awkward fluster that was not characteristic of him. Opening her eyes, Stephanie's gaze met Rachel's face as she again noticed her daughter's — well, her peace. *That's it. She looks so peaceful.* Stephanie smiled more genuinely than before, and they all began eating dinner.

After helping with the cleaning up, Rachel looked at the clock and realized she still had a few hours to do some more research. She opened her laptop and again saw the Bannister quote. She smiled and decided to do a screenshot and send it to herself. It was a bit incriminating, and it was more than a bit "New Agey" as her dad would say, but Rachel thought she could defend the quote as "inspiring" if she got busted by her parents for having it on her phone. Just as she was deciding what to do next, she got a phone call from another girl from church, Amber Duxbury.

"Hi Rachel. Can I come over?"

"Well, it's kinda late." Rachel really, really didn't want to minister to Amber right now. She had a really good feeling going on inside of her, and she just wanted to be alone with her thoughts. Hanging out with the neediest girl she knew wasn't on her agenda.

"Rachel, I promise I won't stay too long this time," Amber whined, pleading her case.

Rachel caved in to her lifelong "denial of self" training, sighed, and said, "OK. I'll tell my parents you're coming over to help me with history or something." The minute she said it, she realized she'd have to come up with a better lie because Amber was not in any way a person one would label "scholar." Amber was never really going to help her with homework — or probably anything else. She smiled, thinking of Bannister, *Yeah, I don't see Amber becoming a 'distinguished neurologist' anytime soon.*

Because Amber lived nearby, there was a knock at the Carson door within minutes. "Who could that be at this hour," Rachel's mom complained.

"It's Amber. She really needs some help right now," Rachel said in that tone of concern just to the right of condescending. Stephanie silently mouthed, "Oh," as she made that face that all but said, "*Again? Am I right?*" Rachel let her mother persist in her derision of the chronically troubled girl, thinking to herself about her own secret counseling session, *If she only knew.*

Throwing the door open, Rachel stood aside, quickly getting

out of the way of the bigger girl as she burst into the living room without waiting for any invitation.

"Ah, hi Mrs. Carson."

"Oh, hi yourself Amber." Stephanie turned to smile briefly before returning her attention to the television, that blessed isle of oblivion.

The two girls headed upstairs to Rachel's bedroom, and closing the door, Rachel asked, "So, what's going on?"

Amber rolled her eyes as if to say, "What isn't going on?" Then, without further prompting, she blurted out, "You can't tell anybody about this. I need you to swear, Rachel. Promise me you won't tell anyone." She waited.

Rachel paused, seeing herself at her first counseling session with Theo, worried about her own privacy. Her annoyance with Amber softened, and Rachel looked at her intently and said, "I promise Amber. I won't tell anyone." "Rachel, I'm pregnant and I don't know what to do. I think my life is ruined." Amber looked even worse than Rachel remembered herself looking as she had started dealing with her own crisis.

Amber continued, "I mean, I know he loves me, but we can't get married or anything right now."

Rachel's head swooped down and forward while one eyebrow went up to ask wordlessly, "Who?"

"Coach Travis and I got really close lately. I love him, and we just let it go too far. I mean, we did other stuff for a while, but it just got too hard for him to keep it, you know, to just oral and stuff. I don't judge him for that."

Rachel's stomach protested at the images conjured up by Amber and her words. She did *not* need those pictures in her head. Swallowing the bile rising up in her throat, Rachel found it was all she could do to just listen quietly. Truthfully, Rachel had always felt creeped out by Coach Travis Williams and had resisted calling the YL youth group leader by his first name the way he encouraged other girls, like Amber, to do. She'd heard rumors flying around about Coach Williams and the girls on the basketball teams he coached. The stories had always been deliciously scandalizing, until Rachel saw him with Amber one time. She definitely did not want any part of the way that the two of them had looked at each other. *Big time creep factor*, she had thought to herself at the time. But following her parents' divorce, Amber had grown increasingly attention-seeking, especially with boys — and now with Coach Williams, who was no boy. Rachel suspected that Amber was as sexually experienced as she was emotionally needy. But rather than being judgmental, her recent experience with her own crisis pregnancy had humbled her, and she found herself feeling far less annoyed with Amber than usual.

"I don't want to be pregnant right now Rachel. Maybe it would be different if I was 18 like you and all together the way you are, you know? But I don't want him to have to face his wife with this. You would not believe how mean she can be to him. She would probably report him, and he wouldn't even be able to coach or anything."

Rachel found herself slightly ill at the thought that Amber, even in the midst of her predicament as a 16-year-old, was so preoccupied with Coach Williams' situation and the potential consequences for his having had sex with an underage student athlete that she was utterly unfocused on coping with her own shattered life.

"Do you think I should keep the baby Rachel, or should I give it up for adoption? I mean, when he divorces his wife someday, wouldn't we want to have our first baby with us? What do you think I should do Rachel? Do you think I should go to the Crisis Pregnancy Center? Maybe the CPC could help me."

Rachel couldn't take any more. "What are you talking about Amber? He's a married man. He and his wife go to our church. You know that because you see them every week at Young Life. They're still ministering there, right?"

Amber nodded her head numbly.

Rachel continued, "They have two young kids, they do YL, they go to church, and he wouldn't even be a coach at high school if Pastor Rob hadn't got him that job. Do you really think he *should* give all that up, that he would give all of that up? Would you even want him to do that?"

Amber burst into tears, "I know, I know. I know you're right." A moment passed before she stopped crying and asked, as if Rachel hadn't said anything, "Do you really think we'll never be together? You could never understand how much we really love each other, Rachel."

Rachel's patience evaporated, and she said in a firm tone, "You do not want to have this baby, and you need to do something about it. Right now."

"What can I do? My parents will never sign off on my having an abortion. But if I don't, I'll probably have to give up...everything." Amber's eyes filled with tears and her voice quavered, "I don't know what to do Rachel. Tell me what I should do. Maybe the CPC?"

Rachel became angry as she thought about the bait-and-switch tactics of CPCs (*Stopping abortions is more important than how many lies we have to tell!*) and their spreading ignorant misinformation like, "Condoms don't really help prevent STIs." She'd listened to their lectures, and that's why she didn't have a condom that day with Rob. She wondered to herself, *Maybe the CPC gave him Bible study sessions like they offered me.* She shuddered when she thought about how many times she'd seen a confused teen led by the nose with lines like, "Do you believe in God? Well then, let's see what He has to say in the Word." *Crap,* she thought, *I've said that myself.*

That's when Rachel became sure that she knew what her friend needed. She leaned toward Amber and said in a slow, soft voice, "Well, there's a way, Amber, there's a way to deal with all of this." Amber's brows raised, and the two leaned in toward one another conspiratorially.

"So, first of all, you need to know that your body is yours and that you are not your body. That it is here to serve you and you are in control of your body. And you need to know...." As Rachel's voice went on Amber's eyes grew bigger and her tears dried up. The next two hours passed quickly as a world-changing secret was shared from one woman to another for the first time.

By age 11, Etsa was already known in the forest as a shaman warrior-in-training. Every day he studied from those around him. Sometimes it was directly from the spirit world in his many ayahuasca journeys consulting with Nugkui and the ajútap warriors who sought to imbue him with their own courage. His favorite lessons were the long days he sat still in the forest allowing himself to learn from whatever the spirits brought him. He was still learning even the most basic life lessons in love and service from his mother and father. His great learning often allowed him to teach those far older than he. Not all of the elders of the forest appreciated this.

One day his father began teaching him how to protect and heal himself and others from the dark magic of chonteros, the sorcerers who use darts to inflict harm on their victims. "Sometimes these sorcerers make their darts from thorns or even the fangs of venomous snakes," his father explained. Etsa asked, "Would they use the fang of the yellow eyelash viper I told you about?" His father replied, "A favorite. They all look for that one."

Chapter 7

Two weeks later, Rachel sat in the metal folding chair feeling untethered to reality. She wasn't sure why she was at Bible study tonight. Pastor Skip, the youth pastor, had encouraged her, but really...tonight? The crowd was larger than usual for a couple of reasons. One was the special speaker, Suzie McSweeney, who was speaking on Sanctity of Life for All. Rachel knew McSweeney probably had a tremendous testimony because she had admitted to having had an abortion, and, of course, knew how that "disastrous and selfish decision" had shattered her life as a teenager — leading to a life of drugs and promiscuity, and some whispered, prostitution. But McSweeney also knew, after all of that, how God had given her another chance to redeem herself, to do the right thing and to prove her faithfulness to God and how God had been faithful to help her. Rachel knew all this of course, but she had also chosen a different path altogether and was in no mood for another session of sex shaming. In fact, she reflected, she'd never felt closer to God than after her trance work.

"Rachel? Do you always go to these?" Amber took the seat next to Rachel and plopped down.

"No, you?" Rachel asked. Then Rachel caught sight of Coach Williams and his wife with all the YL kids. "Oh, Young Life is here for the speaker, right?"

"Yeah. I thought I'd go and try to be open. Since, you know, that night...when we.... Well, I'm trying to go on without the baby and without Coach. You know, it's hard when you're in love. You really just don't know what it's like, Rachel."

Rachel felt unease wash over her. "Are you saying that you're still having sex with him?" She didn't wait for an answer, as Amber's avoidance of eye contact said it all. That night in her home, Rachel had felt as though she was doing the right thing in helping Amber, and now she was beginning to doubt the wisdom of getting involved with the troubled girl. For Rachel, the trance and the connection with nature — with her own inner nature — felt special, really special. So, to see Amber so...muddled, was disconcerting. Rachel shook her head in confusion.

Just then, the worship team leader called for prayer, and after asking for God's blessing, the electric guitars fired up to the sounds of Christian rock. Eyes closed and heads turned heavenward as both adults and teens voiced the familiar lyrics, their bodies rocking in rhythm with the melodies.

After the last song played out and the hallelujahs died down, Pastor Skip stepped up to the mic, his eyes closed as he intoned, "Thank you, Lord, for what you're doing among us right now and for our speaker who has been anointed by you with a message that we all need to hear, a message that is truly life giving in the most meaningful sense. 'N Jesus' name, 'n all God's people said?" "Amen!" the small congregation responded. The young man looked over the crowd of youth, and he saw with a sense of gratitude that Rachel was there and was looking so much more together. Skip thought to himself that referring her to Theo had been a good call. As his gaze swept the hall, he noticed Amber and the expression on her face as she looked at YL ministers Travis and his wife. He thought, "There's trouble," before clearing his throat and saying with his best emcee voice, "Please join me in welcoming Suzie McSweeney to our church."

The enthusiastic teens clapped, shouted a few "Praise the Lords" and whistled a warm welcome, as the speaker walked across· the platform. "Hi, I'm Suzie McSweeney, and I am here to tell you that I know God's Word is Good. And because of His word, I know that all of our unborn babies are God's sacred little angels sent to us for our own deliverance from the sins of selfish and self-centered false pride and the gods of this world. The spirit of our modern age that drives this holocaust has become our nation's undoing! Our carelessness with these precious little ones is linked in a direct line to all of our modern plagues."

Rachel listened as McSweeney continued in the same vein for some time, weaving her own story into her sermon. Rachel had to admit that McSweeney was one of the best — eloquent, but in a simple and humble style that seemed heartfelt. She had heard this sort of witnessing a lot during her years at the church and had usually listened with an expression that she had hoped came across as compassionate piety. And she had felt right with God then, she thought. She wasn't having sex, and she had little trouble with guilt. She felt compassion too for the young women, mistaken as they were, who had chosen to selfishly murder their own children due to Satan's deceptions and the influence of the Democratic Party.

But that Rachel was long gone now. Back then, everything about sex, pregnancy, and abortion had been theoretical, almost like memorizing answers for a test at school. Did anyone really care about things like the Constitution, trigonometry, or physics? But Rachel had since then found out that sex and especially pregnancy had a certain compelling way of making the theoretical matter of morality look very ungrounded in reality. Maybe, she thought with a repressed giggle, Maybe we're supposed to somehow get the two of them, sexuality and morality, to sit down and work things out.

As Rachel half listened and became a bit distracted by her own thoughts, she became aware that McSweeney was wrapping it up and getting ready for the altar call. Thus, the guilt-stricken could come forward and confess their sins — and thereby be not only healed, but also provide evidence for God's great work in paying for people like McSweeney to come to their church.

"Let's pray, shall we? Lord, we come before you as a broken people who have done great wrong. We are strangers living in a strange land, and frankly, Lord, our great nation is truly lost and is becoming stranger by the day. We need you, Lord, we need you and your forgiveness for our careless attitude to the sacred gift of life — and so we confess that we might have your forgiveness, Lord Jesus. There are those in the audience tonight who have considered abortion, who may have even aborted their own babies, there are young men who have paid for these services and right now, O Lord, we cast ourselves on your mercy."

Just then, as McSweeney was coming to the altar call, Rachel heard an audible sob and turned in her seat to see Amber pull herself out of her seat and stumble, eyes blinded by tears, up towards the altar, ascend the platform, and then go to (Oh no, God, please not...) the microphone. Rachel froze in place, not knowing what to do with the calamity unfolding before her.

The spectacle provided by Amber was quite gratifying to most everyone. The young had an object lesson of great clarity in just how horrible it was to sin. Those various ministers of the gospel, the youth pastor, the worship team, and, of course, Suzie McSweeney, were delighted to have been used as instruments of the living God in bringing yet another lost lamb back to the fold.

Rachel, still frozen, finally remembered to breathe— and that act was the limit of her physical ability to cope in the moment. She watched as she saw the needy, messed up girl she knew as Amber hold Pastor Skip a bit more tightly than he'd normally feel comfortable with in public, and then be taken into the sisterly embrace of Suzie McSweeney. Minutes passed, and then, to her horror, Rachel watched Amber take the mic.

"I just need to confess that I have si...sinned (as she began to weep anew) and that I have aborted my own baby. I am guilty, guilty, guilty and I repent. I repent," she repeated. She continued, "I learned how to become unpregnant all by myself, but that doesn't make it any better."

At this point, those on the platform with her looked a bit confused. "Unpregnant? What was that?" seemed to be the consensus.

Just when things couldn't get any worse, Rachel thought, they took a decidedly worse turn as Amber continued her sobbing yet triumphant confession.

"And I just have to say, I'm so sorry Coach Williams, and Mrs. Williams, I'm sorry that I got rid of our baby. I wish I'd never learned how to do this. I am so sorry."

The sudden hush that followed was out of sync with the normally predictable pleasant and sleepy world of good families going to a good church. Eyes popped. People got that look in their eyes that said,, "Did I just hear what I thought I heard?" Pastor Skip rushed the mic, grabbing it from a surprised Amber and then very professionally led everyone in a prayer of dismissal. "And finally, thank you Lord Jesus, for showing up tonight and blessing all of us. 'N his holy name. And all God's people said...."

Normally there would be the enthusiastic call and response here where the whole congregation would say "Amen!" again, only tonight, it came out a bit more like a subdued, "Amen?" People just didn't know what had hit them. Coach Williams? Coach and Mrs. Williams did what? Amber did what?

The only one who looked peaceful in this moment was Amber. Why wouldn't she? thought Rachel. She's got everyone's attention now.

Perhaps the least confused person in the night's congregation, Rachel was understandably the quickest to get the hell out of there.

"A true war shaman must also possess all the skill of a curandero, and he must be competent to cure the wounds inflicted by sorcerers," Ankuash said. Etsa nodded soberly. "I will prepare spirit darts for you, son, and they will go with you when you leave to wage war on the enemies of The People." And so Etsa and his father began fasting, as Ankuash explained, "To maximize the potency of the darts' power. The longer you can fast before I transfer the darts, the stronger they will be. You will be able to cure or to kill as you require, to bring relief or to bring suffering as needed." After weeks of ayahuasca ceremony and three days of fasting, Etsa felt that he was ready. The process was far from easy and would have proven daunting to most grown men, but in the end, Etsa was now walking in a power and confidence that kept jealous sorcerers away from him and The People.

Chapter 8

"And that's when I left," Rachel pursed her lips and blew out the remains of her breath. She looked at Theo to see what he had to say.

Theo said nothing. Therapy sessions were never about making conversation to him — and this one particularly so. Theo pondered how to execute the follow-up stages of his mission, and so conversation — and indeed, Rachel's social norms — were irrelevant. He smiled patiently at Rachel as he waited for her to begin processing her feelings. He didn't have long to wait. A minute passed. Then another. He continued to hold space for her as he waited for her soul to catch up with her intellect.

Finally, Rachel's shoulders slumped as she began to relax. Theo's office had become a safe space before, and she had only just now noticed how rare that feeling of safety was in her insulated world. Theo wanted nothing from her, needed nothing from her. He was simply there...for her. Knowing that he was present in this way made Rachel realize she'd never experienced a moment like this before in her life. As her body relaxed, she realized she didn't have to hold it together anymore, and she surrendered to the tears filling her eyes.

Theo continued to wait. There was no hurry, because in this moment the two had all the time in the world.

Rachel finally felt it and knew it for what it was. For Theo, she was simply that important. He would wait for her. She had never experienced this, what to call it, this *courtesy*. She knew she didn't have to explain. She didn't have to understand. *She didn't have to do anything at all.* She was no longer anyone's "good girl." She was no one's slut. She was not a show pony, there to look just so and to say just the right things. She felt somehow more simply human while at the same time of such greater value than she'd ever known. She thought to herself, "This is what a queen must feel when her subjects attend her."

A quarter of an hour passed while she surrendered to these thoughts, then came to reign over them. She felt herself a queen, who after a terrible and indecisive battle, was in consultation with her minister of war. She was full of a new peace, one that passed her conscious understanding, and then she took some additional and unhurried time mopping up her tears and her smeared make-up. When she'd had enough of that, Rachel said, in a perfectly calm voice, "So now, what do we do next?"

Theo's smile broadened as if he had been rewarded with exactly what he'd hoped for. "Well, it's certainly not the sequence of events I'd hoped for, but if we remain still and simply reflect on this a bit, I have confidence that some great good will come out of this."

Rachel's own smile quickened as she thought to herself a verse she'd heard so many times — yet in what seemed a far more limited way — "...all things work together for good to those called according to a purpose." And then Rachel realized, although sex and sexuality and church teaching would never be the same for her, that the rest of the verse remained as true and was perhaps now truer than ever, "...for them that know the Lord and are called according to her purpose." Now it was her turn to hold space for Theo, the commander who pondered their next strategy.

"OK. I think I have our next steps, Rachel. First of all, what have you learned in all this?"

This was unexpected. Rachel's imagination had run to the external, and here was Theo asking her to go even deeper into her own internal. She paused, thinking, *All right, if that's what he thinks we're needing to do, let's try it.* She said, "This is the third time we've spoken, and I already feel as though I've learned a lot. Are you sure we have time for this?"

Theo smiled and waited quietly, not wanting to take up even one second with answering a question with so obvious an answer.

"What *have* I learned?" Rachel asked herself. She looked up and to the left as if to see the information on a shelf, and then that's where it was. Or at least, that's where it began. "I know I've learned an important new respect for my body and what my body can do. I've learned that I don't need to be afraid of myself, of my own body, my own desires. That's for starters."

Theo nodded along with her and continued to give her room to think without being preached at in the manner she'd been preached at so many times before. Rachel felt so alive, and her confidence grew as she went on, "I know I have a lot to learn. Amber taught me that. I just thought knowing my body the way I do now was like, I don't know, like a new app or something. Watching what she did with the knowledge, I know now she didn't see it the way I do."

"How do you see this new knowledge, Rachel?"

Rachel paused, because the old word worked but seemed somehow out of place here. But, after all, it was the right word, so she said, "Sacred. I see this knowledge as sacred. I think that somehow — and I don't know how — that my body is sacred, too." Her eyes came back into focus, and she looked at Theo and said, "It's a lot to take in." Seeing Theo nod in assent, she added, "But I still don't know what to do."

Theo reminded her, "You're not alone in this. I'm with you."

Rachel smiled.

He continued, "I do believe that we are actually in a better place now than we were before the night Amber came forward."

"What do you mean?"

"Well, I suppose that Amber comes off as a bit...ah...crazy?"

"She always does. She always has. That's why I felt so sorry for her. That's why I tried to help her but...."

"I want to get to that part later Rachel, I do. But for now, can you see that this is not about Amber right now, right here?"

"I don't know what you mean."

"Well, can we agree that Amber is not the problem? That Suzie

McSweeney is not the problem? Not your dad, not your mom, not any one person really. Remember Ephesians?" And then Theo recited,

> *'We are wrestling not against blood and flesh,*
> *but against rulers, against the Archons, against*
> *the Powers, against the Cosmic Rulers of this*
> *darkness, against the spiritual forces of wickedness*
> *in the celestial places.'*

"You remember that?" Seeing her nod thoughtfully, he continued, "We're not here at this time and in this place so we can carry on business as usual, Rachel. God has given us an opportunity to change a world. And, if we're successful, to save a world. Do you see?"

"I like the sound of what you're saying, but I have no idea what it all means," she admitted.

"Imagine a world, Rachel, where a woman can conceive only when she elects to as an act of free will. In fact, that's what this world, right here, right now, is for you. It's just not that way for anyone else. Take a moment to imagine how having everyone knowing what you know would change this world."

Rachel pondered, and then ideas — scary big ideas — began to form. "Well, it would mean that poverty around the world wouldn't be the same problem that it is."

"Yes?" Theo said in an encouraging tone.

"It would mean that women wouldn't have to have birth control to protect themselves from pregnancy. That their babies couldn't be used against them, to hold them back. That they'd never be forced by anyone to have a baby."

"Mmm hmm."

"It would mean that women would be seen more like...mmm, equals or something, I mean, to men."

"Yes!"

"Oh," Rachel said as if surprised by her own thoughts, "It would mean that politics wouldn't be about who was pro-life or pro-choice anymore. It would mean politicians would talk about... us, not the unborn. It would mean that women would never have to worry about access to reproductive health care, IUDs, birth control pills. It would mean no girl would ever have to worry about getting pregnant ever again. It would change the way we think, the way I think, about sex. It would mean that the church would have to find new things to talk about besides always saying, "Thou shalt not."

"Keep going, " Theo encouraged her.

"It would mean men wouldn't have to make women do one thing or the other because having a baby would be the decision of each woman out there and only hers. It would mean women couldn't be controlled. It would mean I, that I...," her voice faded in the depth of her thoughts.

"Yes, Rachel, 'It would mean that you...?"

It would mean that my being a good person or a good woman or a good," and here she choked up a bit before adding derisively, "a good *girl* would have to be based on something other than sex, like, like, you know...actually being good. You know the way that boys aren't judged by whether or not they've lost their virginity? It would be like that for girls, too."

"Yes, Rachel. I agree. It would mean all that and maybe more."

Rachel's head swam with the power of this vision.

"And you know how it all starts, Rachel?"

"I thought it already did start."

Theo smiled, "Yes, Rachel, and how was that? How did it start?"

Rachel thought a bit and then brightened, "It started when I came in here for counseling. I was scared and confused and mad and...and you helped me."

"That's exactly where it all starts, Rachel, because even this knowledge, as wonderful as it is, is only an app so long as it is only a thing separate from the rest of you. Saving this world starts with you and with me. It starts with the proper frame of mind. It starts in the right and safe setting. You came here for counseling. You needed healing. You came to someone who was trained to help you, and you got the first bit of help you needed to get started. But do you really feel like you're done? I think you know there's more to do."

Rachel's expansive mood contracted a bit as she again turned her thoughts inward. She nodded, "I don't know where to start."

"How about we start where it all started: In your family."

Rachel sucked in a quick breath suddenly full of anxiety.

"Rachel, nothing we do here, nothing we talk about here, is

more important than you are. Not even saving this hurting world of ours. You are hurting, and you need some help working through all of that. If what we are doing doesn't really work for you, then how could we have faith that it would be good for anyone else?"

Rachel had listened with her head bowed, looking at the patch of carpet in front of her feet. She felt a rise of panic in her body as she was urged to begin working on herself, to start talking about herself. What was going on?

"I think it would be good if you would let me take a bit more of your history so that we can do a work-up on where things went wrong for you. What do you say, Rachel?"

Rachel was very still before finally nodding. She added, in a small little-girl voice, "I don't know what to say."

"Let's start with your early childhood Rachel. Can you please tell me more about how your mom and dad raised you? We might find some clarity there. And then I have some more questions for you."

"I don't see how that makes any sense? How can I have what was it you called it, Post Traumatic...something?"

Theo smiled indulgently, "I know it's a mouthful Rachel, Post Traumatic Stress Disorder. Most of us just call it PTSD."

"Well, how can I have *that*? I mean, isn't that what soldiers get?"

"Some soldiers get it from the trauma of war — and then, I know it's confusing, but some don't."

"OK, but what does any of this have to do with me? I've never been in a war; I've never been in the army. I've never even been in a traffic accident. I've never had anything bad happen to me. "

Theo took on an expression of openness and said, "Well, maybe I'm wrong." He shrugged, "I've been wrong so many times before, and especially so on those occasions when I thought I was the most right. So maybe I'm wrong. Let's check."

"How?"

"Well, there are criteria for every diagnosis." Seeing her confused look at his jargon, Theo smiled and corrected himself, "Look, it's a science thing, not a revelation thing. You either meet the criteria or you don't. I'm open to checking it out, are you?"

"Well, if you don't mind wasting your time, 'cause I'm sure I don't have anything like that. I came in here the first time because I was scared about being pregnant, and I didn't know what to do. Now you're saying I have a mental illness."

Theo looked at her and then reached to the bottom shelf of his side table for a thick paperback with a purple cover. "Let's just see what we find out. If you have any illness at all, we don't have to worry about it because, He came 'healing every illness and infirmity.' Every one of them. The only thing is, denying the illness means denying potential healing."

Rachel couldn't argue with that, so she waited for the few seconds it took for Theo to find PTSD in what he called the "DSM5." "Here it is. Hmmm. Well, yeah. Here we go." Theo took a breath, and then he said, "OK, you have to have one or more of the following, and I'm editing a bit so bear with me: "Directly experiencing traumatic events, witnessing, in person, the events as they occurred to others, experiencing repeated exposure to aversive details of the traumatic event like...like police officers repeatedly exposed to details of child abuse.'"

Rachel sighed with exasperation, "*See*, I've never had anything like that."

Theo was definitely not smiling now. "Haven't you? I mean, Rachel, you just got done telling me that in your history at home and at church, you were told repeatedly that your having masturbated would lead to your destruction as a future wife, as a mother. You learned that just to be *in your* body was like sleeping with a satanic enemy and that your enemy was your own sexuality. Rachel, you were told that your beauty, your physical beauty, was a stumbling block to men. I wouldn't be surprised to learn that you're always checking yourself in the mirror to see if you're not 'immodestly dressed' all the time."

Rachel looked down, the wind knocked out of her, her former irritation having evaporated.

Rather than being the comforting counselor, Theo's voice became sharper, "Rachel, I don't want to re-traumatize you by bringing this up, so I need you to stay in the smart part of your brain. Can you do that? This isn't a time for a 'fight or flight' response. Can you do that? Can you?"

It was as though Theo's voice had reached into a dark pool where Rachel was drowning and yanked her out just before she went under. "*Yes*," she said in a little girl voice.

"Not good enough, Rachel. We don't need a little girl here, we need *you!*"

Maybe it was because of the sharpness of his tone, or maybe it was because of her established link with Theo in her trance work. But either way, Rachel took in a sudden deep breath and then said in her normal voice, "OK. I'm...I'm all right now."

Theo's gaze met hers, and then, after they'd both really looked long enough to take the measure of one another, he smiled and said, "That was close."

"I'm all right now," Rachel repeated more calmly.

"If it helps you to think of this as a special kind of trauma that's different from what a soldier might experience, try that. Some people even have a special name for this form of PTSD, they call it Religious Trauma Syndrome or RTS. It's what happens when people struggle with rigid religious indoctrination, either in leaving it or even questioning it."

"That...that sounds like something I could be going through."

"OK, then let's go on." Theo looked back down at his book, "It says here that, mmm, OK, you might be having some dissociative experiences, you know, where you're not in the here and now anymore, just somewhere else, maybe like you're watching yourself from way up somewhere."

Rachel remembered how she'd felt when she had had sex for the first, well, for the only time. She didn't feel like she was in her own body but was somehow floating up by the ceiling. It felt weird but she thought, *Hey, maybe it's supposed to be like this.* Aloud she said, "OK, check. What else?"

Theo didn't bother to look up from the pages, "Distressed thoughts or what they call 'marked physiological reactions' to cues that symbolize an aspect of the trauma."

Rachel thought about feeling sick to her stomach whenever in the last year her dad had mentioned anything about going to the annual "Purity Ball" or maybe just noticing she was enjoying a romantic movie a little too much and in a way that just felt wrong.

"Would that include things like movies with too much kissing and stuff? 'Cause that always makes me feel a kind of, I don't know, a kind of 'sexy' feeling, and then I always feel guilty about liking it, I guess. You know, it's that whole 'slippery slope' idea." Seeing Theo's confusion she continued, "It's that if I start with fantasizing about kissing, then I'll be more likely to kiss, and then if I kiss someone, we're more likely to do something more until then we're having sex, and then well, our lives are ruined." She felt sick just saying these words.

"So, you're saying that any romantic or sexual urges are dangerous, right?"

"Exactly. I mean, you can see the trouble I got in."

"But Rachel, what you're describing are normal human feelings, normal human sexuality. Those feelings and your sexuality were never a problem you should have repressed. Now, that part of your brain that picks out boyfriends, that part could use some improvement. Can you see that?"

Usually, Rachel was more likely to be the devil's advocate in these types of conversations, but today it felt better to hear someone else say the words that she knew were dangerous.

"Rachel? Can you see that what you're talking about is just normal? I mean, that the way you are is the way God made all of us?"

"But aren't we supposed to resist the flesh and cling to the spirit?"

Theo looked at her a bit oddly, but it didn't bother Rachel — she'd been staring at the floor again for some time now in this exchange. "OK, Rachel, there's a truth there, but no matter where that truth is, I think we can all agree that knowing God's truth isn't supposed to lead us into mental illness." He smiled again as he set his reference book aside, "Let me ask you something Rachel, and this will be my last question for the day: Is there some way you can see that maybe you've been a bit excessively watchful, what we might call hyper-vigilant, over your sexuality, you know, to where your watchfulness itself causes you problems?"

Rachel's world seemed to, if not crash, at least suffer a significant crack at this point. She remembered how, every month for years now, she had worried that she might not get her period because maybe she just wasn't pure enough. How could anyone really be sure? And then she would get her period and feel relieved for a few days, sometimes even weeks. And Rachel knew this was just crazy because in all those years she hadn't had sex with anyone...so how could she get pregnant? Rachel thought of the countless hours growing to days and then weeks when she'd worry herself sick about being pregnant, to the point she really couldn't think clearly about school or...or anything.

Theo watched Rachel process this, and then he said, "Well, I could be wrong about the PTSD thing, but maybe I'm right. Let's try to stay open to that, OK?"

Rachel came back to earth and flashed a quiet smile. "OK, I'll try. But maybe I do have PTSD. I actually think that I do. What do I do about it?"

"We can work on that, Rachel, next week." Seeing her dissatisfaction with his answer that sounded even a little too 'stock counselor response' to his ear, he added, leaning forward dramatically and sounding more like a queen's minister of war, "I have a plan."

Etsa's mother Chipa had noticed the changes coming over her son as he was becoming a man. As he approached his 13th year, his voice started to betray him, as it alternated between that of the boy he once was and the man he was becoming. She knew in her heart that these important days of becoming sexually mature required as much attention as any other stage of her son's development. She had seen how the invaders treated women, and she hated what all of them, especially the missionaries, had done to The People. She shook her head in disapproval as she thought, "They are always sending messages of shame or behaving in shameful ways. They have no honorable or human path for their desires." With that thought, she determined to talk to her husband, Ankuash, about these things. But whether he agreed or not to give some time to this vital part of Etsa's development, she knew that she was responsible as much as he was.

After talking with Ankuash, the two parents looked for opportunities to offer clarity about this most beautiful part of human life in this world. Sex, after all, was the bridge between the hungers of this world and the miraculous beauty of the spirit world. So Chipa and her husband made a point of redoubling their affections with one another, especially in front of their sons. This affection was in such stark contrast to the types of affection given to the boys that, if there were any confusion between parental love and erotic love, it soon disappeared. This bounty of affection also taught her sons that, in both cases, affection was a normal and beautiful part of being human and not a shameful thing. And Chipa was careful to talk openly with her husband about her own interest in boys as a young woman. Her husband joined in and shared how he'd been attracted to different young women when he was a youth. Together, the two parents shared their own sexual development in a way that helped Etsa remain as free and comfortable with himself as he had always been.

With each conversation, each passing remark about the beauty of an individual girl, and each approving smile at their son's growing sexual interest, Etsa stayed as easy with this new part of himself that he never questioned it. He simply enjoyed his nature as all of The People did. All, that is, except those who had listened to the Christian missionaries.

Chapter 9

Rachel was lying in her bed — giving her life "a good think" as her grandma had described such ruminations — when her bedroom door suddenly opened and her mother, a concerned look on her face, asked Rachel, "Honey, can you come down to the living room? Pastor Rob is downstairs, and he has some questions about what happened at one of the Youth Group meetings. He seems concerned, and he...he was wondering if maybe we could all pray together."

Rachel got up without verbally acknowledging her mother's words and said, "I'll be down in a minute, Mom" as she headed for the bathroom. She wanted to pause the way she'd been learning to do in her therapy, and she wanted to remember how she'd trained in her role-playing therapy with Theo. As she reflected on the scene downstairs, she couldn't help but roll her eyes at the euphemistic use of the term "pray together" — she well knew, from a thousand observations, that this was how church people and especially pastors confronted people. "Is there anything burdening you today that we could pray about?" "Is there anything that would get in the way of God hearing your prayers today?" "Sister, would it be all right if we prayed with you?" All of it was a sham for telling people that they thought that there was something wrong with how they were following, or, not following the Lord. *All of it is just so much...crap*, she allowed herself to think. It lets them stay way up there while their prayer victim is kept below them. Then it dawned on her that this was the kind of, *What did Theo call it?* That's right, spiritual abuse that she'd lived with for so many years. Her earlier resignation, full of dread, to yet another of these mild spiritual beatings was replaced by anger. She breathed again, seeking calm and telling herself, *I need to be in the smart part of my brain now. I need to be thinking.*

Some minutes later, Rachel walked into the living room, the air heavy with —what was it? Concern? Not quite that, but then what? Ah, fear! And Rachel realized that it was not her fear that she was sensing. She could see that on the faces of everyone present there was a look that she could clearly see was a primal level of fear.

Pastor Rob, not an actively evil man, took up the opening lines of the drama as he understood it. "Ah, Rachel, thanks so much for joining us," giving her the same hug he always had, obligatory and nonconsensual at the same time. His voice seemed to pour over those in the living room, "Pastor Skip and I came by because we had some concerns we wanted to review with you." His voice lowered a bit as he more softly said, "And maybe to pray over together. I understand from Pastor Skip that you've been having a difficult time." Rachel could see out of her peripheral vision that her parents both became a bit more focused in their anxiety, their eyes betraying that they knew nothing of this "difficult time."

Rachel met Pastor Rob's eyes in a knowing way she'd never experienced before. And she decided to do something that, as a Christian, she'd learned was dangerous. She decided to simply tell the truth and so she made her disclosure, "Yes, Pastor Skip discerned that I was burdened, and after talking to me and praying for me, he referred me to a counselor." Pausing a moment, she added, "I never told my parents because I thought it was personal."

Rachel's father erupted, "Rachel! You know that as long as you're under this roof and under my covering, you have an obligation to be in submission to my authority. Young lady, you *know* that. We've gone over this. We've had meetings, we've had Bible studies, we've prayed over it."

"Dad! I'm 18 years old. I know all that. I'm not saying I'm right, but I'm not going to say that I'm wrong about wanting some privacy. I think I have a right to that."

Just as Larry was about to talk over her, Pastor Rob broke in like a referee at a boxing match, "Of course you have a right to privacy Rachel, and we're not really here to argue that you don't." Rachel's dad, she could see, was biting his tongue over being overruled. Pastor Rob continued, "Actually we're here about what happened at Youth Group last week. There was a bit of a hubbub from what I heard." He smiled jovially, affecting that "nothing much to see here folks" sort of look. "I'd just like to hear your take on what happened."

Rachel paused a moment to collect her thoughts before asking, "Um, what did you want to know exactly? A lot happened that night."

Her father couldn't resist, and he prompted, "Rachel, just tell Pastor Rob what he wants to...," quieting only because Pastor Rob made a pump the brakes motion with his left hand while never taking his eyes off Rachel. He waited for Rachel to resume, and then, when she remained silent, he said, "There was a lot that happened in front of our guest speaker, Rachel, that frankly, we felt put the church and all of our guests in an awkward light."

Inwardly, Rachel breathed a sigh of relief realizing Pastor Rob was concerned primarily about the church's reputation and appearance, and, by extension, his own image. So, after thinking a minute, she said, "Well, I was listening to the speaker, and I found myself caught up in my thoughts 'cause I had a lot of questions, and then, before I could ask them, she finished, and then there was the altar call, and then everything just got really weird, you know?"

Pastor Skip nodded his head with her in agreement and seemed about to say so when the Senior Pastor preempted him. "Weird how, Rachel?" asked Pastor Rob.

"Well, I feel uncomfortable saying this because it might sound like gossip, and I don't want..."

"No, no, no, Rachel. This is not gossip, but frankly it's a call to you for help — because something serious could be going on, and I don't want people to start talking. I actually want to prevent gossip, Rachel, and you can help. You know, if there's anything to what I've heard, this kind of gossip could set back the cause of Christ in this city and all we've worked for. You can help us safeguard the reputation of the Lord. You know how the Accuser works, Rachel — we don't want to give the Devil any room here to develop mischief."

Again, Rachel was struck by the efforts at, *What else could you call this but 'damage control,'* she thought. She said, "Well, I could see how that could happen, I mean, I got the idea Amber was saying that Coach, I mean Coach Williams, got Amber pregnant."

"What!" Rachel's parents exclaimed in tandem as they looked agog, first at Rachel, and then at Pastor Rob.

"Well, thank you Rachel," Pastor Rob finally said, sighing. "This is pretty much what I've heard from others," and just then he looked knowingly at Pastor Skip, and they both nodded. "I have one more question, Rachel, and then I'm hoping we can all take this to the Lord in prayer. Is that OK?"

Seeing Rachel's nod, he continued, "So Rachel, you've known Amber for a while, and maybe you know her better than anyone really." Rachel waited without saying anything. He took a deep breath before continuing in a tone and with a look that made Rachel think that there was nothing sadder on Earth than the question he had to ask. But when he actually said the words, Rachel had to work so hard to not laugh that she was staring at the carpet for a moment. "Rachel, there's nothing on Earth I'd rather not say but I have to ask, but are you aware of any history Amber has had of being a stumbling block?" He continued, "I only ask, Rachel, because Amber basically accused a good man of the church, a servant of God and a beloved husband and a father, of adultery and fornication. I'd hate to think that happened, I really would, but in trying to hold everyone accountable so we can deal with this in a way that is best for the whole church, we need to know if she's done anything that would explain how a good man, a man who's given so much of himself to the church and the community, became so tempted. I think that this has devastated his wife too, Rachel, and that's why I ask." And here he paused, waiting for Rachel.

Rachel's thoughts were swirling about in her head like a slow-motion portion of a movie where there's a lot going on, but you have all the time in the world to check it all out. She could see how she'd come downstairs expecting everything to be about her, and she could see how Amber's words about Rachel "teaching" her how not to be pregnant were just so out of the realm of everyone's experience that those words hadn't even registered. No, what had registered was the fact that Amber had pretty much called out Coach Williams as the father of their love child. That solitary factor, sex outside the bounds, was what had registered in their minds. They were consumed with damage control over a scandal that threatened the reputation of every leader associated with the church. The whole point of the evening with the admonitions about the sanctity of life, the scriptural answer to the question of when did life begin, and finally, what happened to women who ruined themselves with sex before marriage — turning themselves into soiled tissues no one would ever want to touch, and then, to compound their sin, seeking out the help of an abortionist —all this was really nothing in comparison to the men and their reputations. She could already see that Coach Williams was, at the worst, maybe going to get chastised verbally, but that the drama unfolding here was eventually going to feature 16-year-old Amber as the scarlet woman who'd made the 31-year-old married man do what he'd done. And then, just like that, the slow motion stopped, and real time kicked in as she responded, "Ah...all I know is that Amber has had, like all of us, some hard times too, and she just really needs our love right now."

Pastor Rob flinched at the words he'd used so often, and everyone present looked more than a bit unsatisfied by Rachel's words. But what could they say? She was speaking the very platitude she'd heard countless times from each of them. Nonplussed at being outmaneuvered, Pastor Rob nodded, and then, turning to Pastor Skip, asked him to lead them in a prayer.

Pastor Skip did lead them in yet another in a series of seemingly heartfelt, but ultimately (for Rachel at least) meaningless prayers. Rachel listened with only the smallest bit of attention necessary so she could know when to hum "um hum" and murmur, "Yes, Lord" and finally, "In Jesus' name. Amen." But the rest of her consciousness was aware of Pastor Rob's attention that seemed to her to indicate he was wondering about just what game she was playing. She knew him now as an adversary.

Etsa had traveled far. Not as far as some of the men in the village might have, but Etsa was still only 12 years old, and his foot regularly gave him a great deal of trouble as he made his way through the emerald forest. He had made tremendous strides in learning and was a highly accomplished shaman, but he still felt sheepish when thinking of himself as a warrior. After all, his brother, Kujak, was now the strongest of all his friends and regularly excelled as a hunter. The young women seemed to think highly of him too. In fact, Kujak seemed to have far more confidence in Etsa as a warrior than Etsa himself.

Etsa was seeking his spirit animal that would guide him in this matter. After all, the forest had never let him down so far. So, on he trudged. Today's journey was taking him high into the mountains, and the animals were not the same as the ones he'd grown accustomed to in the riparian lowlands. An armadillo, a big one, crossed his path, and although not on a hunting trip, Etsa considered killing the delicious beast. What stopped him was the deep awareness of the spiritual nature of his journey, and he felt that hunting would detract from that awareness and from the pure intention that drove him. He considered that perhaps the armadillo was his spirit guide and found himself laughing too much to really consider it. Besides, he could see no parallel in his life to the primary feature of the animal – his armored hide.

He passed a deer and saw a sloth and briefly considered both before instinctively going on. He felt as though he'd know when he found his spirit guide, and he didn't see himself as fleet of foot or as delicate as the deer – nor as slow and lumbering as the sloth. As twilight began, he noticed an ocelot lying in ambush for whatever came along the trail below its perch on a low-hanging limb. Seeing the ocelot made Etsa think of the powerful jaguar and the smaller pumas that lived in the forest, but again, there was no spirit guide that seemed right for him. He wasn't powerful physically, and he certainly wasn't as graceful as any of these. He carried on until it was nearly too dark to see anything.

And then he saw it, just barely, high above and nearly invisible. It was a cloud-forest pigmy owl. He had heard of these birds from other travelers, but he'd never seen one. The mere fact that the bird was far from its normal haunts seemed to underscore the spiritual significance of its meeting. Just then the little owl's head turned, and Etsa realized he'd been looking at the back of the owl's head. He had been fooled by the clever owl's false eyespots. Etsa pondered how this probably fooled other creatures into thinking the owl was aware of their presence, even though he was looking the opposite way. The light was fading, but there was still plenty enough to appreciate the cryptic camouflage of the bird's overall plumage that allowed it to become nearly invisible even in the day. The bird was small, short, muscular, nearly invisible, cleverly misleading, and as Etsa knew, the harmless looking little bird was an opportunistic ambush predator who dropped quietly down from above on its prey in the daytime. Etsa thought of his foot and how disarming that was to people who didn't see his spiritual power. Now, in watching his spirit guide, Etsa learned to cherish his foot as an owl might cherish his plumage, as a wonderful bit of predator misdirection. To that he added his short stature and the rounded face that he'd been so often teased about. He would become invisible in the land of the enemy. Etsa thought of how the owl's habitat had been degraded by the ignorant invaders who would come to the forest and see only one thing rather than the whole of it, the interconnectedness of it. He thought grimly of how in his upcoming war with the barbarian nation of the north, that he was fighting as much for the endangered owl as for The People.

And then he smiled, and Etsa allowed his spirit to meld with that of the fierce little predator. Together they observed the larger world around them. Together, they watched everything. Together, they were perfect.

Chapter 10

Theo came home from work, quieting steps already quiet for a man with a cane and a limp, until he was satisfied that no one had heard his entrance. He paused to really hear the heartbeat of his home. Then and only then, he planted himself and loudly announced, "Hi, everybody, I'm home!" He waited a second, and then he heard his wife Jessa's call, 'I'm in the kitchen!'" A moment later, he heard his son Chris yell from his bedroom where he was probably doing his homework, "Hi, Dad!" Theo listened to these heartbeats of family life and then smiled, for all was right with his world in at least this one, small way. Everyone was safe, and everyone was home.

Entering the kitchen, Theo noted that his wife was busy making lumpia, the spring rolls native to her Philippine island homeland. Her hands were wet from preparing the food he loved so much, and she became helpless with giggles at her inability to return his affection as he hugged her from behind. "Hi, honey," he murmured into her ear. Then, noticing the duck eggs cooling away in a corner of the counter he added, "Hey, we're having balut too?"

"Not too many American men like balut. I always like buying it for my adventurous husband!"

Theo grimaced at her words.

Jessa never noticed his discomfort or his lack of buy-in to her observations. As an emigrant from "the P.I.," as she called the Philippine Islands, she was so satisfied with the miraculous turn her life had taken in her having married an American that this fact was the central fact of her existence — and to her own personal happy ending to the fairy tale that was her life. For her, being married to Theo meant as much as being married to a movie star — or even more, as she often told herself, because of Theo's faith. Theo's faith, and the way he lived it, meant to her that she would never be divorced and never have to put up with a mistress like so many of the women back home. He was still a celebrity to her, and to them, as she often reminded her family back home. And now they had a child together, a son!

Over the 16 years they had been married, Jessa's fawning over him had proven a bit cloying to Theo over time. He'd often ended up feeling like a trophy husband, not because of any particular ability or his income, but simply because he was white, an accident of birth. For him, his ethnicity had never been significant before coming to America. For him, now his white skin was merely useful to him in the pursuit of the great strategy that informed his every moment.

Just then, as the two were each lost in their own thoughts and in their ritual hug, their son Christopher came into the room. Unlike his father, the 14-year-old was strong and healthy and had never in his life experienced anything like the trauma Theo's patients had because Theo had made sure to protect his son from anyone who seemed likely to be abusive. With this goal in mind, Theo had limited his son's involvement in church — where, Theo knew, some of the greatest dangers to one and all lurked. Instead, Theo encouraged his son to play baseball and run track at school and to use his son's love of sports to motivate the boy to hang in there with the more boring parts of a young man's life such as sitting in a classroom and doing homework.

So far, everything Theo had planned and hoped for his son had come to pass. The boy loved sports, video games and desperately wanted to learn to drive, but he was also good at school and he was kind — at least, as kind as a teenager was capable of being without the benefits of the ayahuasca medicine Theo had been given back home. Nevertheless, Theo was utterly grateful for the miracle that was his son.

*****

Elizabeth Carter worried. As a single mother, she told herself, she had a right to worry. Her children both depended on her so much. It's not that their father, now remarried three years after the divorce, didn't love them. He does love them, she told herself, but not with a mother's love. It never occurred to her that there was anything out of balance with her utter devotion to her children. Yes, she had been confronted about using her kids to avoid — what, men? Intimacy? Sex? A professor at her grad school (And a Christian school at that! she reminded herself) had firmly insisted, after reading Elizabeth's required sexual autobiography, that she still needed some work on her own sexual issues so that she could avoid bringing her own sexual pain into her professional care of others.

Elizabeth felt that the professor was a bit presumptuous in believing that Liz's zeal for the Lord could possibly be evidence of... what, a sexual hang-up? Just now, thinking of this bit of history, she snorted derisively to herself, As if!

True, she hadn't felt comfortable with her sex life in marriage, but that was only because her former husband seemed so into it. Not for the first time she remembered how he seemed to take such pleasure in having sex, and that he seemed to like the sex more than he liked her. That just felt wrong in Elizabeth's world. It felt, and here she had to silently shake her head in how wrong-headed it all was, that he took pleasure in his sexuality or just being sexual. Like he could have enjoyed sex with...well, maybe not anyone, but at least, anyone he was in love with. No, for her, she mused, sex was only made OK because she was in love. Sex, in and of itself, was just...if not dirty, then at least suspicious. *That's it*, she thought, *sex is redeemed by love, by Jesus' love, just like I am.* Comforted as she was by these thoughts, Elizabeth recalled how she'd gotten going on this train of thought: her office mate, Theo Van Prooyen.

Theo's expressed views were certainly *loving*, she had to admit, but there was more to walking with Christ than just loving people as they were. There was the message too, the message about right living. *OK*, she thought, *righteousness.* She knew that the word may not be popular outside the church, but Elizabeth felt a responsibility to hold up the lessons of right living in Christ to her clients. She tried to be gentle about it, because, after all, she was a counselor, not a preacher. Nevertheless, she thought, "People need to know that there are consequences for stepping outside of God's will." Liz felt as though she'd be derelict in her duty as a sister in Christ to not speak up, say, when a sexually unhappy wife would confide in her that she'd been masturbating to try to take the edge off her loneliness and sexual frustration. She shared the same kind of tough love with men who'd gotten used to looking at pornography. She also counseled those wives who felt as though they had "a right" to take care of themselves with masturbation, or, far more troubling, the occasional wife who complained her husband was "a little heavy handed" or who "sometimes got too physical." With those women, she'd reinforced the same lesson that she'd been told from every pastor she'd ever known: "Remember, you're his helpmeet, a daughter of God and his sister in Christ. It's your job to win him to a more Christian walk by being a godly and submissive woman. In Jesus' name, you are a handmaiden of the Lord, and in Jesus' name, your husband will repent if you are faithful." Elizabeth had had to shake off certain personal doubts about how this approach hadn't really had the desired outcome in her own marriage. But, she reminded herself, *he's the one who got the divorce attorney. That's totally on him.* Having recalled how she had suffered in silence, well, most of the time, she felt more confident in herself, and she returned to the comforting harbor of the familiar words of submission. *Someday,* she thought, *I'll meet a godly man.*

Again, she realized that she'd allowed her own history to crash in on her thoughts about the situation with Theo. She had to do something, she realized, or, *People are going to think that he and I are of the same mind and I'm not like him. I'm faithful to the Word in a way he just doesn't seem to be,* she told herself. And with that, she made up her mind and placed her call to Pastor Rob Barton. After sharing at length her thoughts with him, Elizabeth felt a lot better. *Pastor will know now that I've got nothing to do with any soft soaping of the Gospel message.* And what she thought then was not only would her referral stream of clients from the church continue — and here she giggled to herself for how silly it sounded, but it was true after all — *I've been a good girl, too.* More soberly, even though Pastor Barton had assured her that he would keep their conversation entirely confidential, she reflected that she and Theo might have a conflict over this. She became frightened for a moment, thinking Theo might no longer share their office, as she considered how paying the office rent entirely on her own would add some level of financial burden. But, she mused, *Who knows, I could end up getting more referrals from the church because Pastor knows I've been willing to take a stand and that I wasn't wishy-washy.*

Etsa's 14th birthday was just a few months away when his father, Ankuash, came to him one day and began talking to him of the shaman's role in romantic feelings, sexual desire, relationships. Etsa knew that the quiet intensity of his father's instruction indicated the utmost seriousness of the subject before them. After speaking at length about the protocols, the ingredients, and the various spiritual forces at work in the hearts of the lovelorn, his father cautioned him, "Above all, my son, as a war shaman, you must maintain your purity if you are to be successful in your battle with the barbarians who have descended on our forest. There is a danger in failing to see the line separating doing good and doing sorcery. Men and women will never fail to want what they want and to seek it out. But you must remember that simply because someone wants someone, that does not mean you are responsible for helping them. People often want what is bad for them. You yourself may find that you can easily fall in love with someone who may simply be the wrong partner for you.

He went on, "There is an older and deeper magic than learning how to bend people's feelings to your will or to manipulate others for your own ends. I will see that you know what you need to know of these matters. I will see that you may know when and how to abstain from them so that someday you may have the domestic harmony we all want. There is nothing wrong with loving whom you love or desiring whom you desire. But the use of magic to overcome the will of another is a great evil. You must never try to overcome the will of the one you desire, because even if you are successful, such a beginning cannot last."

And with that, his father allowed Etsa to listen in as he provided consultation to the many people who sought his knowledge in obtaining love charms from animals, plants, and minerals. He listened as his father advised those who sought out the powerful anen – or magical songs used to enchant the will of the desired one so that their admirer would become irresistible. And in all of these matters, Ankuash spoke respectfully of the feelings, the desires, and the loneliness of The People. But he also spoke of the power of this magic – and how it was not only a magic against the will of the other, and so could never bring real love, as that can never come from anywhere but the heart. And finally, Ankuash always offered to teach anen to the men and women who sought him out so that the women might sing in their gardens to implore the spirits to help them grow in love and maturity, and the men might sing on their hunts so that, just as anen could attract game, the spirit world might attract the right partner to them in the right time. Such incantations respected love and others and oneself, he explained.

Some took Ankuash's words to heart and lived by them. Many more left unhappy. They clearly intended to seek out sorcerers because they wanted what they wanted, and they were already possessed beyond thought by their neediness.

Chapter 11

Rachel put her face in her hands and growled. "I can't believe the situation I'm in. Everyone is either mad or disappointed or just crazy! I can't believe this!"

Theo had listened patiently while Rachel poured out her frustration about all the drama following the guest speaker's pro-life presentation at the church. He sat in his chair listening, somewhat unreadable in his stillness as Rachel disclosed how creeped out she had felt with her father. And finally, he had smiled during her account of Pastor Barton's visit and how she'd skirted telling him about her trance work.

"This is such a mess. What am I going to do?" Rachel looked at Theo and seemed to believe he would know how she could put all these pieces back together.

Theo smiled a tad too long for Rachel's patience, and as her face took on a look of exasperation, she spun the single syllable word into several, "Well?"

Theo volleyed, "Well?"

"What am I going to do?"

"Great question. What *are* you going to do?" Theo seemed to be mocking her, and Rachel became confused. She said in a quieter voice, "I mean what *should* I do?"

"That's the real problem, isn't it, Rachel?"

"What do you mean?"

Theo's smile faded as he sighed, "I mean, that's what you always do, isn't it Rachel? You try to find the most moral way to achieve your real goal: Taking care of everyone else." he paused to allow his words time to sink in before he continued, "In this case, Amber, we have to include your dad, Pastor Barton, and, well, maybe the whole church, right? You're certainly wanting to know what you should do with Coach Williams and with his wife, right?

Rachel nodded, her head swimming with the mess she'd created.

"And you probably think that this, ah, this mess is something you created. Isn't that right?"

Rachel looked at him, wide-eyed again with wonder at how transparent she was for him.

Theo laughed, "Rachel, don't worry, I'm not reading your mind. In fact, any counselor who couldn't make that call should probably be taken out and horse-whipped." He laughed at his own humor and then noticed how confused Rachel looked. "OK, what I'm saying is that, for you Rachel, taking care of the needs of others has been the singular focus of your existence." "And," he added, "you're pretty good at it for such a young person. In fact, you're too good at it."

Confusion layered over confusion for Rachel. "I was taught that was what we're supposed to do, I mean, as Christians." She looked down, red-faced, "I mean, I know it's weird for me to say that, I mean about being Christian, I mean after, you know...."

"After all your trance work in letting your body help you with your pregnancy? Is that what you mean?"

"Yeah, I mean, maybe I don't have a right to ask, but isn't loving one another part of being a Christian?"

"Sure. But that's not what we were talking about, and that is precisely the problem. You confuse loving one another, not a bad idea at all, with providing caretaking for everyone."

"What's the difference?"

"Let me use an example outside of anything we've talked about. Would that be OK?"

Rachel nodded quickly.

"So, if someday you get married and your husband turns out to have a horrible drinking problem and one day he passes out after, say, vomiting all over everything, including himself, should you do your best to clean him and his mess up?"

Rachel sat still for a moment, taking in a scene that would have seemed unthinkable — but she knew that millions of women, millions of people faced situations like this all the time. Hesitantly she said, "I don't know. I mean, I suppose so, because if I ask myself what Jesus would do, I think he would clean him up — as gross as that sounds. I mean, it would be hard, but, yeah, I guess I should."

Theo smiled as if she'd gotten the answer just right. She couldn't have been more wrong. "OK," he continued "then let's say your future husband" and here he smiled more broadly, "went on to have this 'get drunk, throw up, then pass out' cycle regularly, say, once a week. For months. Or years. What do you think you should do?

Theo's emphasis of the word "should" did not go unnoticed by Rachel, but she had to respond with more confusion, "I don't know. I guess...."

"That's it, Rachel, now you're guessing. But let's say you guess you should, and then you do clean up after your beloved future spouse. Let me ask you: If you clean up after him, instead of letting him wake up in his cold, dried vomit, is he more or less likely to be aware that he has a drinking problem?

Rachel's head sank to her right as she widened her eyes, acquiescing, "Less."

"I agree. Now, is he more or less likely to address his problem if he's allowed by you to become aware that he's got a problem?"

Rachel remained still for some moments. "Oh. I see."

"Maybe not quite yet." Theo leaned toward Rachel as he said, "So, when you 'take care of someone,' it really isn't always helpful, is it?"

"No, I guess not." Seeing Theo's eyebrows rise in collective skepticism at her answer, Rachel committed, "No, it isn't helpful."

Theo's smile became more relaxed. "So, do you think it's still what Jesus would do? I mean, would the Jesus you know actually engage in a pattern of behavior that would contribute to robbing someone of facing the consequences of their actions?"

"No, he would not," Rachel said in that more determined tone.

"So, Rachel, what has happened in your young life is that you've normalized taking care of people by calling it love, and then you've guilt tripped yourself by calling it a moral duty, and that's why you overuse the word '*should.*'"

Rachel was silent as she took this in. "Are you saying that's what I'm doing with Amber?"

Theo stared at her and began gesturing clockwise with the index finger of his right hand as if to say, "And?"

"And Pastor Barton?" And again, that hand encouraged her. "And Coach Williams." This time it wasn't a question and the hand continued. "And my dad," Rachel said heavily before she finally added, "And everyone." She sank into the armchair with the sheer gravity of her new perceptions.

Theo watched her, seeming ready to wait until she was prepared to continue.

Tears filled her eyes as she said, "I am so messed up. I've been taking care of people my whole life. It's...my religion!"

"And now you can see that this, this caretaking business, has nothing to do with Christ." Theo summarized her thoughts and waited.

"I am so messed up," Rachel repeated.

"OK, so, do you know the story about Thomas Edison, the inventor of the light bulb? He was asked about how he felt about his failure in making the light bulb, an invention that he'd been working on for a long time. He said, 'I haven't failed. I've succeeded in learning 10,000 ways how not to build a light bulb." Theo smiled, waiting for Rachel to come around.

"So, I haven't been stupid. I've spent 18 years learning how not to have a life."

Theo nodded and waited. His eyes, made more owl-like by the rounded frames of his glasses, watched and continued to wait for Rachel's thoughts to move along.

Rachel took a deep breath and let go for a moment of how insanely she'd lived her life so far, and then, after taking a deep breath, she asked, "OK, so what do I do now?"

"Do you remember our last session, when I told you I had a plan?"

Rachel nodded affirmatively before asking, "When do we get started?"

"About five minutes ago when we started this conversation." Seeing her eyebrows mimic his own earlier incredulity, Theo continued, "The first step in changing is realizing the need for change, don't you think?" Theo paused, looking rather cheery, Rachel thought, considering the serious business she was facing.

"I guess so," she said conversationally, and then, seeing his eyebrows go up as another silent request, she again committed, "Yes. I agree."

Satisfied, Theo picked up the rhythm, "Now for the bad news: You're not going to be able to stop taking care of people." Then, seeing Rachel's jaw grow slack with dismay, he added, "At least, not for a while. And there's a reason for that Rachel — you take care of people the way people with a drinking problem keep drinking. Only now you see that your caretaking is just as compulsive. You are so good at it because you've practiced for so long that I don't want you to get discouraged if it takes a minute to change."

"But I already see what I'm doing, why can't I just stop?"

"Because, Rachel," and here Theo's voice slowed and became somehow more resonant in Rachel's mind, "because your caretaking behavior, sick as it is, serves you. It helps you avoid so much. And this behavior of yours, what some people call 'codependency,' is only a symptom of a larger problem. Like abusive drinking, your codependency has its own set of problems; for example, when you're so focused on others, you are failing to take good care of yourself, and so your life has more problems because you're so distracted. You have more serious problems that you're avoiding."

Rachel was intrigued, "What problems?"

Theo smiled reassuringly, "Don't worry. This is a problem that we've already talked about, remember? Post-traumatic Stress Disorder, PTSD."

"I don't see what you're talking about, I mean, I remember our conversation, but I don't know how all that stuff about," and here she gave an involuntary shiver, "about sex and my body and whatever, affects this other stuff."

"Long story short," Theo explained, "you use people-pleasing as a way of coping with your shame, which is a result of the trauma." And here he gave her a gentle look, "Make sense?"

Rachel nodded, her breath suddenly stolen from her.

"And all we need to do is rewire your brain."

Rachel laughed with the silliness of the idea, "Oh, is that all?" Then, seeing the serious look on Theo's face, she asked, "How do we do that?"

"Time and practice." Theo explained, "A long time ago, you became aware that you were really different from boys in ways other than your anatomy. Sometime, and I think it was before puberty, you learned that your body was both holy and somehow dirty, that men would consider any beauty you had as 'a stumbling block,' and that it was your job to make sure that you didn't allow whatever beauty you had to lead others astray. You learned that there was 'a slippery slope' from thoughts about boys, or kissing, or romance and the ultimate sexual sin which is?" And here Theo stopped in a sort of therapeutic 'call and response' waiting for his congregation of one to respond.

"Sex outside of marriage," Rachel whispered.

Theo nodded to encourage her before adding, "And what do we call that in church Rachel?"

"Fornication," Rachel said, looking down, no longer able to make eye contact. Her breathing grew shallower until it went still, and for a moment, Rachel felt as though she might faint. Theo seemed so far away and...

"Rachel!"

Rachel shook her head and glanced at Theo as he went on, "You see, we only have to talk about this sex 'stuff' a little, and your brain says, 'bye bye.' That's what we call dissociation, and you do it whenever this subject comes up in our conversation."

Rachel nodded, lost in her own thoughts for a moment. She knew there was something so spot on about what Theo was saying. But as clearly as he was right, she nevertheless felt as though she was going in and then out of two different states or two different places.

"So, are you OK if I continue? I need you to say out loud that you're OK and that you want to continue having me explain what's happened to your brain."

"No, I'm...I'm OK."

"I need the whole thing Rachel, please repeat what I said."

Rachel looked confused.

Theo repeated, smiling, "I'm OK and I want you to explain what's happened to my brain."

Rachel felt as though she had to shake cobwebs from her brain as she thought, "What were we talking about? Oh, yeah." Aloud, she said, "I'm OK."

Theo waited until she laughed and added, "And I want you to explain what happened to my brain."

Then Theo allowed himself to relax as he joined in with a chuckle. "OK, I'm going to make this a bit scientific just to help keep you in the room. We're not going to be processing any feelings for a while." Taking a deep breath, he continued, "You know what neurons are?"

Rachel nodded, "Cells in my brain, right? They transmit electrical impulses, and that's how the brain works."

"That's right, Rachel. And a long time ago, in the late 1940s a man named Don Hebb came up with a way of explaining what I want to talk about, and it's called 'Hebb's Law.' Some people call it 'Hebb's Axiom.'"

Rachel interrupted, "What's an axiom?"

Theo laughed and quickly added, "That's why we're gonna call it Hebb's Law." Seeing Rachel first furrow her brow and then relax into a smile at his joke, Theo continued, "So, you know how specialized parts of the brain do specific tasks?" Seeing a bit of confusion on Rachel's face, Theo added, "Like when you think about a movie, it's not like the whole brain is working on that movie or you'd forget to breathe." Rachel smiled indulgently and Theo went on, "So, when you taste something, a different part of your brain lights up compared to when you do math."

"OK, I think I'm with you."

"I think so too. Pretty simple so far, right?" Again, Rachel nodded, and Theo continued, "So when you feel guilty about something, a different part of the brain is activated, compared — well, compared with enjoying your food." He paused, waiting for Rachel to signal him with a nod of understanding. When she did so, he continued, "But what if every time you ate food and you fired up the circuit that said, 'Mmm, delicious,' someone else was guilt tripping you about eating too much, and they always told you to watch out for being fat or no one would like you."

Rachel spoke out, "That would be horrible!"

"Yes, it would. And, you see, that fear and guilt would be a different part of the brain from enjoying your food, a different circuit, right?" Seeing Rachel following along, Theo continued, "So, imagine this horrible thing happened repeatedly. Like, over years and from a young age. You have the 'Yum, food!' circuit firing up and every time it does, the 'Be afraid, fatty, you shouldn't eat that' guilt and fear circuit fires up. Over time, can you see how you'd only have to bring up food as a thought and that thought alone would light up the guilt circuitry?

Rachel nodded.

Theo concluded, "And that's what happened to you with sex." Rachel was very still with understanding, "Whether it was a thought about your body or holding a boy's hand or kissing or even thinking about kissing. You see, Hebb's Law states that, 'Neurons that fire together, wire together.' You can't even think about anything related to normal human sexuality without feeling guilty."

Rachel was speechless for some time before quietly murmuring, "Like brain-washing."

"Right."

"So, what do I do? I mean, I see what you're saying, and I see how totally messed up it is to do that to someone but, once it's done, what can you do?"

Theo got that minister of war smile on his face again, the one with the dangerous eyes, "We turn Hebb's Law loose on itself."

"How do we do that?"

"Well, every time you think of a sexual thought, whether it's about your future sex life or just how you like someone or want to kiss someone, no matter how small or how silly, you have that brain bomb go off."

"Brain bomb?"

"Sorry. A brain bomb is a thought that should be normal, but that instead explodes in your brain, wreaking havoc and destruction of the good and normal parts of you. Like a car that's designed to carry people around, and instead, is planted with a bomb to kill people. We are going to disarm your brain bombs, like a couple of bomb disposal specialists, by rewiring your brain circuits so that when you have a sexual thought..."

"Yes?" Rachel burst out impatiently, her eyes bugging out for effect.

Theo smiled before continuing, "When you have a sexual thought, you are going to pair that thought with another thought that taps into a very powerful set of emotions. Instead of guilt and fear messaging, you're going to use gratitude and love. You're simply going to say to yourself, every time you have a sexual thought or feeling, "Thank you Lord for making me a sexual being. I am perfect in this way, just as you made me."

Rachel had some trouble speaking, "I, I don't, I don't know what to say. First of all, really, that's it? It sounds too simple and easy. And second, I, I don't know if I can say that. It sounds... (and here she blew out her held breath) sacrilegious?"

As her minister of war, Theo's gaze became intense. "You must. It is your only hope. Indeed, it is the only hope of the world. Rachel, consider truth for a moment. Truth, real truth, is simple, isn't it? You were so messed up by a very simple application of Hebb's Law as used by others to, well, save you from yourself, from your nature. But, just like the rest of God's natural world, your nature is both wild and beautiful. You never needed to be saved from your nature. You have been robbed of your God-given sexual nature. It's time to take back what belongs to you."

Whether it was the tone or the words themselves, somehow Rachel felt a power come over her, a power that felt truly regal, that felt somehow, oddly remembered.

"I'm gonna do this. Now, how do I say the words again? Teach them to me." Theo honored her request and repeated the words, "Thank you for making me a sexual being." And after she had that, he added, "And I am perfect in this way, just as you made me."

Rachel repeated the whole phrase until she knew it in her bones. She left the office and got into her Lyft to go home, mindfully repeating her new sexual litany until it felt wholly hers.

Etsa and his family knew their time together was winding down. Indeed, all the senior advisors in the war council knew that the time was short. Etsa had become a living weapon and was soon to descend, like the little cloud-forest owl, into the heart of the enemy's homeland.

Ankuash announced a final ayahuasca ceremony before Etsa's departure so that they might all benefit from what most assumed would be the end of any travels into the spirit realm on the wings of the medicine. No one expected the barbarians to have any such medicine. But provision had been made for this eventuality, and Etsa was adept in the use of sacred breath work to return to the spirit world.

Falling into the earth after taking a particularly strong dose of the medicine, Etsa was swiftly met by the Queen of Tears. They communed in their spirits and Etsa felt the better for it because he knew she would always be with him one way or the other.

"You will never be alone, Etsa. You will feel alone, and you will make mistakes in your journey, but this is always true of every warrior, of every shaman, and of every war shaman as well. You are a man, after all. But hear me when I tell you that in your future trials, there will be both great heartache and great blessing. Yes, even in the land where ignorance rules, there are shamans and you will find them and receive comfort from their songs, their anen. You will find great comfort and great wisdom in them. And there is a special blessing, a surprise waiting for you to confirm all that you have learned: you shall learn to fly as your spirit animal flies. Believe it. And remember, remember everything. The war will be long, but you will prevail."

Chapter 12

As Theo left his office for the day, his mind was filled with the thoughts of his session with Rachel. He was aware, in the midst of all the stress of his client, that he too was growing increasingly full of tension. As he breathed to calm himself, he recalled his own much needed private litany, part of a larger liturgy he had developed to sustain him spiritually in his lonely outpost. He had discovered these words, those of the poet William Carlos Williams, with great joy shortly after he'd come to America and learned the language of these hostile, destructive people. Continuing to monitor the road as he drove, Theo spoke the words aloud, letting them cleanse him:

> "There is nothing to eat,
>> seek it where you will,
>>> but of the body of the Lord.
> The blessed plants
>> and the sea, yield it
>>> to the imagination
>>>> intact."

He repeated the lines, reveling in their magic, feeling the tribal medicine flow through him, until he pulled into the parking lot of his gym where he retrieved his gym bag from the trunk of his car. Once he started his labored trip to the entryway, again favoring his forever aching foot, he again picked up the litany.

"There is nothing to eat,
seek it where you will,
but of the body of the Lord.
The blessed plants
and the sea, yield it
to the imagination
intact."

He marveled how a man born in *this* country, in 1883 no less, could possibly write such words. *Maybe being an artist and a physician helped him bridge the distance between this violent American place and people to the unseen realm of the web of life,* Theo mused, not for the first time, as he smiled at his mind's worrying at an idea until he was satisfied. *Someday, and soon, I will know,* Theo said, thinking of his own death as he recited another of his comforting thoughts before returning his focus to the lines of Williams. He walked through the doors, greeted the desk attendant with a nod, and made his way to the locker room.

There, he nearly groaned at the pleasure of taking the weight off his clubfoot as he sat on a locker room bench. Unlacing his shoes and first pulling off the easy one was, for Theo, a sort of saving the "best for last," as his son used to say when he was little. Easing the orthotic shoe off of his clubfoot was painful — but oh, so full of relaxing ease — that he savored that moment and those sensations for a space.

As Theo changed into his swimsuit, he maintained his chanting of the poetry, feeling the words in his mouth as he continued to hold them in his mind. He had always felt each syllable just this way as he welcomed and wondered at the manner in which the words came to hold him, comforting him like a mother singing a lullaby to her beloved child. Comforting him like the Mother, as he remembered the medicine. Theo felt beloved. He was relieved to hear his mind's voice speak his Awajún name now, he was again Etsa, beloved of all in the universe.

Making his way to the pool, every step filled with throbbing pain, Theo smiled indulgently at the young swimmers who were unfamiliar with him and too young to know better than to stare at his foot. Still, the words he recited held him as he grabbed the

railing of the ladder at the edge of the water, "The blessed plants...
yield it to the imagination...intact," and with this final repetition,
he eased his swollen foot, his "sacred wound," as his adoptive father
called it, into the welcome buoyancy of the pool. Theo loved these
moments where he transitioned from one world to the next. It
reminded him of home with The People, which was funny in a way,
because The People had nothing like America's swimming pools.
What they did have was the medicine, the Mother, and he had
known a more abandoned floating in that world than he'd ever felt
while swimming. *But swimming,* he reminded himself, *is still pretty
good. No, it is a miracle for me to fly like my brother, the little cloud-forest owl.*

Theo savored the sensations as the wetness enveloped him,
Ah, just the right temperature! Swimming in indoor pools was an
unexpected wonder that Theo had never experienced at home with
The People, of course. At this point in his life, he knew that the
whole world knew of such things and that there were likely to be
pools in Peru, *Although,* he smiled to himself, *not in the jungles of Peru.*

Theo gently made his way to the end of his lane in the pool.
Holding onto the side, his forearm resting in the pool's perimeter
gutter, Theo reflected on how quickly the battle had been engaged.
He was not surprised, but after all these years, he was sincerely full of
gratitude to finally see the beginning of the end. Theo was grateful
to have been chosen for this role and grateful to the Mother for
allowing him to live in this time and place. "It's harder here, but the
sacred surrounds us wherever we are led," he thought as he pushed
off and began to swim down the lane to the other end. There, he
turned mindfully because of his foot — for him, there would be
no fancy flip turns like so many of the more athletic swimmers
who were training next to him. For Theo, dipping his head back
into the water as his trailing arm's weight came down on his head,
remembering to use the right foot to push off, was just part of his
ritual of swimming laps.

Theo had discovered repetitious movement as a gateway to an
altered consciousness as part of his readings in Buddhism. For
some, tea ceremony or archery was the path, but for the man with
the clubfoot, swimming and the trance breathwork were portals to
the spirit world. Theo sensed without thinking about it the slowing

hand of time. And as Theo began to feel the slowness creep into his consciousness until time seemed to simply stop, there was no more distraction, no more worry, and no more pain. He became simply a conscious particle in a universal consciousness. He could stay there forever. Flying. Flying through the forest of the universe.

Lap after lap, Theo continued to swim. Turns became as nothing, in fact every bit of consciousness of this particular time and place became irrelevant, as Theo became increasingly aware — not only of the vast web of life ("The blessed plants"), but of the vast web of all existence, of every molecule, of every atom. He reveled in the consciousness of the universe and of all time. This pool with its aggregate finish and perfectly heated water became his sea, watering the blessed plants of The People's medicine.

> The blessed plants
> and the sea, yield it
> to the imagination
> intact."

Yield it? Theo asked as a familiar sort of private "call and response" spiritual exercise. *There is nothing to eat but of the body of the Lord,* was the response. Theo had long felt it helpful to renew his vision by achieving this precise state where the tribe's medicine, Ayahuasca, became one with his Christian faith. Theo lost his sense of self in the joy of their union. An hour passed, and still he swam.

When Theo felt it was time, he finished his workout and completed his meditations with his closing salutation inspired by Paul's letter to the Ephesians, "One God and Father of all, who is over all and through all and in all."

Thus armed with his renewed awareness of the infinite oneness, Theo lifted himself from the Mother's embrace, saying goodbye to his sacred time in the pool and goodbye to the sacred water itself. He was filled with a knowingness of the sacredness of all things, and he was determined to bring all the world into this knowledge.

******

Pastor Skip sat in the Senior Pastor's office, uncomfortable as a spider monkey aware of a large snake. Not that the armchair itself was uncomfortable, but things were just too weird for the inexperienced youth pastor to know what to do. Just then, Pastor Barton entered wordlessly. He settled his weight into the office chair behind his desk, and then and only then said, "Thanks Skip, for coming in."

"Oh, no problem, glad to do it, you know I've been wondering…"

Pastor Barton continued as if he had heard no conversational banter. "I've asked you to be here today to discuss what has been happening with the youth group, Skip."

Skip Houton looked miserable. He had just bought a car (not too showy but still, it was new) and was making payments that were just the smallest little bit beyond his budget as a youth pastor at the bottom of the church's pay scale. He had only bought the car because he'd believed his position to be secure, and now, well, now things didn't feel secure at all. Not that the Lord wouldn't provide of course, it's just that….

"Well, Skip, what do you make of what's happened?" Pastor Barton's baritone voice wasn't raised, but the tension in his tone was unmistakable as he continued, "First of all, the church was very much in the position of being embarrassed by what happened last week. We were embarrassed in front of a nationally known speaker with a national ministry — and don't think everyone she runs into from now on isn't going to hear about what happened at that service."

"Well, it wasn't exactly a service Pastor, I mean, it's not on the schedule or anything as a service and…."

Rob Barton interrupted with a warning hiss as if talking to a dog, "Not the point, Skip! You should know that by now if you're going to be a pastor in this church."

There, thought Skip, *I definitely heard that.* His inner spider monkey was overwhelmed with fear by the hypnotic eyes of the boa constrictor before him. Instead of fleeing for his life, he wasted precious time thinking about his latest shiny object, *I wonder if I can still take that car back.*

Barton continued irritably, "You don't see, I suppose, that an embarrassment for this church is an embarrassment for *every* single person on staff here? For *everyone* who attends our church?" Seeing Skip nod nervously, Pastor Rob continued before Skip interrupted him again. He was in the mood to lecture, and he wanted an attentive audience. Reading other people and their faces had always helped

Rob Barton know what to do and what to think. "So, you see then that although the church's embarrassment is an embarrassment to the whole staff, most of all, Skip, it's an embarrassment for me as Senior Pastor." Skip nodded again and then stopped out of worry that he might appear too obsequious. It was hard to gauge sometimes how to get just the right amount of fawning without losing one's credibility. Pastor Barton continued, still annoyed at the head-bobbing idiot in front of him. He was only a peccary, but he felt confident he could devour this young spider monkey.

"OK, so besides trashing our reputation nationally, it seems that we have a bit of a problem with Coach Williams from Young Life. What do you know about that?"

"News to me Pastor, and frankly, I'm not even sure we can believe that there is a problem. Sometimes young women just get a case of puppy love or a crush or something, and the next thing you know they're fantasizing and then accusing good men, married men in the church, of the worst possible behavior."

"I know, I know. You're so right about that, and usually I'd just chalk all of this up to that. He's a good man, his wife is faithful and at his side in all this, and it would be a disaster for the church, worse than the gossip that McSweeney woman is spreading around the country." He glared at Skip and set his jaw implacably, "It would be in the local news Skip and *that*," and here he paused for emphasis, a trick he'd learned in Bible college hermeneutics class, "is simply unacceptable. You see that, don't you, Skip?"

"Well, I…"

Pastor Barton continued. His question was rhetorical, and he didn't want to lose his rhythm, "The *entire* cause of Christ would be set back in this city, *in this state*, for years to come. You do see that, don't you Skip?" Pastor Rob was starting to sound desperate as he felt the sensation of falling, falling into a very empty space. "They'll all be laughing at us, and there'll be nothing we can do about it then."

Skip wasn't stupid. *I mean, I was the quarterback of Tillman High's football team, after all…*

"So we need to get that girl, we need to get that girl and her — *situation* — under control. Thank God there's no baby on the way to make more of a stink out of this whole stinky mess. Speaking of that, do we know if she got an abortion? I just can't believe that could have happened because of the state of her family's resources, or lack of, should I say? And we've been very effective at closing down the local abortion clinics, so I just don't see that she could have got an abortion." Pastor Rob's voice drifted off as he became lost in his thoughts.

"That's exactly what I was talking about, she's a bit high strung, even for a girl, and she probably couldn't have had an abortion, and she probably wasn't even pregnant. As for any suggestion of Coach Williams having an affair, well..." and here his voice trailed off.

"Holy Family Skip, we're past that. His wife, or should I say, his *pregnant* wife is staying with him, and that's not our issue anyway. We can let YL deal with that, and if they don't deal with it, well, we just won't reschedule any activities with Young Life for a while, OK?"

"Sure, Pastor Rob, I was thinking the same thing and I..."

"But what about what she *said*? What was her name anyway? Amber, right. OK, what she said about learning how to become *"unpregnant,"* what the heck was that, and where did she get it from? I know, I know, we asked her, and she finally gave up Rachel Carson, but going over to the Carson house went nowhere. Rachel's dad's such a good man. Going to make a great elder. Anyway, there was something about her words that felt, I don't know, just a bit slippery, like she wasn't really answering my questions. It just feels like there's something going on."

Pastor Skip was thinking about high school and wondering whether he'd made the right decision about giving up going to college to work in ministry. The spider monkey within him knew how dangerous it was to be apart from the other monkeys; so easy to miss predators, they all seemed camouflaged into near invisibility. But he managed to nod his head thoughtfully before finally shaking it slowly, covering his bases with something verbal but noncommittal, "Well, I don't really know..."

"Now I get this call from Elizabeth Carter, Theo's partner at his office. She's expressing concern that Theo has been spreading false doctrine about Christian love and maybe even abortion. He's been a son to me," he added almost at a whisper.

Pastor Skip realized instantly that he'd never been like a son to Pastor Barton and that he was never likely to ever enjoy such a relationship with the man.

Looking up at Skip, Pastor Rob asked, "Did you ever send any of the girls in youth group to Theo for counseling? I mean, specifically, did you ever refer Rachel Carson to him?"

In a small voice, the soon-to-be former Pastor Skip said, "Well, yes, I mean you've always recommended him highly, and I knew she was depressed, and I just thought...."

"OK, well then, I guess Theo and I need to have a conversation." Looking at his desk and shaking his head, Pastor Barton sighed. "That's all Skip, you can go." Skip was worried, afraid, and filled with a weakness he'd never known on the football field. He somehow managed to push himself up off of the chair. Gee, he thought, I really liked that car. The spider monkey within him felt so much more comfortable with picking up shiny objects rather than spiritual ideas. After all, spider monkeys have no thumbs.

****

Theo entered his home as silently as always. He stood, knowing that in a moment he would yell out his usual announcement about being home. But before he did, he savored the utter peace he felt within every atom of his being. The war was going well.

Because of his mother and father's nurturing of Etsa's sexual development, he had always felt comfortable in his own skin. He liked being a man. He liked enjoying the sight of beautiful women. He liked the give and take of flirtation, and he had learned how to touch himself in order to take care of some of his sexual needs. He had always been taught that to be a successful war shaman, he would have to have these pleasures rather than their having him.

The Awajún, The People, had always, with a single voice, encouraged this approach to sexuality — that it was neither to be fought nor to be feared. For The People, sex and hunting were inseparable, linked in spirit. By extension, they taught Etsa, why not sex and war? Etsa had been trained to consider hunting, gardening, singing, magic, and sex all as spiritually charged. This teaching helped him greatly, but alone, this teaching was not enough to protect him.

Chapter 13

It was after Rachel had returned from her counseling appointment that her father came home from his work at the mine where he was a shift foreman. He was a hard man, but a fair one he hoped, who was used to giving and taking orders related to getting the job done. He struggled at times with bringing his workplace attitude into his home. His daughter Rachel seemed to find it increasingly irritating. He was confused because this attitude, so successful at work digging up the tons of material it took to make a profit, had become strangely self-defeating with his little girl. Larry sighed as he thought, *It is not easy raising kids in this world.*

He shuffled into the kitchen where his wife Stepahnie was at the stove preparing the family's dinner of spaghetti and broccoli. To Larry's mind, staring at this vegetable reflected the disappointment he felt about the way things were going in his home life: like it or not, you have to take what's offered. Approaching her from behind, Larry stumbled past her with an awkward pat on the shoulder. "Hi Hon," he said softly. Stepahnie was surprised at his unexpected touch, as she hadn't heard him arrive. Her body stiffened at his touch, but her startled response quickly gave way to a forced smile, "Hi honey, how was your day?"

"Oh, you know, the usual. Bored as can be one minute, and

then everything is a matter of life and death, at least for upper management. Say, Rachel home?" He added, "How's it going with her?"

Stepahnie smiled and said, "She seems fine, why?"

"Oh, I don't know. She's been acting and saying weird things about not going to the Purity Ball with me, and then there's this thing with her friend Amber. Boy, isn't she a piece of work?"

"Well, Larry, you know we shouldn't judge. You remember how her mom was? Back in high school? I think everyone slept with her."

Larry grunted in agreement and then tried to steer the conversation into safer territory. His wife, Steph, had never cottoned to any rumors of his own experiences with Amber's mom Luanne. Luanne *Burns* back then. Larry didn't believe for a minute that Stepahnie would be so invested in not judging people if she found out that he'd been playing around with Luanne when he and Steph were going together. "Yeah, but what about Rachel? Do you know anything? I just get the idea that things are somehow different for her lately. I don't understand what's going on."

"Oh, Larry, you get so worried about things. She's fine. Why don't you stop at her room and say hi when you go up to take your shower? She'd like that," she said brightly.

Not an effing clue, Larry thought about his wife. What he said was, "Yeah, maybe I should." He looked distracted for a moment, and then he made himself smile and added, "I will." His wife smiled and turned back to her domestic labors, and, just like that, he was dismissed.

Larry shambled up the stairs, his fatigue a weight he'd grown so used to that he was no longer even aware of it. He paused, briefly, listening for a moment to learn what he could. He heard only the clicking of his daughter's keyboard as she typed away on her computer. He knocked, paused a second, and then opened the door and walked in.

"Dad! I wish you wouldn't just walk in like that! I need you to respect my privacy," Larry took note of the fact that Rachel had protested before she'd even said hi to him. It irritated him.

"Well hello to you too," Larry grumbled. "What's up?"

Rachel rolled her eyes at her father's ignoring her and became resigned to the inevitable, thinking, *Not my will but thine be done*, as she closed her laptop and turned to face her dad. She sat silently, intuiting that this was not likely to be a pleasant conversation.

"So...what's up?" Larry repeated awkwardly as he settled his weight against Rachel's desk, towering over her.

Rachel got up from her desk chair and crossed her room to sit in the window seat, where she put her stockinged feet up on the cushion. Her room was, for Rachel, a place to escape her parents, and her window seat was where she'd spent innumerable hours of her young life reading. She settled in for whatever it was her dad was bringing. "Nothing special," she said.

Larry sighed again. "I was hoping to patch up whatever had you worked up the other day about the Purity Ball. You know you've made a lot of sacrifices keeping yourself for your future husband, and I think it's important for you to honor that. We've both put a lot into this, Rachel, and I want to support you through the years that you are under my covering."

Rachel was used to this kind of language — implying a woman was in need of a man, either father or husband, to "cover" her. I should be used to it, she thought to herself, I've been hearing it my whole life. She took a moment to consider her words and then gave truth a try. At least, some of the truth. "Dad, I'm just not feeling it anymore. I don't really believe in it. I don't really believe that a girl's virginity is all that." When she saw her father's facial expression of alarm, she added, "Sure, for some girls, whatever they want is OK with me, but I'm tired of being judged for whether or not my hymen is intact. I can't do this anymore."

Larry couldn't contain his exasperation, "I don't get it Rachel. What happened? You were all about this not that long ago, and now, it seems overnight, you seem to be backsliding in a big way." Larry couldn't help remembering his wife's remarks about Amber's mom and wondering about some sort of generational curse. Had he somehow set this, this rebellious attitude, in motion years ago?

As if reading his thoughts, Rachel said, "This is about me dad, and no one else. I'm going through a lot of growth right now, and I'm seeing things differently than I did when I was a kid."

Larry couldn't help himself, and he gave in to angry sarcasm, "Oh, when you were a kid? Like you mean maybe a month ago?"

Rachel felt herself grow icy calm. Must be the therapy, she thought with a private inner smile. Her next words were measured and calm. "I think I've been feeling different for a while, Dad. I guess I was just too intimidated to talk to you as honestly as I should have."

"Who *are* you?" Larry stared at his daughter as if he'd never known this person before. He was right in this.

"Dad, I've been learning a lot about boundaries and respect for self, and I just think it's important for me to speak my truth to you so that...so that I could grow in my integrity."

"OK, now I know where this is coming from. It's that therapist of yours, isn't it? He's the one who's filled your head with this nonsense. Young lady, you are supposed to 'Honor thy father and thy mother.' That is God's Word, and there is no limit on obedience to that Word so long as you are under my covering and living in this house. That's why there's no lock on your door and never has been. Your mother and I have the right to come into your room whenever we want and look at whatever we want. That's how we found that note that boy wrote you at school. Remember that? Privacy? Are you kidding me? Where in the Word of God does it say anything, I mean anything, about privacy? That is New Age crap that is contrary to the will of God, and don't you ever forget it!" This last sentence was said with such feeling that Larry's spit was flying out of his mouth. He continued speaking, but with his jaw clenched so tight that his words had barely enough space to escape his lips, "Rachel, I am very disappointed in you, and I'm taking a stand: Not in my house! 'As for me and my house, we will serve the Lord.' Joshua said it, God wrote it, and I believe it." Larry's breath was labored as he finished reciting the words he'd heard at church so many times.

Rachel sat quietly. When she was younger, she remembered how afraid of her father she felt whenever he talked to her like this. Today she wasn't feeling afraid. She felt as though she'd never be afraid again for the rest of her life. To the consternation of her father, Rachel smiled indulgently.

"Oh, you think this is funny?" Larry spat the words out, and before he had a chance to tell her just exactly how not funny this matter was, Rachel closed for the kill shot.

"It's not funny, really Dad, and I see that," Rachel said calmingly.

She continued, "But I don't think you're going to the heart of the matter. I think something else is going on that I don't think you want to talk about." Rachel spoke these last words in an even voice, but they hung in the air like a challenge.

Her father stared at her, only his eyes betraying his fear, as he said coldly, "I have no idea what you're talking about."

"I know you and Mom haven't been happy for some time," Rachel started.

Her father stalled, "Don't be ridiculous, Rachel. Your mother and I have a good marriage in Christ, and besides, this isn't even about us, Rachel. It's about you and your attitude."

"Dad." Rachel's tone was all she needed to make that one word a death knell. "You've been using me as a substitute for what should be going on between you and Mom. And it's still not going on between you two. But I don't care anymore. I don't care how lonely you are, how sad you are, or how much you need me. I am not ever going to be that person in your life, Dad. I can't take the place of Mom, even if she doesn't want that place, and I have officially stopped trying. I'm not going to be your little girl going on dates with you. You are not going to be my prince who makes my world so special. I will make my own world special, and I will find someone to share that with, or I'll just enjoy my life alone. But you are never going to be that person. What we've had in this, this *fixation* on my virginity and on my sex life or the lack of it, is feeling like some sanitized version of incest, and I can't stand it anymore. I want you out of that part of my life, and I want you out of my room!"

All the words, all the Bible verses, all the preaching from all of the rallies, the men's retreats, and the Promise Keeper meetings all fell crashing to the floor of Larry's mind. There was nothing to say to Rachel's charge of the word "incest" that Larry couldn't bring himself to repeat. He looked at the floor. He swallowed several times. In the end, there was nothing. He walked away, beaten.

Rachel sat quietly for several minutes, hugging herself and rocking in the window seat. A few tears fell down her cheeks. Then, after a long and deep breath, Rachel smiled a bit and walked back over to her desk and opened her laptop. She had to reenter her password, and then she ran her eyes over her earlier work. She had never pictured herself a writer before. *Dang, and I used to hate English class*, Rachel mused. Now she couldn't get enough of writing because she felt finally free, on the inside, to say what she'd been thinking. All she'd had to do was use search terms like "women," "recovery," and "fundamentalism," and a whole new world came alive. A world of powerful women who actually liked to think, to talk, and even to argue. About *ideas*. Her fingers flying over the keyboard, Rachel thought, *This is going to be good.*

She typed for another hour and then went to bed with her heart so light that she didn't even pause for a moment to consider the silent heaviness weighing on the others living in the house. Her father, wide awake and in utter dismay, lay next to his wife. Larry Carson felt sick. At least, that's what he told his wife when she'd asked him if he was all right. Larry was definitely not all right.

****

Rachel's sense of joy and purpose in writing her inaugural blog posting on the Fundamentalist Women in Recovery site was the most alive she'd felt in a long time. Her effervescence had somewhat fizzled out after hearing her mom remind her, "Don't forget tonight's Bible Study honey. Pastor encouraged us all to go, and your father and I are going with you. Won't that be nice for all of us to do together?"

And here they were. The ride over to the service would have been a quiet one because both Rachel and her dad were preoccupied with their own thoughts. But for Rachel's mom, it was just a grand opportunity to chatter on without interruption, and she somehow managed to catch her family up on all the many details of her life that seemed to her of the utmost importance. Now that they were seated in the auditorium, the torrent of words ceased as the worship team began warming up for the service. Just then, Pastor Skip came out to give the usual invocation, and to Rachel's surprise, there was Pastor Barton quietly sitting in the front row. He never comes to these, Rachel thought, *I wonder what's going on.* Precisely 20 minutes of worship later, she found out as Pastor Rob, and not Pastor Skip, took the lectern: "Let's pray for God's blessing on tonight's study of the Word." As the prayer ended, Pastor Rob used a peculiarly heartfelt tone of gratitude as he closed, "And thank you, Holy Spirit, for having led us into tonight's special service. And all God's people said..." "Amen," responded the congregation. And only then did Rachel notice that this particular Bible Study seemed to have a much heavier attendance than usual. There was an atmosphere of, *What*, she wondered. *expectation?*

Pastor Rob opened with a brief couple of announcements before he said, "Tonight's lesson from the Word may seem a little out of sequence for those of you who have been studying discipleship with Pastor Skip, but we've had some very special events occur recently, and I believe that tonight we could afford a break from the usual to reaffirm some of our most cherished beliefs." And with that, Pastor Rob called out, "Everyone, please turn in your Bible to Psalms 139, starting with verse 13, and he commenced to read,

> "For thou has possessed my reins; thou has covered me in my mother's womb.
>
> I will praise thee; for I am fearfully and wonderfully made: marvelous are thy works; and that my soul knoweth right well.
>
> My substance was not hid from thee, when I was made in secret, and curiously wrought in the lowest parts of the earth."

After pausing, Pastor Rob closed his King James Bible, "The one Jesus used," as he liked to joke. He placed his hand deliberately and dramatically on the closed book's worn leather. Then, he gave an audible sigh, as if he couldn't help letting all the world know that he had been greatly moved by this passage of scripture. He closed his eyes and moved his head from side to side a bit. "So grateful," his facial expression seemed to say. Then, opening his eyes, he smiled ruefully at everyone, and after a moment of quietly surveying the congregation, Pastor Rob took a deep breath and said, "I know unbelievers..." And here he shook his head both sadly and very condemningly at the same time, pinching his lips together, "Unbelievers cannot know the meaning of these words. They cannot know it, or they would not be able to continue their reign of terror on the unborn."

Rachel took a deep and calming breath, *Oh*, she thought, *it's going to be one of those kinda nights.* A year ago, she would have been transfixed with devotion. Three months ago, she would have felt so guilty. *Now,* she mused, *now I just feel...detached. I want to know what he's up to.*

"But *God's* children know, don't they?"

Scattered choruses of "Amens" were heard. Not good enough.

"But *God's* children do know, do they not?"

The chorus of "Amens" was stronger this time, as the congregation came to understand what Pastor wanted of them.

Ask and you shall receive, thought Rob as he felt his own confidence grow knowing that everyone wanted him to succeed, *They need me to succeed. In Christ's name.* Aloud he said, "Some of you may have heard rumors of what took place last week with our special speaker." Some of you," he intoned with gravity, "may have heard gossip. Not that you knew what you were hearing," as he offered broad dispensation to those who might have suddenly felt uneasy about what they'd heard. "But tonight! Tonight, you will hear Christ working among his people in truth and in justice." Here he paused and gave a more human, that is, relaxed smile before saying, "Young Sister Amber, please come forward."

Rachel watched in revulsion as Amber Duxbury, her head bowed in devotion and penance, walked down the aisle past Rachel's family. She stepped up on the stage and came to the lectern to join Pastor Rob, who put his arm around her protectively.

"We have a young sister in Christ who would like to begin her life anew tonight. And, yes, she has something to confess and yes, we will stand with her." He paused again as if daring anyone to disagree, and then, turning to Amber, Pastor Rob said, "Amber, I understand you have something you want to share tonight with God's family." He handed Amber the hand microphone.

Amber paused as if perhaps she was too shy to speak, and then she looked up, her eyes shining, and said in a contrite but strong voice, "I need to confess to everyone here." Here she smiled as she paused — just the right amount of time before continuing in a more joyful tone, her eyes aglow — "To my family in Christ." Here she paused, waiting for the cries of "Amen, sister" and "Praise God" to die down. She continued, "I misspoke last week when Suzie

McSweeney came to speak. What I need to say, what I should have said, is that I..." and here, her voice cracked a bit, "I got pregnant outside of marriage, and then, against everything I've been taught by Pastor Rob and Pastor Skip and Young Life..." Here Pastor Rob looked initially indulgent, and then, just for a moment, annoyed that he had to share the moment with Pastor Skip, much less YL. But Amber, after smiling up at Pastor Rob for a moment, returned to her performance, "I got pregnant, and rather than face God's consequences of my sin, I aborted my baby." And here Amber broke down, *Very effectively*, thought Rachel as she heard the gasps from the auditorium and saw her mother's head cock in sympathy as she looked at Amber and mouthed, "Ah, God bless you."

"I knew the narrow path, and I knew I should say no to my lust." And here some of the men in the auditorium squirmed to think of the teenager's lust. "And then, when the Lord gave me a child, I turned away from him and sought an abortion. I only hope God...and you all can forgive me." Again, Amber broke down in tears.

Pastor Rob, his face appropriately somber, squeezed Amber's shoulders in a modest, and decidedly not lustful, side hug. After a few minutes of "Bless you sister" and "Thanks be to God," Pastor Rob addressed Amber, using the mic so that everyone could hear, "I understand you want to do something about, well, to show your remorse and your repentance, Amber."

The young girl, still crying, nodded her head 'yes,' and then took up the mic like a pro. "I have named my baby Joshua, because his name means 'Savior,' and I believe Joshua has saved me." And here Amber raised the arm not on mic duty and addressed heaven, "He saved me!" And she repeated this again and again as the crowd looked up with approval and voiced more cries of "Praise Him," and "Thanks be to God." Finally, as the volume began to die down, Amber added, "And tonight I just want us to pray in a memorial for my baby Joshua, who died for me and for every other one of God's girls who is tempted to sin and then to cover up their sin with murder! Praise God!"

At this last bit, Pastor Rob looked a bit startled before he recovered — and remembering how all this mess had started with Amber's penchant for public address systems, reclaimed his mic from her. Looking at the whole auditorium of worked-up folk filled him with the gratification that he'd done the right thing in handling things this way. Finally, his eyes focused on Rachel for a moment, and his jaw tightened just the littlest bit. Regaining his concentration, Pastor Rob said "And now, let's get the worship team up here and thank God for what he has done among us. Mighty are his works." And as the musicians rallied, he finished up, "And let today be an annual day of memorial to Joshua and all the little Joshua's God is calling us to save!"

Rachel heard her parents join in the spontaneous shouts of praise as the electric guitars picked up the melody of a familiar song and all God's people sang the words projected up on the screen. Everyone was amazed. Rachel's own feeling was of horror at her part in this, *this whatever it is*, she thought. The wedge that had started separating her from her childhood, her family, and now her church was tonight unexpectedly taking even more from her familiar life. Rachel felt herself falling away from her old beliefs, falling away from what she used to know as true, but what so clearly was no longer true for her at all.

When the day of Etsa's infiltration into enemy territory arrived, Chipa held him and wept with joy and sorrow at what he was to do. Ankuash and Kujak walked with him into a small town where they found one of their trading partners. After making a costly trade, their trader, whom they'd known for years, agreed to take Etsa into the city of Lima. There the enemy had a forward base camp known as the American embassy.

Etsa's blue eyes and blond hair spoke for themselves, making it clear that he was neither native nor mestizo. The trader shared with the Americans the story Ankuash had given him about how the boy had been found as a baby some 15 years earlier and had been cared for in the remote jungles of the Amazon. Checking historical records, the enemy's agents were amazed to discover Etsa's origin story as the boy whose parents were naturalized Americans, missionaries in fact. It took some days, but eventually through some detective work, they were able to contact the mission agency and share the miraculous recovery of the child who'd been presumed long ago dead. By the end of a week, Etsa's footprint on his birth certificate had provided positive identification. The mission organization called his parents' home church and the leader of this church, Senior Pastor Rob Barton, insisted on what he called "bringing our boy home."

After seven hours of flying through the sky, Etsa landed in America. People from another sister church met him and guided him to his last gate and final flight to his parents' home city. Pastor Barton, his wife, and their own children were waiting at the airport. There were embraces. There were tears. There was terrible food.

He was in.

Chapter 14

"Thanks, Theo. Have a seat," Pastor Rob paused, smiling. "Thanks for coming in on such short notice, I know it's... inconvenient," he continued as he watched Theo moving unusually slowly, his cane nearly bending from the weight it bore, as Theo appeared to do his best masking the pain his clubfoot was giving him today.

"No problem, I'm always glad to accommodate you in any way I can, you know that. After all, I can never repay you for all that you and your family did for me when I came to this country."

Pastor Rob was only too glad to begin this conversation with a trip through memories of the past. He and his wife Charity had, after all, given the boy a home when he showed up. Not that it hadn't been good for him too, he thought, and not for the first time. "You know, I still feel the wonder I felt when I first saw you. It was like some sort of modern-day miracle. After your parents had been reported dead, we'd given up all hope of seeing the baby we'd blessed and prayed over ever again. And then, there you were. It was really a Bible story that came to life. Bringing you to America was something we all felt guilty about, you know, that we should have somehow done sooner." Theo's face broadened to allow for his typically warm, but noncommittal smile. Pastor Rob had seen this smile many times before, and he always found Theo's, *What was it?* he thought, before landing again on a word more New Age than he felt comfortable with, *Centeredness. That's it, he continued to think to himself, He's got this detached way of speaking as if it's not really a conversation we're having. Like he's waiting.*

Theo finally spoke, "Well, you've always had a hard time understanding that no one actually *brought* me to America. I chose to come." And then, speaking quickly to mitigate any potential conflict, he added, "And I owe everything from then on to you and Charity. Having a home from day one, getting an education, even my place in the community. I owe you both so much, and I know I can never repay that debt." And here his eyes shone with a sincere and untroubled gratitude toward his adoptive family.

Disarmed, Pastor Rob's voice took on a gruffness uncharacteristic of his role as pastor, "You know Charity and I prefer that you call us Mom and Dad."

"I know," Theo agreed, nodding his head, smiling in his gentle noncompliance.

Pastor Rob sighed, knowing that still, even after all this time, maybe especially now, Theo was never going to call him 'Dad.' "You know, when we got that call from the embassy in Lima, we just couldn't believe it. And then when we saw you, and we saw what looked like the image of your father's face on this 15-year-old boy, we knew it was true. You had somehow survived, and we had a chance to do something for two of God's children who had so selflessly sacrificed their lives trying to bring the Gospel to the Peruvian jungle. But you said you 'chose to come.' That's confusing, because I just assume everyone in that hell hole of ignorance would want to come to America."

Not for the first time, Theo indulgently tolerated the ignorance of those who presumed that The People were ignorant, but this time he did not smile. "I know I didn't speak English when I first came here, but even after I did, you never talked to me about — you never asked me about — my life in the jungle after my parents disappeared."

"Theo, I think we all wanted to spare you that trauma. And then, you have to remember that your days were pretty busy with learning

English, learning how to be an American and then becoming a believer. And then there was college. We had our work cut out for us, and we were all a little too busy to go over the nightmare of what happened to your parents. It just felt counterproductive, like, you know, living in the past. We were just relieved you were as normal as you were." Here Pastor Rob worked hard to not stare at Theo's clubfoot. "I didn't mean that you weren't normal," he said apologetically.

"Well, I wasn't normal. I wasn't considered normal even by the Awajún or even the shaman's family who adopted me and raised me," Theo's eyes took on a farsighted look as he thought back to the earliest days of his mission, and as Pastor Rob remained silent while his eyes became more focused, he revealed himself in a manner Pastor Rob had never imagined existed.

"I was always clubfooted, of course, and that meant a limited amount of play compared to the other boys who would dare one another to go hunting for *sajinos* so that they could practice with their blowpipes. Those *sajinos* were delicious," and here he sighed for the comfort food of his youth, thinking of the little peccaries in the jungle. "The other boys would wrestle and fight and try to get strong enough to be ready to defend the village against others. They were always thinking about being warriors, and for a long time, I really wanted to be just like them." Here he laughed, and seeing Pastor Rob's raised eyebrow, he explained, "I just think it's funny that I ended up becoming a shrink, you know, a therapist." Seeing the older man's continuing confusion he added, "In our tribe, it was the norm for warriors to take the heads of the enemies of The People and to shrink them, using them as warning signs to others considering an invasion." He laughed, "I was so amused to find that Americans called therapists 'headshrinkers' or 'shrinks.' I never thought I'd take my place among the warriors in such a spiritual way." He continued, "And then when I read about headhunters in the Bible I thought, OK, they were doing this even in New Testament times, you know like Salome getting John the Baptist's head."

Pastor Barton was listening with both horror and in rapt attention, hearing for the first time about a life so alien he never imagined it could be home for anyone who, well, who looked like

Theo. He didn't want Theo to stop talking, but some of his pastoral training must have kicked in because he stated, "Well, thankfully God had other plans for you. He had a beautiful plan for your life."

Theo pulled himself out of his reminiscences to acknowledge the remark, briefly making unflinching eye contact with Pastor Barton before saying with uncharacteristic firmness, "Yes, He did." Then Theo's thoughts returned to his beloved forest.

"But I knew I would never be like them in the way I first wanted to so much. You can understand how someone might want to fit in with the kids around him, right?" and here Theo glanced for a moment at Pastor Rob's nodding head. "So, when the shaman raising me told me I was chosen to be his disciple, I was surprised but happy."

"How old were you? How could you be happy about being a pagan's apprentice?"

"I must have been about 10 years old. I was happy because all my life I'd been raised by the Awajún, and they have a custom, no, an *ethic* I suppose you'd call it, that they call "*ipáamamu.*" It kind of means "mutual aid," like when those who are able help those who need it and then later, maybe sooner or maybe years later, the help is returned. It was a beautiful part of being in that community, but I always knew I'd never be able to aid anyone physically, you know, with my foot crippling me the way that it did." And here Theo became a bit sad at the remembrance of his sense of being so apart from The People at first, because he could never share ipáamamu with them, at least not until he became a shaman in his own right. Although no one would ever be so needy as to need the help of someone who could barely walk, much less run, Theo had discovered his own spiritual path of *ipáamamu* that allowed him to help his entire tribe far more than merely helping them bring in a crop or build their houses.

"But by the time I was maybe 12 years old, I knew so much about the web of life that sustained the tribe, the foods that we needed to live and all the medicines that the forest brought us, that I became something so much more than just another warrior. More than anything I'd ever imagined."

And here Theo's gaze became so otherworldly that Pastor Rob

had to ask, and he did it quietly because he felt so afraid, "What did you become?"

Theo's owl-like gaze returned to this world, and in the web of life he could see the mind of the large prey animal shining out of the pastor's eyes. *Yes, this little one knows something is wrong, but he doesn't know an ambush raptor is stalking him without moving, without even trying to do so,* he thought as he remembered details of the commanding vision he had received. Inside himself, Theo became happier in remembering the spirit world so clearly. He said, with authority, "I became a war shaman. Noting the uncertainty in his prey's eyes he continued, "I was trained in all the medicines of the Awajún, I know the *anen*, the sacred songs that help bring healing and wild game and love. I came to know how to help the young men in their spirit journey because I brewed the hallucinogenic *ayahuasca* liquor as my father, the shaman, had taught me, and I stayed with the young men until they returned, the fear of death no longer in them. Of course, I couldn't do this until I had completed my own journeys through the spirit world."

Here Pastor Rob could no longer contain himself, and he leaned forward, extending a finger toward Theo, "That is witchcraft! And that is all it is Theo. I can't believe I'm hearing you talk about this like you were taking a kid to Disney World. This is real Theo, and it's witchcraft," he repeated in his shock.

"We might have to agree to disagree on that. You once taught me that saying, remember?" Before Rob could explode in volcanic anger as he looked he would, Theo sniffed, "Besides, I am a new creature in Christ. I believe. And I am become God's righteousness. But that being said," he added, "I'll never be untrue to the spirit world or the beautiful plan for my life that both my visions and my Lord have confirmed."

Barton was confused and utterly nonplussed by the experience he was having. Theo had never before spoken to him in this way. On the one hand, he thought, *He's talking about drugs!* On the other hand, he heard the familiar words spoken by a true believer, and he could see that Theo was at peace with God and his beliefs. Rob Barton was going to need some time to digest these words and figure out how this conversation had gotten to such an unexpected spot.

"But that's not why you asked me to come in today, is it?" And there was the old Theo Barton had known for the last two decades — polite, soft-spoken, and eager to resolve conflict.

"Ah," and here Pastor Barton looked around trying to shake his head clear of the intrusive thoughts that had driven out all others, "ah...no, it's not Theo. Ah, I asked you to come in today to discuss an unrelated matter (*At least I hope it's unrelated,* he thought) that has some of the people in the church confused." Here Barton again paused, trying to catch his emotional breath. "You see, a young girl in our church, underage actually, mmm...Amber Duxbury, has come forward recently with a story that she'd recently become pregnant. She confessed that she'd had sex out of wedlock and that she'd somehow procured an abortion. After talking to her at length, Pastor Skip and I got the idea that she had some crazy belief that she'd terminated her own pregnancy, by, well, what sounded like some voodoo or magic and therefore nonsense." At least," he concluded, "that's how it sounded until I heard what you had to say today."

Theo continued to listen attentively, nodding his head to indicate he was following along, until he raised his right eyebrow in an economy of communication that conveyed the query, "So what are you asking?" and the accusing sequel, "You're really buying into this?" Eyes gently lidded, the cloud forest owl watched as the underfed snake spirit of the pastor became immobile. It was only then that Theo became aware that Pastor Rob was only underfed because, his conscience conflicted, he both served and fed on the flock who'd entrusted themselves to him.

Hopelessly, Pastor Barton finally blurted out, "So we're wondering if there's anything to that? I mean, come on Theo, you counsel a lot of people in this church, and I've referred half of them at least. People go to see you because they know you're a believer. For most of the church, even the idea of going to a therapist is like giving up on faith, and they're scared that to get mentally well they're going to have to give up their salvation and their eternal security." Here the boa paused for a breath, thinking he'd slithered beyond the danger. He continued, "I just need to know you're not promoting abortions, Theo. You didn't tell Amber Duxbury how to get an abortion, did you?"

Theo's eyes expanded in disbelief as he paused before answering. He let out a big sigh, mostly for dramatic effect, as his father had taught him, as he answered, "No Rob, I've never encouraged anyone to get an abortion or showed them how they might obtain such services." And as Pastor Rob let out his own breath that he'd been holding, Theo added, "I've never had any need to." The little cloud forest owl had good eyes but even sharper hearing, and he could hear the scales of the small boa constrictor scraping against the synthetic carpeting of the pastor's office. The little owl was watching in wonder as the undernourished serpent below him was so out of touch with the spirit world that he couldn't see, much less hear, the threat impending upon him.

Normally Theo's answer was the sort of "Neither hot, nor cold" kind of equivocating that Pastor Rob liked to hack down with as many Bible verses as necessary. Today was not a normal day. Not by a long shot. *But everything is going to be OK*, he believed without even being aware of the words. Theo looked at his prey with new eyes as his own spirit guide swelled to the size needed to ambush the narrow-eyed snake creeping up to his death — at least his death in Theo's world. The little owl, no longer so little, continued to breathe in as he grew into his attack.

"You see, here's the problem, Pastor Rob. It's the way the church talks about sex. And not just our church. All churches." And here Theo paused before declaring his orthodoxy, "I love Jesus, I love the Word, and I love praying," and here he smiled at the owl's pun, "and I have never seen a greater unforced error in human history than that of a great religion in conflict with a normal and inescapable part of human nature. Our sexuality deserves its own hymns and praises, and instead, we've turned it into an obstacle course that no one ever can complete. Our message, from as early an age as kids can understand, is that sexuality is shameful. We've got this list of 'Thou shalt nots' that doesn't stop until all possible ways of getting one's sexual needs met honorably and legally just evaporate. Our doctrines on sex are really just a form of abstinence porn, because clearly, we're so preoccupied with sex that we can't stop looking at it. We can't stop trying to control it."

Here, Pastor Rob took the party line, "I think we have a responsibility to uphold Biblical standards, Theo, and..." The owl's talons took a firmer grip on the predatory snake's throat.

"Biblical standards? You have to be kidding right? We're actually highly selective with the notion of 'Biblical standards.' Don't think I didn't notice how carefully you've avoided the subject of who got Amber pregnant. She's underage, and I've heard about the coach — and isn't this way of handling his abuse of her typical of us? Isn't it? Like any bully, we focus on those weaker and more vulnerable than ourselves, and often enough it's the women. Sort of like the story of the woman taken in adultery who was about to be stoned; I've noticed that very few people seem able to commit adultery all by themselves. Where's the 'Biblical standard?' now?" The cloud forest owl's beak shifted ever so slightly upward for his death blow that would peel the snake's scales from the soft meat beneath. There was no need for hurry.

"And the funny thing is, it's not just the women's sexuality that we're trying to control, it's everyone's. That's what makes abortion the big deal, so big that outsiders can see our preoccupation with abortion for what it is: A bunch of sexually repressed people obsessing over the money shot of control issues. How many people get to control another person's business with their doctor? We do. We claim the power of life and death over these people and their private lives. But never once did Jesus say that was to be our path. People can't even touch themselves because they've been so shamed about sexuality. And where's the Bible verse against masturbation? There isn't one, and you know it."

Rob offered weakly, "But Jesus said, 'Whosoever looketh on a woman with lust in his eye hath committed adultery in his heart.'"

"Yes, he did. And teaching those words of Christ the way that you do has always meant that people couldn't even trust the normal thoughts and feelings of attraction to one another because even the thought of wanting to be with someone, to touch and to be touched, is itself a sin."

The serpent twisted to face death's transformation. "Well, Theo,

I'm sure that your undergraduate work prepared you for a proper theological exegesis of that verse. I can't wait to hear it."

"No, they repeated everything I'd already heard from you. But when I started seeing how sick we were about sex, I started looking at the scriptures in context, and I realized that in that passage of Matthew 5 you just referred to, that there was simply a repetition of one of Jesus' most common teachings: Before we start looking down our noses at others and judging them, we would do well to remember that we have all failed in many ways. We've all been full of hate toward our brothers, we've all patted ourselves on the back for not being as bad as some, and we've all looked at others with sexual desire. You know I've had clients over the years who are so bound up with even their heterosexuality, which you think would be the easy one (and here Theo arched his brows) that they can't even say they're attracted to someone. They see a hot girl, and if they're attracted, they say, 'Oh, I would *so* marry her.' Everyone in the entire world, *everyone* except the religious knows that this is nonsense. Eventually even our own young people figure out what kind of nonsense it is too, and in the marketplace of ideas, they will move on. You've seen the stats, Rob, there are more pagans in the U.S. now than there are Presbyterians. People are already moving on." To say the cloud forest owl punched through the serpent's scaly hide would be an exaggeration, because the feathered predator didn't need speed. His beak was strong enough to pull the top off a car now. The butchery of his prey continued. "What we have done is create a religion that is utterly divorced from the reality of nature, of our own human and sexual nature. We no longer provide meaning and context to the most intimate part of human existence. Instead, in our control of others, we have raced toward irrelevance."

"When we reached for political power, we sold out our values. And now, no one is even listening anymore. And we don't deserve to be listened to. We are utterly irrelevant to the way people live and the decisions they make. And this situation has nothing to do with Christianity or Jesus or the Bible. It's about our becoming a sex cult along with our favorite political party."

Pastor Rob said nothing. His eyes became vacant as the forces that had always animated him bled into the polyurethane carpeting of his office. The spirit owl feasted on his fresh kill until gorged on the soft tissue. Then and only then, Theo rose from his chair and limped into the hallway for home. First blood. The battle lines had been drawn.

The first year away from home was difficult, but not without gain. His foster parents found one surviving picture of his parents. They were holding the little baby he once was before they left for the jungles of Peru. He stared at their happy faces and their hair, blond as his own. He took after his father in the shape of his face and his mother in his short stature. Etsa also had a new name, one chosen by his birth parents he was told. So, from then on, he was known as Theo. By the time he was 16, Theo spoke English well enough to attend high school. What little celebrity he had by virtue of being "the boy who came from the jungle" melted away quickly when his fellow students realized he wasn't strong, wasn't personable enough to be compelling, and worst of all, when Theo revealed himself to be, unforgivably, an intellectual.

Voracious for knowledge, the young man soon outgrew his need for language tutors and advanced to where he was able to go from regular classes to advanced placement ones. It was in AP English that he was stunned to discover the shamans foretold by the Queen of Tears. In America they were called "poets," and their songs were called "poems." Theo experienced a shock when he realized that this entire people seemed to be spiritually deaf to the magic in the poetry.

One day, Pastor Rob took Theo and his own children to the water park. The experience reminded Theo of his early stunned experience of travel in the spirit realm. There was water but not a single animal: no fish, no birds, and best of all, no snakes or caimans hiding in the shallows. Clinging to the edge of the pool, letting go for moments where he fluttered his legs and his closed palms into the water as he'd been taught, Theo realized he was flying through the water. Weightless, Theo was no longer crippled, but felt free to fly like his spirit guide, the owl. He watched the other children. Some were swimming a clumsy crawl. He determined he would learn to fly in the thick atmosphere of clear water. He would fly here for the rest of his life.

Chapter 15

In the weeks following his confrontation with Pastor Rob, Theo wasn't surprised to see his referrals from the church dry up. Cancellations from his current clients also increased, as the word somehow got out that Theo was no longer the golden child of the church's leadership. Even his referrals from the national group Focus on the Family had dried up when, Theo assumed, Pastor Rob had withdrawn his endorsement of his practice. Just as Theo's ability to earn a living deteriorated, he couldn't help notice his office mate Elizabeth's practice seemed busier than ever.

Theo had known this was coming, and although he wasn't happy about seeing his income shrink, he felt good about the way his mission had finally begun. He sighed thinking about how very long ago he had been charged with waging this war. He had spent his adult life studying his enemy, after all, and even he had wondered if he would be ready when the time came to begin the enchantment that would end America's war on The People, and, in fact, the entire web of life. Taking stock at this point, he felt that not only was the war progressing satisfactorily, but that he had reaffirmed who and what he had always been, even in the spirit world before he was born. All was going according to the visions of his shaman father and confirmed by his own journeys through the spirit world.

Just then his son's voice broke in upon his thoughts. "Hey Dad? Can I interrupt you?"

Theo looked at his perfect, perfect boy and felt again the bright infusion of love he always did whenever Christopher and he were together. Where Theo was a pilgrim of the spirit world, Christopher seemed altogether thoroughly planted in this one. Where Theo sought meaning, his boy, he noted, was never more alive than when he was playing sports, moving, running, jumping or even wrestling other boys. Christopher didn't have as much interest in cars as some boys, but he certainly could hold his own in any of the latest video games. Where Theo as an infant had presumably lost his parents forever, his son had never experienced any significant trauma.

It wasn't the case that they had nothing in common but some mutually shared DNA. The two were at ease with God, with the opposite sex and with one another. In fact, although each had his own life, both father and son savored their times together. Christopher was well aware of the fact that his father adored him, but rather than a selfish feeling of entitlement, he only felt an immense sense of reassurance from this knowledge.

Can we go swimming?" Christopher asked.

Theo smiled at the thought. Of all the sports and activities Christopher liked, many of which were just sources of physical pain for Theo, only swimming offered the two the opportunity to experience what Theo imagined other fathers and sons experienced when playing a game of hoops or going on a hunting trip. With his own adoptive father, the tribe's shaman, Theo had been free to share the lessons of botany, philosophy, religion, and of course, their travels through the spirit world. The two, Theo reflected, had a closeness that Theo could feel sustaining him every day even now after so many years apart. Despite the fact that he was now as busy as any commanding general with an army in the field, Theo would never say no to his son's asking to go swimming. *Besides*, he thought, *I can spend some time in the spirit realm.* What he said aloud was, "That sounds great son, I have a pretty light day at work, and I don't have to go into the office until later this afternoon."

In the car all the way to the pool, the two talked about the sort of unimportant things that seemed inconsequential, but in reality, wove the two together even further in their bond as father and son. And then, finally, there was the water itself, a place where conversation ended, and the cloud forest owl could fly at will through the infinite web of existence where even ideas had life. As hard as Theo had worked to blend in with the world of the invaders, he never could nor would relax as fully as he did in the water.

Although the young boy was incomparably more athletic than his father, that difference was minimized in the water. Theo had, over the years in this alien land, become a very competent swimmer. Once he realized the utter privacy offered by planting one's face in the water for lap swimming, he quickly mastered taking only the briefest moments on alternate strokes to sip a bit of air before plunging his head back beneath the wet medium. Theo never lost his identity in his spirit journeys, but instead became more intensely himself. He smiled to himself, flying through the water. He remembered that the jaguar spirit also loved to swim, and that the forest jaguar was a strong swimmer. Once, he had even watched a limping jaguar plunge into the water of the river to sink his powerful jaws into the vertebrae of a caiman twice his own size. Dragging his prey up onto the bank, the predator glanced across the water in Theo's direction, and their eyes seemed to meet. Then Theo knew that this jaguar and he were closely bound, and that someday this lesson of predation would repeat itself. Indeed, it was repeating itself now in his own fatherly lessons to his young and perfect son. Theo took a deep breath and shoved off from the pool's edge. Life was as it should be.

****

After showering at the pool, the two swimmers headed home. There, Theo dropped off his son, who had the rest of the day off from school to play video games and hang out with his friends, while his dad went into the office for a couple of appointments.

Theo arrived an hour early because he realized he had some case notes he really needed to make while his memory was fresh. He was at the standing desk when Liz came out of her office with a former client who'd canceled his appointment with Theo a few days earlier. He looked both sheepish and defiant as he barely glanced at

Theo on his way out. Theo gave an inward sigh at the development and then made eye contact with Liz.

Liz looked as though she were teeming with so many ideas and feelings that she might explode. She was aware of how it must have looked to Theo to see one of his clients come out of her office. Normally she would have merely shared a superficial smile and tried to pretend to be normal – her preferred way of living in recent years. Today she would have been open to the idea of putting off explaining to Theo what was going on with some sort of plausible deniability, perhaps something like, "Well, I don't really have a release of information to talk about that right now Theo. You understand don't you?" She knew Theo would understand because he was a professional and because, well, because he was Theo. Liz knew, deep within herself, that Theo was the least judgmental person in her world. Feeling the truth of this knowledge, Liz made her decision on the spot.

"Theo. I need to talk to you. Would that be OK?" Theo looked at Liz – her tone was unfamiliar in some way, and then he placed it. It was a genuine tone, without any guile. Intrigued, he set aside his patient's chart and turned his whole attention upon her, asking simply, "Sure, what's up?"

Liz hurriedly said, "Can we go into your office for a minute?" Theo gestured with his outstretched hand to say, "Ladies first," and then followed Liz out of the records room into his counseling office. Theo, like his spirit guide, never expected anything but was instead an observer of everything. He sat down and waited attentively, his round glasses making his face look all the more owl-like.

"Ah...I have something going on that I need to talk to you about, and I don't know where to begin, and I feel horrible about asking you for help because of some of my actions lately. This whole thing feels unbalanced and weird, and I am just not prepared to deal with it all."

Theo paused, knowing he had no need to say anything because he knew Liz was in too deep to stop now into her, whatever it is. *An entreaty? A confession?* he thought. But, although guarded, Theo remembered that she was not his prey. Recalling what he knew of Liz's life, he remembered that, long ago, she had already been preyed upon. He spoke reassuringly, "Please, Liz, you know we can talk about anything, and I'll do everything I can to help you."

At this unexpected and thoroughly undeserved kindness, Liz's face went from that of tense rigidity to utter childish helplessness. Tears sprang from her eyes involuntarily, and after glancing heavenward for strength, Liz began, "I, I have no right to even ask you for help, Theo. Much less to expect any. I have done something terrible, and I know that you'll probably never forgive me for it, but something even worse has happened, and I don't know what to do about it." There she froze for a moment as tears, mucous, and shame filled her face's every cavity.

"Whatever it is Liz, we'll work through it."

Liz recognized Theo's tone for what it was, a calm and confident statement of faith. Faith in himself, in her, in the God they shared in common. He, not she, was the one with faith here, and as Liz reflected on that truth, she cried all the harder. After blowing her nose, hard, into the tissues she'd carried into the office, she continued, "I've been such an idiot, Theo, I don't know how you stand me."

"Please Liz, let's get to what is really upsetting you," Theo encouraged.

Taking another deep breath in a day of deep breaths, Liz blurted out, "My daughter Bree, you know she's only 13?" Here she paused to gather herself before blurting out, "Well, she's pregnant. And Theo, she *cannot* be pregnant. You know what I mean? She's too young for her life to be, to be...ruined." And here Liz again broke down for a few moments before composing herself. "I know we got into a discussion about this just the other day, but it's different when it's real. And Theo, this is getting pretty damn real for Bree and me. It's not a theology discussion anymore."

"So," he teased her with a smile, "you're saying that the discussion we had recently about abortion and how clear the Bible was isn't so clear anymore?"

Liz sighed, "I figured you'd hold my feet to the fire on that Theo, and I don't even blame you. I'd probably crow too if I were in your place."

"No Liz," Theo interrupted, "that's not what I meant at all. I'm not nearly as concerned about being right as you seem to think.

It's just that I wonder how you will live with yourself if you do anything to interrupt this pregnancy. I mean, I know you'd be OK if God Himself brought a miscarriage, and maybe you've even been hoping for that?" He noticed Liz's guilty look as she turned her face away before he continued, "I mean, whatever you do, you and Bree would have to live with your decision. You would have to take responsibility for your choice, and I know that can be hard for some people when it comes to managing their sexuality."

Liz realized that they were no longer two colleagues having a conversation, not even a personal conversation. She had become the object of Theo's intervention, and he was qualifying her for her suitability for that intervention. She centered herself, "To be honest, I don't know. I mean I don't know how I would handle an abortion, or how Bree would for that matter. She's just so young..." and here her tears again interrupted her words.

Theo noted and then disregarded her pain now as he pressed ahead, "Liz, I know you're familiar with the usual choices: Have a baby and raise the baby, or have a baby and then go for adoption, or have an abortion. Am I right in thinking those are the options you're reviewing?"

"Come on Theo! I know all that, but I, I don't know, I thought maybe there was something, I don't know, something else."

"Maybe there is Liz. Maybe there's a way for you and Bree to take a different path that doesn't include abortion. Something personal. A really personal decision that no one could make for you, and no one could make for your daughter. What if there was some way that your daughter could choose for herself whether she wants to be pregnant right now?"

"Well, I'd say that train has already left the station. At least that's what I heard Pastor Rob say the first time I heard him talk about the pro-choice position." And here Liz looked up as if trying to remember that moment before intoning the words in a remarkable imitation of Pastor Barton, "The time to make a choice is before a woman has sex. By the time a woman has decided to have sex, she's already exercised her pro-choice option."

"Yeah, I've heard him say that too." Theo nodded, "But what if it was just up to your daughter? What would she choose to do?"

Liz reflected, "I, I don't know Theo. I really don't. If I'm being honest with myself, I know I can be a bit pushy." Glancing at Theo's enlarged eyes and his forefinger pointed subtly upwards, she laughed and admitted, "OK, I can be really pushy."

"You realize that, for there to be a real option, a real choice, no one can control anyone. Specifically in this matter, Bree, young as she is, is faced with a situation that is rather more adult than she's used to, and normally in the church, we all are taught that parents should make this decision for their children and that decision should be to complete the pregnancy. Always. No matter what. No matter who or how this decision will affect others. In matters such as this, the Church has a track record of teaching us that it is our duty to serve the Lord and to carry a pregnancy to term."

"Well, that sounds right. I mean that's what I've been taught. Isn't that right though?"

"Well, Liz, was the Sabbath made for man or was man made for the Sabbath?"

"Huh? Theo, come on, this is serious, I don't have time for theological puzzles."

"Elizabeth, I'm not playing," Theo said sternly. "I'm asking a question that was asked in the New Testament and you need to answer it before you make a choice. Is it our job to serve our faith or is it our faith's job to serve us? He paused, wordlessly, as if he had all the time in the world and he was just giving it all to Liz.

"I guess that I've thought for a long time that God wanted us, no, needed us to serve him. So, I guess I thought that meant we were supposed to serve our faith. Now I'm not so sure." Liz looked thoughtful as she continued to ponder the question.

Theo nodded his head, "OK, well Liz, consider this: Does God have needs? Does God have needs that we could meet? Does He have needs that we might deny him and thereby ruin His day?"

Liz laughed quietly at the thought, "No, I guess not. No, I guess God serves us, now that I think about it, not the other way around." She looked sheepish to consider how confused she'd been in answering such an easy question.

More somberly, Theo continued, "It matters Liz. It matters because this is a choice that your daughter can make, and you as her mother would have to deal with that choice because it is entirely about her. You can't decide for her one way or the other. Can you live with whatever Bree decides for herself?"

Liz was still for some minutes, thinking it all through. Thinking about a future where she could hold such a decision over her daughter and guilt trip her for the rest of her life — and a different future, where she was not her daughter's judge, a future where her daughter wasn't even hers but belonged to herself. And then she realized that loving her daughter had nothing to do with her daughter's choice, because loving her daughter was about her own capacity to love. Liz didn't know what Theo knew, but she did know that after today she was a changed woman. She cleared these thoughts out by shaking her head and said, "I get it Theo. My daughter was never mine, I don't own her, I just...love her. This is up to her, and, I suppose, up to Him. I mean, if there is a way to do this that doesn't involve abortion."

Theo smiled and breathed for a moment. "OK Liz," he said in a workmanlike tone, "You know I've done a lot of training in hypnosis right? Well, I have something to teach you that only you can teach your daughter. From then on, this is all in her hands. Are you OK with that?"

Liz nodded her head.

Theo continued, "OK Liz, have you ever done any trance work before?" And as Elizabeth began talking, Theo started matching her breathing and the pace of her speaking as he started the initial training induction. The slow day he thought he was going to have turned out to be pivotal in the battle ahead. "And Liz, as your breathing slows and your face continues to relax, you find yourself aware of your own rhythmic heartbeat. Can you hear it now? Indicate 'Yes' by simply smiling.

Theo waited until he saw Elizabeth's smile grow significantly before continuing, "Now you can relax your face and just enjoy feeling your body's lifeblood as it's pumped through the body. And as your body stills and becomes quieter and quieter, as your listening becomes clearer, you can feel your blood pulse through your extremities, starting with your neck. Smile when you feel that pulse. OK, you can relax your face. And now I ask you to turn your mind's eye to your arms and the blood flowing through them." After he saw her smile, he continued to direct Elizabeth to be aware of her entire body's blood flow through her legs, and finally, down into her womb. Elizabeth, twice-over a mother, was an ideal candidate for this work, and she quickly learned how to increase and decrease the flow of blood to her womb.

"And now Liz, please direct your attention to the blood in your womb and begin drawing that blood back into the body from the womb. And as your womb's blood supply drops Liz, and you become aware of that, please allow your smile to form." Minutes later, and after additional direction, Liz smiled. Success.

"And now Liz, with the remaining blood still in your womb, I'd like you to send a message of stress from the womb, a message that sends a clear message that you and your womb are not ready to host company just now." Theo knew that this task was quickly accomplished by the smile on Liz's face, and then he guided her, "Now please hold your focus on this feeling and remember this feeling. When you choose to come out of your trance, you will remember everything we talked about today, and you will remember exactly how you found your body and learned to be master of it. You will remember, and you will have confidence sharing all of this with your daughter at a time and place of your choosing, should you decide that she too has a right to her body and all of its gifts.

Liz was smiling before Theo had even finished, and when she came out of her trance, she was calm. She took a deep breath and asked, "Where did you learn that? That was amazing!" She didn't wait for an answer, and Theo didn't offer one. He simply listened, and then Elizabeth said, "I see no reason to be afraid of any of this. This has to be of God, or He wouldn't have made us this way." She smiled warmly at Theo, and then, just before their goodbyes, she laughed, "I never thought I'd be thinking of myself as 'born this way,' but it's true, isn't it?" And with that, she gave Theo the most authentic, warmest hug she'd ever shared — and then headed home to her daughter. The two of them had things to talk about.

Every Sunday morning Theo accompanied his foster family to church. Ditto for Sunday night and Wednesday night, too. Pastor Barton would have insisted on it, but he discovered to his delight that he never had to resort to spiritual strong-arming his foster son.

Initially, Theo attended the services to study the enemy's culture and habits, looking for an advantage. Then, over time, his interest became more academic, as he read scripture and studied church history. He found much to admire about the person of Jesus and grew to first like and then love this shaman, God's son, who taught the unity of all and that all were children of God. In the end, in spite of all the services, the church itself and the pastoral staff, Theo came to believe in Jesus as the Anointed One.

Pastor Barton was again delighted to see the young man stand up and go forward to publicly acknowledge his commitment to Christ. He would have been stunned to think that Theo thought of Jesus as a fellow shaman and spiritual advisor on how to destroy the insanity that was killing the planet.

By now, Theo was swimming laps regularly at the YMCA. There, as he logged his miles, he used the sacred breath work to talk to the Queen of Tears and their new friend, Jesus. Theo thought of the word "conspire," and its meaning "to breathe together." It fit. The three of them were breathing together, conspiring together.

Chapter 16

Stepping inside his home, Theo planted his feet as he usually did before bellowing out to one and all, "I'm home!" Normally, Theo's son came to greet him, and his wife would call out from the kitchen, beckoning him to come and give her a hug while she cooked. Today, Theo was greeted only with a silence punctuated by the unfamiliar sound of a furious sort of kitchen industry. Curious, Theo made his way to the kitchen, where Jessa was using a spoon to murderously scrape at the inside of a bowl. The sound of the metal spoon against the metal bowl was disturbingly percussive, even militant. He recognized his wife's expression and knew instantly that she was angry. He knew just as quickly that her anger was directed at him, because if it were anyone else, she would be venting with him instead of ignoring him.

Theo took a single sharp breath as he assessed the situation and recalled the routine he'd developed over the years of his marriage. His earlier life in the forest had prepared him perfectly for his true purpose, but like many other men, he found that domesticity was still a bit of a mystery to him. He'd never encountered any women like Jessa. She did everything he'd hoped for from a life partner, but then there was this. No matter how much love he'd poured into their relationship, no matter how many blessings, no matter how much material wealth graced their existence, none of it mattered when she was hurting. She was in her own private world, and God help the man or woman who didn't join her in acknowledging her pain.

In the past, Theo had attempted to solve whatever problem or problems seemed to provoke these domestic dramas. Over the years, 15 of them altogether, he had learned a lot, and he approached his wife as he would a beautiful but very dangerously wounded forest creature — perhaps even a spirit from another world that was lurking along a well-trod path, looking for something, anything to devour in a mistaken belief that doing so would fill her belly and so her pain might end. Theo had long ago accepted that some sort of distraction would only temporarily assuage the emptiness that lay within his wife. Theo knew what was coming: Jessa would likely attack him, at any moment, as she usually did when she was in this kind of mood. Learning this had helped him understand that like himself, Jessa had a home in another world — only her world was one where there was never peace. Reviewing all that he'd learned took but a moment, and as always, he smiled. After getting a drink of water from the fridge's door, he sat down at the breakfast bar.

He opened the battle, "So, what's wrong?"

Jessa had been angry before Theo arrived, but she became even angrier at Theo's calm presentation. "Nothing," she said in her clipped tone that dared him to believe *that*. The more Jessa thought about Theo's calm, the more eager she was to see that placid face become as enraged as she felt.

Knowing that Jessa's one-word answer was only the opening nod of acceptance to a long and dangerous dance that lay ahead of them, Theo took his time, nodding his head. In these opening moments of the dance there was always an unspoken argument about, well, the argument: Who, after all, was leading the dance? After waiting just long enough to quietly sip his water and convey his first iteration that he was to lead this conversation, Theo answered, "Are you sure?"

"Of course I'm sure, why wouldn't I be sure? Nothing's wrong," Jessa said angrily. She hated Theo, *When he's so...so, like this*, she thought. She had tried to be a good wife and a godly one, but she knew in her heart that she really didn't love Theo the way she thought others might have expected of her. Out of guilt, she had tried to love, but she'd never really had that warm feeling of kind adoration she sometimes observed in other women. She wasn't sure she was even capable of having such a feeling for anyone really. But she liked it when she was angry with Theo; her feelings felt more real, more "legit" as her son liked to say.

Theo knew his wife didn't really see him and also understood that she was incapable of loving him. He'd come to accept that marital love was not to be his lot in life, at least not for now. *And that's all right*, he thought, *considering what's at stake in all this, and besides, she's given me a wonderful son.* Theo had come to see that his wife was ill, and over time, he had come to accept her as she was. He smiled at the sense of familiarity as the dance continued. After all these years, he knew every rock, every stump, and every pitfall of the familiar dance by heart. *Next up*, Theo thought, *she'll be attacking me from the position of victim.*

As if on cue, Jessa stopped trying to destroy every kitchen implement she owned, and staring hard at Theo, her eyes filling with tears, she barked, "Why do you do this, Theo? Why on earth can't you get along? Why do you have to make everything so hard? You know what this does to me. I am so ashamed."

"I don't know what you're talking about."

"Really? Really? You don't know that the whole church is talking about us and how you're caught up in that girl's abortion?" And here Jessa just glowered at Theo as if to say, *You know exactly what you did, and you're responsible for the reaction to it!*

"OK, so what's happened?"

Theo's calm voice and warm eye contact meant less than nothing for Jessa, because she knew that if he really cared about her, he'd be as angry and upset right now as she herself was feeling. So she spat out, "Nothing! Nothing except an hour ago I was on the phone with Pastor Rob's wife, and Charity was telling me about the hurt and the scandal that the church is going through over that girl and her abortion, and she said you had something to do with it. I know you're at the bottom of all this Theo. I can tell. And you know I hate it when you do things like this!" And, with that, Jessa threw her spoon across the room at the wall.

Theo became very still. He had spent years pondering Jessa's words in these situations. He knew his wife was unable to give or receive love, and he knew that this sickness was taking a heavy toll on her, slowly it was true, but still. *She will always be hungry for something no one can give her*, Theo thought, *but she's not entirely wrong in what she's saying.* He wondered at his wife's uncanny intuition and knew it as one of the enemy's magical weapons.

"So, what did Charity say?"

"She asked me if there was anything we needed prayer over, Theo. Then she offered to come over and pray with me. For me! And there's nothing wrong with me here!"

Theo thought about that last disclaimer for a moment and resisted the urge to smile at the idea that "there's nothing wrong with me" was said with enough anger to suggest that Jessa was angry enough to hit Theo. She'd done that in the past, but that had been long ago.

Theo regarded his wife's enraged face and knew her anger for what it was: *So afraid of abandonment. Social stigma is no red badge of courage for her, no matter who it is or why it is that she's getting the message that she's somehow 'just not good enough to be loved,* Theo thought. Then he decided to make a small disclosure.

"Maybe I am somehow involved. That girl Amber was never a patient of mine, and I don't know her, but she was a friend of one of my patients. Maybe something I said was taken out of context or something. But I've never advocated abortion, Jessa. You know that, don't you?"

Jessa remained glowering at him, skeptical at best.

Theo continued, "Pastor Rob called me into his office and asked me all about this too, and I told him the same thing. I'm working within man's law and God's law, Jessa. I have nothing to feel bad about."

Jessa's shoulders slumped for a moment, and then her rage returned, reanimating her, "I don't know what you've done or what you haven't done, Theo. I just know you've put me in this situation, and not for the first time. It's always something with you. In the early days, it was about your crazy views about the environment, and

I'll never get past how you became known for helping those whores who get pregnant without even being married."

Theo realized that the life he'd offered Jessa wasn't easy for her. *But then,* he thought, *no life would have been easy for her. No one could have brought her everything she needs because her needs are bottomless.* Aloud, Theo said softly, "I know being with me hasn't been easy, Jessa. I just don't know what else to say when people talk about the whole planet like it's theirs and they can do as they please with it."

"OK Theo, now we're getting into it. Pastor Barton calls that 'Dominion Theology.' And you know that we're to 'Fill the earth and subdue it.' That's in the Bible, Theo, and for a guy with a theology degree, you should know that," she added in condescension.

"Actually, my degree was in Christian Studies," Theo said quietly. He could otherwise ignore the insult about his undergraduate degree, but he couldn't resist reacting to the slur about the women he'd helped, "And women who've gotten pregnant and who don't want to be pregnant aren't whores," Theo continued, his voice taking on an edge. "They are just like you or me; they've had some rough times, maybe made some bad decisions, but they are human beings who are as worthy of God's love and professional care as anyone."

"But you use *hypnosis* to help them Theo." Seeing his surprised look, she said, "Yeah, I know you don't talk about your work at home, Theo, but I've heard those women saying, 'Oh, Theo, he's so great' and 'Oh Theo, he helped me so much' and 'Oh, and I didn't even know that Christians could use hypnosis.' And guess what Theo, they can't! You should know that by now. I know you were raised in the jungle, Theo, but come on! You can't do magic here in America!"

"Do you really think you know about magic, Jessa?" Theo said calmly but with a growing anger inside him. "Besides, everything I do in my office with my clients is accepted by my licensing board. As a professional, I am bound by the rules and ethics of my profession. I don't do magic, I do therapy."

"Well, if your hypnosis therapy is so powerful, and you can help so many people with it, including those whores, then why don't you heal your own clubfoot?" Seeing Theo become suddenly silent, Jessa sensed weakness and so pounced. "Huh? Theo, why don't you heal your foot?" she asked, her voice dripping with contempt.

Theo had fallen silent because he was ashamed of allowing himself to get sucked into yet another insane argument that solved nothing and went nowhere with Jessa. Gathering himself and feeling solid ground beneath him again, he patiently explained, "Jessa, trance work is a science thing, it's not a miracle thing. I can't hypnotize a new foot into existence."

Frustrated by her tantalizing closeness to a now very much evaporated chance at victory, Jessa gave up trying to provoke Theo. "Just go away," she said bitterly.

Theo made his way, painfully, toward the back of the house to his son's room. He sighed. It wasn't just his foot that was hurting. After knocking and then waiting a moment, he opened the door to his son's room, where he saw his son at his desk, presumably doing his homework. But despite his father's nagging, his boy had his headphones wrapped around his head. Theo watched as the 14-year-old's pencil scribbled its way across the page and then began again on the next line. His angry heart calmed, and his irritation faded as it always did when he watched his son *Being...being perfect*, Theo thought, and he again recalled the Bible's description of sacrificial lambs and thought the phrase applied to his beautiful son. "He is without blemish, without any defect whatsoever."

Oblivious to his father's shutting his bedroom door, the teen worked away at his algebra, his homework nearly completed. He was looking forward to a night swim with his dad.

Theo had approached his Christian faith as he did all of his spiritual instruction. As a Christian Studies major after high school, Theo gave himself over to deeper studies of scripture and church history. "How," he wondered, "had such a beautiful message become so corrupted in this country? The variety of perversion is nothing short of stupefying. How on earth did they learn to embrace the materialism of the prosperity gospel and come to believe that financial wealth is always the will of God and that it is always a sign of his approval? Jeez, he thought, didn't anyone ever read Job? Then he researched the church's position in the culture wars in America. They've made it all about sex. He began a mental list as he saw that Christianity in America had become a sex cult, outlawing and repressing homosexuality, contraception, abortion, masturbation, sex education, divorce, the reality of the transgender phenomenon, non-binary couples' adoption of orphans, keeping gays out of the military, fighting marriage equality, premarital sex, and, midway through the 20th century, even labeling oral sex between married couples as perversion. No wonder they need so much money, they have so little love and so much hate for their own bodies. They need something to fill that empty place.

But Theo, as knowledgeable and open as he was, was in many ways still an immature young man with no viable path to getting his own emotional and sexual needs met, at least, those beyond what masturbation could satisfy. In this world, he was alone in his battle planning and without any real friends. Despite his learning and his wisdom beyond his peers, his neediness grew within him, and he remained naïve regarding love.

Then he met Jessa, the daughter of a Philippine immigrant family who'd brought their only daughter with them to the United States when she was 14 years old. In addition to simply being attracted to her beauty, her looks were also comforting to him because she somehow reminded him of the women back home. She was in his college, so clearly her faith was very important to her. And although Theo didn't think of it at the time, the two easily bonded through sharing the wounds they had in common. They were both "strangers in a strange land," living the reality of Exodus 2:22. Their peers considered each of them a bit odd, and both were doing all they could to fit into a culture that was so different from home. Neither had anyone who was more than a casual friend; both were alone, and both were very horny – although Jess hadn't had the language to even begin thinking about her sexual needs, much less discussing them in any but the most moralizing of terms.

But none of this was the undoing of Theo's first effort at domestic bliss. He had fallen in love, and she had professed her love for him. And Theo was still so young that he irrationally thought that their love was enough, that it was all they needed. He never doubted it for a minute. He was so very wrong.

Chapter 17

Monday morning, still muscle weary from another late swim with Christopher, Theo slowly got ready for the office. He was not possessed of a great deal of enthusiasm this particular morning, because he was still emotionally hung over from his conflict with Jessa. He shuffled from bedroom to bathroom, from shaving to showering, from the mechanics of getting ready for work to the reality of his practice having crashed and turned to rubble. Theo didn't need to review his appointments for today because he knew that he only had one, an older couple who didn't attend the same church that he did. He thought for a moment and then realized that he really didn't know anything about their church affiliation whatsoever – or even if they had one. A rueful chuckle escaped his lips, as he realized that for all their self-absorption, the evangelical church as a whole had an influence far outstripping its actual numbers in America. He thought of the millions in this country who didn't worry themselves for even one second about, "But what does the Word say?" He gave another dark chuckle and shook his head.

Before even coming to this country, the medicine had revealed to him the grand strategy needed to save The People, and, indeed, the entire world. Theo had never lost his focus on that strategy. If anything, after living in the States for so many years, Theo had found the evangelical church to clearly reveal itself as the enemy's strategic center of gravity and the true heart of darkness in America. Without the moral cover given by the church, the attacks on the environment would have long ago been given over to the idea of being stewards of the earth. It was true, he thought, without the moral misdirection on social issues, America would be looking a lot more human, even kinder. Theo, absorbed in this line of thinking, gave a third grim and knowing chuckle at how the evangelical church, along with a lot of other churches, had become caught up in what Theo called "The Sex Wars."

Theo, in his mind's eye, ticked off the many fronts on The Sex Wars as if they were each an all too familiar worry bead. *Controlling whether gays can marry or adopt a child, whether trans citizens can serve in the military, whether the poor along with the rich can get abortions, whether kids can have a sex education, whether women will ever truly be respected as equals.* He shook his head silently in disgust, *They've learned absolutely nothing since the Civil War and their support of slavery as a Biblical plan for civilization. And even then,* he thought back to his history classes, *they still did their best to control whether or not people could marry outside their race.* Then Theo came back to the present and realized he was going over all this familiar ground as a welcome diversion from thinking about his marriage. Taking a deep breath, Theo straightened himself up, stretched his shoulders back, and said aloud, "Time for breakfast."

Marching with a bold limp out to the kitchen, Theo was surprised to find that his son was sitting alone and seemed unusually focused on his bowl of cereal. He asked, "Where's Mom?"

Without looking up, Christopher said, "She said she needed to get out of here. I think she's meeting someone for breakfast. Maybe Mrs. Barton?"

Confused, Theo stood still for a moment before remembering that Charity Barton hosted a women's prayer meeting every first Monday of the month. "Huh. That's different. Mom doesn't usually go to that. Does she?"

Christopher shrugged disconsolately, still avoiding eye contact.

"Chris, what's wrong?"

Christopher's eyes were already filled with tears, "I don't want to talk about it."

Theo was speechless. He knew of no reason why his son would be so upset. Then, looking more carefully at the boy, Theo gently took his son's chin and said, "Look at me." There it was, the red handprint on his cheek that Chris was trying to hide.

"So Mom hit you. You know that's wrong, right? She had no right to do that."

"I know, Dad, I know. We just got into it, and then she got mad. I know you talk all the time about having an abuse-free home, but I don't think Mom gets it," and as the boy was speaking, the tears flowed down his cheeks.

"What happened?"

"She was saying stuff about you, and I just disagreed with her. I wasn't being a smart ass or anything. Really," he reassured his father.

Theo took a deep breath and sat mulling over the morning's events. He nodded his head, "I think Mom gets that from the way she was raised." Then, seeing his son dart a look at him, he added, "That doesn't make it right. It just helps me, at least, to understand her. I think she's pretty scared right now."

"She said you were a useless failure, Dad, and then she said I was just like you," more tears flowed as the mucus filled his son's sinuses.

"Do you believe I'm a failure? Or that you are?"

"God no, Dad. I just didn't like to hear her saying that."

Theo pondered for a moment how he was going to help his son over the years ahead deal with the emotional abuse that was sure to eclipse the physical abuse the boy had experienced over the years. Jessa's behavior was their family's dirty little secret, Theo mused. *Maybe that secret needs to come to its end.* Aloud he said, "Hey, you know I feel the same way. If you give me a minute to eat something, how would you like a ride to school?"

Christopher loved being spared the two-mile walk to his high school. "Yeah Dad, that sounds good," he said as he began putting away his tears and composing himself for his day.

Theo limped over to the refrigerator and opened the door to try to get some inspiration for breakfast. He would be very early for his one appointment, but a ride was the best he could offer the boy right now.

****

After dropping Christopher off at school, Theo glanced at his watch and saw that he was still well over an hour early for his first appointment. *It doesn't matter,* he thought, *I don't really have anything else I have to get done today. Maybe I'll clean up around the office and get some filing done.*

His mind was still filled with trying on the mundane details of what looked to be a very uneventful day, *Unless bankruptcy is an event,* he thought and then added in a flash of good humor, *No, it's more of a process Theo. Bankruptcy is a journey, not a destination.* He laughed at his own humor before rounding the corner to the hallway leading to the counseling suite, where he saw a sight that stopped him like an invisible wall. A dozen people or more were milling around his office door.

Oh God, what now? Theo thought, dreading some new attack from the sorcerers in this evil land. Theo made his way through the crowd of strangers, "Excuse me. Excuse me, excuse..." and here his voice drifted off. Theo was never surprised in this country of unending evils, until suddenly, he was. His office waiting room was packed with more strangers, some seated, others standing about. Some were talking excitedly in hushed tones, and one or two, he noticed, seemed so invested in avoiding people that they seemed to shrink in upon themselves.

Still wondering what was going on, Theo caught sight of Liz, waving to him, "Hi, Theo," as she squirmed her way through the crowd of, Theo finally noticed, all women. At the mention of Theo's name, the electricity in the room pulsed larger, and suddenly everyone was conjoined by an unusually focused interest as they all stopped talking or trying to look invisible while Elizabeth explained, "Theo! All these people are here to see you!"

"Ah...what...what are you talking about, I don't understand," Theo stammered.

"Come with me for a minute," Elizabeth took Theo by the elbow and excitedly drew him into her office, "Excuse us...excuse us...thanks," where she closed the door. "I got here this morning, Theo, and a bunch of them were already waiting for the office to open. When I asked what was going on, they all started talking at once, and it took a minute to sort out that somehow, they've all learned about you from the internet, and that's where their stories all diverged. Some said it was Instagram, some Snapchat, and some of them said they'd found out about you on YouTube. But, Theo, they're all women, and they're all wanting to talk to you about taking charge of their bodies." And here Liz leaned in and lowered her voice, "Theo, they're all here because of some pregnancy issue. I think they want or need the same work my daughter and I did."

Theo was pushed back on his heels for a moment. He knew. He'd known that the strategy was going to work, and he knew that he'd been told to be patient and wait for the moment the universal mind would bring to him, but...the moment was now. He was so moved that his eyes misted up as he stammered, "Liz, I...I don't know what to do with this. I have a 10 o'clock in an hour with the Raymond family, and I don't have anyone to...and I don't know where...or how...." Elizabeth laughed at his consternation.

"I know, I know, Theo. So look, here's what I suggest, if it's OK with you. I'm going to take a minute and call my clients for today to reschedule them to later in the week." Seeing Theo's eyes widen, Liz added, "It's no problem, really. None of them are emergency cases. They'll be fine." Then, showing him her clipboard, she said, "You go ahead and take the first name on this list." Seeing Theo's confusion, she explained, "When I saw them and heard what the first few wanted, I knew there had to be some order to it all, so I asked everybody to sign in. You go ahead and see the first one, and I'll call the Raymonds and tell them that you need to reschedule them if it's all right." Theo nodded, all business now that he saw how much order Liz had carved out of the chaos, as she continued, "I am going to do you a big fat favor here Theo." Grinning, she continued, "I'm going to schedule everyone else for their intake appointments, and some lucky few will stay or they can come back later today for their appointments, and, well, a lot of them will have to schedule another day. How does that sound?" Liz was practically chirping, her mood was so bright.

Theo nodded and said, "Thanks, Liz. I so owe you."

"No Theo, you have no idea how much I still owe you. Now

let's go out there and help some women who don't want to have 'a crisis pregnancy.'" Seeing the questioning look in Theo's eyes at her use of the term used by the anti-abortion groups that sponsored "Crisis Pregnancy Centers," Liz said, "In all of the internet links, the term "Crisis Pregnancy Options" kept coming up for these women searching for help. Plus, this is weird, a lot of them said they had learned about you under #Polliwog. Weird, right? So...we're good?"

Theo looked thoughtful for a moment as he began to understand what had happened, and then he smiled. Taking the clipboard from Liz he said, "Yeah Liz. We're good."

As Liz walked out with Theo, she again took charge and announced that she would be taking appointments for everyone, and if they'd all just get comfortable, she had some calls she had to make. People started breathing more easily once they knew a competent woman was running things.

Theo took a breath, and glancing at the first name on the list, he asked, "Is there a Ms...ah, is there a Ms Woodward here? Rebecca?" Just then, Theo saw a young woman in her 20s waving her hand in his direction. "OK, please come into the office, and let's get started, shall we?"

As the two of them walked into Theo's own counseling office, the waiting room full of women began to fill with the quiet buzzing of business.

"Please take a seat," Theo said as he always did, "and make yourself comfortable. I look forward to helping you today, so tell me, what made you think you might need to come in for counseling?"

****

It was a long day, and when Theo, exhausted from his work, emerged from his office, he was surprised to see that Elizabeth was still there, seated at the reception desk.

She looked up from her book, smiled and then, setting it aside, said, "Hi Theo, how'd it go today?"

Theo couldn't remember the last time anyone had asked him about how his work had gone and spent a moment savoring the feeling. "I want to say this without exaggerating, but Liz, honestly, it was one of the best days of my life."

Elizabeth smiled and said, "Theo, I am so happy to hear that. I kind of thought it was. In fact, it was a great day for me too." They both smiled, and the silence between them was a comfortable one. Then Liz remembered, "Look, Theo, we have some unfinished business that we, and by 'we' I mean I need to take care of."

Sorry to see the moment they'd had slip away, Theo rushed to accommodate Liz and said, "Oh, sure Liz, please know I respect all that you've done for me today, and I commit to compensating you for all of what you've done. I would be glad to work out..."

"Shut up for a minute, would you, Theo," Elizabeth said, still smiling.

Disarmed by her relaxed charm, Theo realized that he had no idea what Liz was talking about.

Liz laughed, "Wow. That's the first time I've ever seen you caught completely flat-footed, Theo."

"Well," Theo smiled and then looked down at his foot, "It happens more often than you might think."

Elizabeth's face instantly sobered, horrified that Theo might have thought she'd been insensitive about his clubfoot before seeing Theo's eyes dancing with mischief at his little joke.

"OK, Theo. I need you to be quiet for a minute while I tell you something. I have a confession and an apology, and I hate making apologies. But, anyway, like I said earlier today, I owe you, so here goes. Do you remember, and I know you do, our argument the other day about your beliefs?" Seeing Theo nod, still smiling annoyingly, Elizabeth took a deep breath and continued, "Well, I did something really bad, really foolish, and about which I am deeply ashamed. I called Pastor Barton and repeated to him everything I said to you. I felt extremely satisfied with myself when I did, and I hope that's the last time I take such satisfaction in self-righteousness. I was quite the snitch and very much a spy, Theo," and here, tears came to her eyes as she continued, "I'm sorry, Theo. I'm so sorry. But the reason you had all those clients cancel and all your referrals dry up was because of me. I did it because I was afraid, I was afraid of being all on my own, I was afraid of not having enough money, and I'm so afraid that I'm going to be alone for the rest of my life, and that's why I'm still so mad at Bree's dad for going on with his life and leaving us,

I mean leaving *me* behind. But none of that matters, Theo, what I did was wrong, and I can never undo it and I am so sorry." Then she focused her attention on Theo and saw that he was looking down at the floor, and in that moment she felt so wretched, and she continued, "And you were so kind to help me when I needed help with Bree's situation, and Theo, Theo, I just feel so awful. I don't know what to say. You must hate me. I tried to destroy you."

Theo was quiet, allowing Elizabeth the space she needed to purge her conscience. The seconds ticked by until he felt the time was full, and he said, "You know, Liz, I utterly and completely accept your apology. Thank you. Thank you for being so bold and so good to say all of that. You know, some people might have reason, good reason, to doubt me and even my faith, but ever since I came to this country and heard about Christ, well, I realized the words of Christ were of the same spirit that I'd first heard in the forest as a boy in Peru. I'd heard those words, the whole world has heard those words and the eternal truth of them. Even the people living in the most absolute absence of kindness or love or joy know that his words have a truth that transcends our individual moments in the passage of time. I knew right away I could never walk away from Christ because, like Peter, I have to say, 'Where would I go, you have the words of eternal life.' It would be like walking away from my own body, unthinkable, He's that much a part of my being. I was surprised when I came to this country, because I hadn't believed it was possible that any of your people knew such words. When I came here, I really didn't see how anyone in this country held anything sacred. But you and your actions and even now, this moment, this is a Romans 8:28 kind of thing, isn't it, Liz?"

"All things work together for good?" Liz smiled skeptically. A big part of her had already begun to pull away from the church since her daughter's pregnancy, and to hear Theo quote scripture to her was...nice?

Theo smiled such a warm and embracing smile that Liz's doubts melted away, and then he leaned in, as if to share a secret, and said, "I know *who* brought those women to our office. I know why we're hearing about #Polliwog." And as he explained about his use of the metaphor to explain how a fertilized egg or even an embryo is not a human being, Liz felt herself become more comfortable than she had felt in many years. She felt the beginnings of an odd feeling she had never felt before. She thought it might be what people feel when they talk about feeling free. *That's it. I...feel...free.* She savored the moment before getting busy again with Theo's new clients.

There were many good things that came out of Theo's misstep in marrying Jessa. He finally had a legit way (according to the church) for him to get some of his sexual needs met. No, they were never able to enjoy true sexual companionship or genuine sexual intimacy. But they did have affection and sex, and when you're starving, some food is better than none.

The war shaman knew also that his marriage to Jessa was a powerful addition to the cryptic plumage of his spirit guide. He was now all the more forgettable and hidden from any suspicions as he continued to conspire with the Queen of Tears. Taking additional counsel from Jesus, Theo was relieved to know how much his fellow shaman agreed that the gospel message had been perverted, and finally, destroyed.

Chapter 18

Pastor Barton's face twisted with annoyance. Through a supreme effort, he — almost but not quite — managed to keep the hiss out of his voice as he spoke into the phone, "What do you mean he's got people lined up outside his office?" He listened for a moment while at the same time shaking his head to share his exasperation with the well-dressed man sitting across from his desk. "OK, then, thanks. Please let me know if you learn anything else. The Lord bless you for helping me with this. I know this is deeply personal for you. Yes…I am so with you on that, we do need to look out for the children. Thanks again. Bye."

Hanging up his office phone, Rob Barton sighed heavily as he looked down at his desk, seemingly focused on the photo of his wife. "OK, well, that's it then. That little problem we were just talking about is definitely not going to take care of itself." He raised his gaze to meet the dark eyes of Michael Juanarena who, along with his wife, had been a strong and faithful member of the church for the last ten years. Their family was the sort that Pastor Barton wished he'd had more of in the church. Michael was a lawyer, and then five years ago had become the local district attorney in his first run for office. The rumor was that Juanarena was eagerly looking forward to running for a statewide office in the next election. Maybe attorney general, maybe even governor. Pastor Barton knew these rumors, and he had encouraged Michael to consider a shift in his career that would put a godly man in the very corridors of state-level politics and power.

"Well, I've been listening to you talk about the scandal the church is facing, and I agree with you: This situation has got to be contained. You've put too much godly effort into the Lord's work to let it all go now. I'm just glad that you trusted me enough to bring me in on this," Juanarena said in the unctuous tones that had served him so well in court, and he hoped, in future endeavors of the political sort. "Before I share any of my thoughts with you, Pastor Rob, I guess I should know more about this Theo...what's his name? Van...?"

"Theo Van Prooyen. It's a Dutch name. His parents were Catholic. Jayden and his wife Jana converted and were born again before coming to the States. Our church got on their radar, and they wanted to make this their church home, so they did. Jayden and Jana (Pastor Rob pronounced their names correctly as "Yayden and Yana") Van Prooyen were two of the most loving and intelligent Christians I'd ever met. They were truly spiritual folks too, not just some sort of libtard snowflake types. They were zealous servants of Christ. That's probably how we lost them to the mission field," he said ruefully.

"What do you mean, 'lost them?'" Juanarena's dark eyes held a steady bead on the pastor. The heavy bags under his eyes only seemed to add to the gravity the man carried with him into his every conversation. How does he do it? Pastor Barton wondered as he again considered the man's heavy frame that he knew to be north of 320 pounds. Gravitas, that's it, thought Pastor Rob, wishing he could maybe get a little more gravitas in his own life.

"The church here was good for them in so many ways, but they had a need...a need for something more meaningful, I think. Simply being here just didn't seem to be enough for them. I mean, they were smart and highly educated; Jayden already had a degree in ancient Greek literature. Classical, they call it. It's a lot harder than Biblical Greek," he explained. Juanarena sat impassively, listening intently. Motionless, his heavy eyelids seemed to have a life of their own, sometimes closing for a bit longer than most people would have expected. He seemed to have a reptilian stillness to him, and he almost disappeared when his eyes shut.

"His wife had a degree in art history. She was a sharp one," Rob Barton remembered, half to himself. "But anyway, they just had a hunger to share more. They also had so much to give, and eventually their thoughts turned to a more dedicated form of service to Christ and the church. When Jana read about a tribe in the Peruvian jungle that had never been evangelized, well, they just caught mission fever. The only thing that slowed them down was that Jana was already pregnant, and so they decided to train in the language and the tribal culture, and they waited until Jana's sixth month of pregnancy before leaving. Not that the church wasn't behind them 100 percent. We were..." and here his voice drifted off in his memories, "100 percent," he repeated softly. Then rousing himself, he added, "It was probably that degree in art history – or maybe it was the pagan Greek stuff of Jayden's – that planted the seed for what we're dealing with today." Pastor Rob, taking note of the expression of confusion on Juanarena's face, explained, "Jana insisted, and Jayden himself supported her in this, that the child's name was to be, get this, Prometheus. I hadn't even heard that name until then, and so I looked it up, and I'm here to tell you that I did not have a good feeling about that name. You know where it comes from?"

Not one to lose his flinty focus on a prey animal, Juanarena simply shook his head lazily. As he listened to the pastor prattling on, Juanarena's loathing of the man's weakness raised in him, as male weakness always did, a strong urge to vomit in disgust. He picked up the thread of the man's droning on.

"Well, I didn't either, so I looked it up. It's come back to haunt us after all these years too. Just so you can know, 'cause I think it matters, 'Prometheus' isn't a Dutch name; it's a pagan one. Prometheus was the guy...the being, who broke with the gods of the ancient Greeks and stole fire for mankind. He's said to be all about reason and science and, well, really, everything in competition with real piety and simple faith. I confronted Jayden about it too. I didn't want to tangle with his wife, but I thought I could reason with him, and then he could hold her to be in submission and maybe fix that name. And you know what? He actually sided with her. He had the nerve to laugh, and he said something, I'll never forget...." and here his voice drifted off again into his memory of the distant past before he became silent, lost in his thoughts.

"And he said?" Those heavy lids almost seemed to sweep Pastor Rob into the orbs they covered. The man was reminding Juanarena of his father more and more, as he continued his passive reminiscence. *Impotent fool,* he thought, *he might as well be senile.* He smiled at the pastor.

Pastor Rob looked away to regain his train of thought. "Jayden said, 'No one loves God more than I do, Pastor Rob, but none of us can ever forget our loyalty to mankind, can we?' Weird, right? I've never heard anything like it in my life and I've never forgotten it. Still don't know what he meant though."

"So how'd he get the name 'Theo'?" Juanarena's ability to carry on small talk while watching a man have a meltdown was something he had had plenty of practice with as a child. Throughout his childhood, he watched as his mother relentlessly dominated his father. At last, he had grown to savor a good dressing down, but he had vowed at a young age to never allow anyone, man or woman, to control him. *Might as well be a castrated hog,* as he remembered his father's years of humiliation. He missed nothing of the pastor's report. He never missed anything.

"Well, all that happened after we brought Theo back from Peru, I mean we couldn't call him Prometheus, could we?" Here he laughed adding, "So I took a bit of his name and decided to use Theo as a nickname, the name means God and it worked better for us, and in the long run, I think, for him. People just accepted it, and it was only after Theo was well established in the faith that I told him the little story I told you. I had to, anyway. I knew he'd eventually need to look at his birth certificate: Prometheus Van Prooyen. Lord help us. Names matter, Michael, and now I can see this one, although he's never used it, seems somehow prophetic, you know, like a Bible name. And there I was, changing his name. Over the years I've come to feel maybe something like King Herod must have felt, you know, how hard he worked at trying to avoid seeing prophecies come true. You know, when he...with all the babies in Bethlehem."

"You mean when he killed them all?" Noting the frozen look on his pastor's face, he murmured benignly, "You, in contrast, were doing what you thought was right." Juanarena's dark eyes glinted before the lids fell again. People never really consciously noticed, but his way of speaking, his peculiar tone, was quite disarming, even hypnotic in its own way. "So, is that it?"

"Well, up until a month ago I might have said that that was it. I mean we brought him to America, or," thinking of his last conversation with Theo, "he came to America, learned English faster than you can imagine, spoke it perfectly after a couple of years, finished high school and went off to one of the best Christian schools out there, Baptist Missionary Association Theological Seminary." He paused, savoring the long-winded name in his mouth before continuing. "That's where he met and married Jessa, his wife. I really never understood why she bothered going to college at all except to get married. Anyway, he majored in Christian Studies, and I guess we all thought he was maybe going to become a missionary or something. Maybe even a pastor here in this church." Shaking his head negatively he added, "We dodged a bullet on that one, considering how things have worked out."

Juanarena could see how a closer association between Theo and the church might have blown up the local congregation. But at the same time, he wasn't so sure that there was much to celebrate in dodging a bullet like this when there might be something even more disruptive coming. Something more like a tactical 12-gauge shotgun blast. *But I'm going to put an end to that possibility*, he thought grimly.

Pastor Barton continued with Theo's bio, adding, "Well, he didn't become a leader in the church. Instead, he went to grad school. Never did trust those. Never knew any good that ever came out of a grad school." He drifted for a moment before reminding himself, as if for reassurance, "At least it was a good Christian school again, Abilene Christian University. Never heard anything bad about it. The church paid for all of it too, I mean, the parts that weren't covered by his scholarships. Did you know he got a scholarship from Christian Missionary Alliance? I think they just felt guilty about getting his parents killed. Then again, they had plenty of other stuff to feel guilty about, what with the boarding school scandal. That was before your time here. The story is that the missionaries who were in the field had their own children in the CMA's boarding school, and those kids came out saying that they were emotionally abused, severely beaten, sexually molested, and some were even raped. Can you imagine? Again he drifted mentally and said, mostly to himself, "At least we, I mean, we all had a hand in sending them out there to those blood-thirsty heathens. Did you know that they still had cannibals in that area? Headhunters. What were we thinking?" he asked no one in particular.

"So how'd he get to be a Marriage and Family Counselor?"

Coming out of his troubled reminiscences, Pastor Rob had to force himself to return mentally to his office before he continued, "Well, he got his degree in Marriage and Family Therapy in grad school in Abilene. Oh yeah, and he did some post-grad work at a place called...what was it...Milton Erickson something...yeah, that's it, Milton Erickson Foundation. Once I asked him what he was studying there, and he told me something about hypnosis or something. Then he did a couple of years of his internship, and he opened up shop."

"You said *hypnosis?*" It wasn't a real question, it was said only to draw attention, suspicion, and fear to the notion. It was the sort of question that had served Juanarena very effectively in court.

"Yeah, I mean, you know, he helped people quit smoking and lose weight with it, and we were all for that so..."

"Excuse me for interrupting you now Pastor, but, and I'm just asking, doesn't *hypnosis* put people in a trance? I mean, isn't that like opening a portal to demonic influences?" The glint in his eyes held Pastor Rob's attention.

"What? Oh. Well. I know that a few people consider it to be part of the occult, but because of Theo's good standing in the church and his attendance of only Christian schools, well, it seemed harmless enough. Now, I don't know. Maybe you're on to something."

"Well, I've gone to enough Bible study on the subject to know that it's a violation of the Word. Just check out Deuteronomy 18:9-

12," and here Juanarena's voice took on the timbre and throaty projection he liked to use in court,

> "'When you enter the land the LORD your God is giving you, do not learn to imitate the detestable ways of the nations there. Let no one be found among you who sacrifices their son or daughter in the fire, who practices divination or sorcery, interprets omens, engages in witchcraft, or casts spells, or who is a medium or spiritist or who consults the dead. Anyone who does these things is detestable to the LORD...'

It goes on, but the message is pretty clear to real Christians, at least to those of us who aren't Catholic or Lutheran. I mean, my parents, you know, were Basque Catholics, and they probably don't even have an opinion on the matter, but ever since I became a Christian, I have turned my mind to understanding the mind of God. With help from the Word, and you of course, Pastor Rob, I feel like I really do understand God's will, certainly in this matter."

Pastor Rob hadn't known anyone in his own circle to feel so strongly about the subject of hypnosis, but he had committed his life to being in the forefront of being against everything anyone else was against and then some. Once again, he thought, *Gravitas. Having his photographic memory sure would help with that.* When he considered how close he'd come to missing Theo's heresy, he said, "In Jesus' name," his thought a cleansing one after such a near brush with Satanism.

"My own eidetic memory helps me share God's Word with those who might be more prone to forgetting. I hope I haven't gone too far with this. What do you think, Pastor?"

"Oh absolutely, brother. Thank you for reminding me of that verse. I seem to recall a long past conversation on this, and I'll do some research in the Word to see if there's any new thinking on the matter, but I'm sure you're right. In fact, I know you're right." Privately, he made a mental note to himself, *'Eidetic.' That's got more gravitas than 'photographic.' I'm gonna remember that.*

"Well, then," Michael Juanarena drew himself up to his fullest possible height in his chair, his eyes no longer sleepy looking, "since we know that Theo Van Prooyen," and he took his first whack at pronouncing the name as loudly and oddly as possible to emphasize its foreign origins, "is outside of the will of God, I think we can zero in on him as the source of the undeserved ordeal that the church has been dragged through. I need to know more about this girl... what's her name, Pastor?"

"Amber? You do know she wasn't a patient of his, right?"

"That doesn't matter one bit, Pastor. I just need to know all about her. I need to know all about everything." And here he stared at Pastor Barton. The old caiman knew he could close his jaws on this little boa constrictor anytime and then drag him into the river to devour him at his leisure. Pastor Barton shivered involuntarily as he considered the formidable attorney and the look in his eyes, and then he gave a silent prayer of thanks that Juanarena was on the same side he was. *Poor Theo*, he thought. Aloud, he said, "Go ahead. Ask away." And, with that, the boa nested into the old caiman's jaws.

****

An exhausting hour later, Pastor Barton felt as though he'd been on the witness stand. He had been questioned and then questioned about his answers and then questioned about them repeatedly until Juanarena felt that he'd gotten as much as he could out of the man. Juanarena was particularly interested in the last discussion Pastor Rob and Theo had and the whole notion of shamanism. He made a note of Rachel Carson's involvement at the scandal's periphery and the fact that Skip had referred her to Theo. Finally, when he was done and after looking down at the copious notes he'd taken, Juanarena took a moment to allow his lids to rest on the bags below the eyes, and then suddenly, those eyes opened so fully that Pastor Rob was startled by how fast the eyes seemed to appear.

"So, Pastor Rob, if you wouldn't mind, I'd like you to arrange for me to interview Amber and her mother. I think that would indeed be the next step. I'll also want to talk to Pastor Skip and then with Rachel and her parents. "

"Ah, sure. You mean here?"

"No, I think that as the chief law enforcer in the county, it would be more appropriate if they came down to my office. There I can take an official statement and decide more clearly where to take what I think may very well be a criminal prosecution and certainly a civil prosecution in terms of Theo's licensure."

The pastor was dumbstruck. He'd seen heretics come and go, and he'd seen church splits and false teachers, but he'd never in his dreams imagined that any church matter like this could go as far as criminal prosecution. *Sure*, he thought, *Catholic priests and kids and Jehovah's Witness parents denying blood transfusions to their children but... us? Here?* and then he wondered about any blowback to his ministry and the church. "You really think this is that serious?"

"You introduced me to the notion of Prometheus, Pastor Rob, allow me to return the favor and introduce you to the Greek idea that I think describes what we have here." He paused as if in court before a dramatic reveal. "A Trojan horse. A Trojan horse is what we have here. You remember the story, Pastor Rob. The Greeks fought for ten long years outside the walls of Troy in order to regain Helen, the famous Helen of Troy. At the last minute, just as they appear to have been defeated, Odysseus, one of the Greek commanders, comes up with a ruse to finally overcome the enemy. He had them make a giant horse capable of holding several men inside, and they left it outside the gates of Troy. In the morning the foolish Trojans pulled what they thought was a Greek tribute to them back behind the walls of the very city they were defending. That same night those Greeks inside the horse climbed out, opened the gates, and the Greek army poured into the city. They destroyed everything in their rage. Theo is a Trojan horse that you have brought into the 'city on a hill.' Matthew 5:14," he added, speaking like a machine gun, "and he won't stop until he has destroyed everything we have built. You brought this catastrophe upon us, and you are going to help me burn that horse and everyone in it down to the ground."

Pastor Rob Barton, so used to being in control and so accustomed to the respect of those around him, didn't know what to do with Juanarena and the crusade that now electrified the man. He found himself unable to speak, and so he simply nodded as if the DA had hypnotized him. Within minutes, what remained of him started making calls. The old caiman had swallowed him whole and was now digesting him as the pastor was beyond consciousness at this point.

Theo remembered one of his father Ankuash's last warnings before he left the forest for America. "No matter how careful you are, how successful you are, every war leader suffers loss. You will suffer loss, and you must not fear this or even seek to avoid it because fear will contaminate your strategic focus. You must embrace the future loss and master it, making it your own."

There were dark spirits at work in the world. Theo knew this and had often had to fight them and their attacks on behalf of his own people. The worst attacks came from the Cocama tribe, who had once been a proud people but who had been reduced through disease. They now spurned any suggestion that they were also natives and that they'd lost anything in the invasion. They had gone so far as to aggressively position themselves as brothers of the foreign invaders. Their remaining sorcerers possessed evil wisdom. Theo knew that the so-called Christians who loved the god of prosperity were the spiritual kin of these people. He knew they loved the rules of God more than the people the rules were meant to serve. He knew that they would strike him and that he would truly be struck down.

In his mind, he worked to embrace this fate. He was not even close to successful in this.

Chapter 19

It had only been a single week since Theo's discovery of the crowd spilling out of his office, but already he could see that this rate of work was unsustainable. Sure, word was getting out, and his calendar was full — but at this rate, it would take the rest of his career to just take care of the needs in this one small city. Theo felt trapped in his small success. He shook his head, "What seemed so wonderful a week ago is just not going to cut it." His financial worries were over for now, but besides the opportunities that he knew were...somewhere out there in plain sight, he had not worked out any accommodation with Jessa, who still wasn't talking to him and who seemed to be working even more closely with her new best friend, Pastor Rob's wife, Charity.

Just then, Elizabeth came into the office, and after greeting Theo brightly, said, "So, what's going on with you? You don't look so good for a man whose practice is booming and who's working on the kind of issues he's always dreamed of."

Theo gave a small, sheepish grin, "I guess I should be careful what I wish for, right?"

Elizabeth looked at Theo closely and ignored his attempt at distraction, "No, I mean it, what's going on?"

Theo made another decision, "OK, Liz, I'll let you in on what

I'm thinking. I'm overwhelmed with the immensity of what I see needs to be done. It's not enough to help the wonderful few who make their way to my office when I know that there are at least hundreds of thousands of women in this country who need the same help. Probably millions across the world. I want to help all of them, not just a tiny handful." Seeing Liz listen attentively, Theo continued, "There's another matter, and it's personal. I love my wife Jessa, but we're not getting along right now, and it's not because of the work I'm doing — but the work has certainly stirred things up in my home." Thinking of his son Christopher and the slap Jessa had given him, Theo quietly added, "I think that situation is worse than I've allowed myself to see."

Upon hearing this, Elizabeth's eyes softened as she nodded compassionately, "That's how it was with my marriage too. You'd think two MFTs would have this part of their lives a little more together, wouldn't you?"

Theo laughed, "Yeah, you got that right. I can plead youthful ignorance — I mean, I was only 20 when we met and 21 when we got married. I had no idea what I was getting into. I probably shouldn't have gotten married at all. In hindsight, I should have just focused on my mission."

If Elizabeth noticed his unusual word choice in using the term "mission," she didn't show it. "Sometimes, Theo, no matter how much we know, there's still going to be an infinite amount that we don't know and that we can't know until we go through some painful experience."

Theo nodded, reflecting. "Oh yeah, and there's another thing. It's not really a big deal but still...." Theo drifted off into embarrassment over even giving the matter a second thought.

"What is it?"

"Well, I got a death threat the other day, and..."

Elizabeth interrupted explosively, nearly coming out of her seat, "What?"

"A death threat. It was a message on the office voicemail. From a man who said his daughter was coming to the office, and that he was warning me from talking to his little girl...or else."

"What did he say?"

"He didn't really say anything after warning me. It's just that, well, I heard the sound of a revolver's cylinder rotating, you know, like he was holding his gun up to the phone to do that. It was a bit unnerving, but maybe I'm making more out of it than I should I suppose..." Theo drifted off lamely.

"Are you out of your mind? Men!" She shook her head at Theo, and he could feel a scolding coming on. "Theo, if I got the same kind of death threat, would you want me to keep it to myself or ignore it?"

"Of course not Elizabeth! I know I'm not much good to anyone with this foot, but still, I would want you to tell me and to call the police and to...." And here Theo stopped as he saw Elizabeth's beginning of a smile.

Holding up her hand in the universal gesture for, "Just hear me out," Liz said, "Look, Theo. The difference between what you've done for yourself and what you would do if it were someone you cared about...like me," and here her eyes crinkled in mirth, "...is what we counselor types call 'denial.'"

Theo sat for a moment, absorbing this. He knew Liz was right. "You're right. So, what should I do? Call the police?"

"Sure, for starters. But now that I know that this has happened, I should tell you a little secret of my own." She laughed at seeing one of Theo's eyebrows arch upwards, "I don't know what that look means, but here it is: I decided, after my divorce, that my children needed me, and I couldn't allow myself to get hurt. By anyone. So, anyway, I got a CCW and...oh, a permit to carry a concealed weapon. I've had a .38 in my purse every day since. I always bring it to work, Theo, and maybe I should have told you, I know, but...tut-tut Theo, I know you probably don't feel good about it, but today I'm glad I have it," and here Elizabeth patted her purse appreciatively, "and you should be glad too Theo, because I've already decided to defend myself and the people I care about. I've only shot targets so far, of course, but I'm ready to kill someone who comes in here to hurt one of us."

Theo had been raised by a people who routinely used blowguns with poisonous darts to hunt game or kill attackers. Some of the Awajún, especially those who lived closer to towns, had even acquired shotguns, truly a second choice when stealth was of the essence. He wasn't uncomfortable with weapons or death, including his own, but he was surprised at Elizabeth. *There's more to her than I thought*, he silently mused. Then, as he looked at her while nodding his head, he was hit with the sudden realization of Elizabeth's true nature in the spirit world. He thought of the spectacularly bejeweled hummingbirds from the forest at home. The smallest of birds, he had spent enough time observing them to know them for the fiercest defenders of their territory. His thoughts turned briefly to the gun in her highly decorated handbag and to how he'd seen hummingbirds use their small, pointed bills as daggers to drive off or even kill their enemies. Reassured as to Elizabeth's true nature and ready competency, he said, "Well, OK. I feel better knowing that, Liz. Thank you for your offer of protection. I know we both hope never to need it."

Elizabeth felt something break free within her. She didn't know what it was, but she liked the way she was feeling. "So what about taking this show on the road?"

Theo was confused, "What do you mean?"

"Well, you have a problem. You can keep doing what you're doing, but that's not enough for you, so you have to reach out to people, Theo."

"Easy for you to say, Liz. I have thought so many things through, but here, at the precise moment when I need a bigger plan, I find myself coming up empty. I don't know what to do," sighed Theo, "But I have a full schedule this afternoon, so I'd better get going."

Elizabeth smiled, "Well, don't worry, Theo. I've never felt more trust in God than now, and I have faith that this is all going to work out." She patted her purse again and smiled.

****

Theo hadn't looked ahead in his schedule due to the pace of his workload, so when 4 o'clock rolled around, he had no idea that he would be face to face with Rachel Carson.

"Hi Rachel! How're you doing?"

"Hi Theo, I'm doing great, how about you?"

Theo simply smiled before saying, "Well, I have a few things on my mind, but what brings you around today? I mean, I'm happy to see you but..."

"I have an appointment to see you, Theo." Seeing him look at her somewhat bug-eyed, Rachel laughed and added, "You know... for counseling?"

"Oh my gosh Rachel, I am so sorry, I didn't look at my calendar very closely, and I just knew I had an appointment with someone...."

Rachel laughed, "Ah, you wouldn't have known even if you had looked, Theo, because I used a fake name." She took a deep breath and said, "Can I sit down? I have a lot to talk about and I'd like to get started."

Theo noticed that Rachael carried herself differently. Not just because she felt relieved about not being pregnant anymore, but there was a new...*confidence, that was it*, thought Theo, *What's happening to these women? First Liz and now Rachel?* Aloud he said, "Please, do sit. So what brings you to counseling Rachel?"

"I'm here to talk about a number of things, and first I guess I should bring you up to date. I started a blog, and I called it 'Rachel's Tears' — you know the reference, I'm sure."

"Jeremiah?"

"Yeah. 31:15. You know what it says. It's kind of lame I guess, but I wanted to reclaim the whole faith thing for me, it was like the only way I could stay a believer, and I wasn't going to give that up. I felt, and I still feel, that it's important to not let people get away with acting like they own God and like He's not for the rest of us."

"OK, so what did you blog about?"

"Well, to tell you the truth, I gave up the blog pretty quick. It was maybe a mistake, but it helped me to write down my thoughts and organize them. I was going through a lot. Anyway, it helped. You know a lot of people use that reference to Rachel's tears to talk about abortion, but I had something different in mind, you know? Like, um, tears of joy, tears of relief, tears of 'OMG, I'm finally in control of my life, my body and even where my faith is going.' Oh, and I was writing anonymously, and I was writing about my experience with you in counseling and how everything has become so different."

"Wow. I don't know what to say."

"Good. I'm not done." Here, Rachel smiled at Theo and added, "And, if you're going to keep interrupting me, I'll never *get* done."

"Agreed. You have my word." Theo liked what he was seeing, and he thought, *So long as she's blogging anonymously, how much harm could it do?*

As if Rachel had read his mind she said, "Well, it didn't stay anonymous very long, 'cause my mom and dad found out. I think they went through my computer when I was still logged on, and they figured it all out. My dad exploded."

"Oh, that's...upsetting," Theo murmured"

"You think? But it's all worked out. First, after yelling at me for a long time, my dad threw me out of the house."

"You're kidding. He wouldn't do that."

Rachel smiled, "Theo, it hurt...a little bit, I guess. But really, there was a gap between us for a long time. Yeah, sending that little polliwog along may have been the fatal blow to our relationship, but there was lots of other stuff there, and it was there for years. Where do I start? The Purity Movement, remember, "True love waits!" She finished sarcastically. "Then there was the way he treated me and my mom, like God had explained everything to him and we were supposed to get it secondhand. I hated that. But anyway, I used some of my thoughts to start a Twitter account, then an Instagram, then, well Theo, I'm on about seven different sites with #Polliwog. I have a YouTube channel now! I mean, I started with Snapchat because I liked the idea of disappearing media, but that just wasn't enough. Anyway, I'm getting ahead of myself."

"Rachel, how do you find the time to do all of this? Wait a minute, where are you living? Are you OK? I mean, I was adopted by a people who took heads as trophies and shrunk them up to put up as 'No Trespassing' signs, but they would never have thrown out one of their children from their home."

Rachel sighed, "I know, right? Well, and that's what they mean by 'respecting the sanctity of life.'" She laughed, "*Anyway.* I was saying...*hello?* Anyone home?"

"No, I'm listening Rachel but, you have to admit, it's a lot to absorb."

"Well, try to keep up Theo, 'cause there's a whole lot more."

"You're kidding."

"No, I'm not. Long story short, before I got kicked out, I was getting not hundreds, not thousands, but tens of thousands of followers."

"On Facebook?"

"Oh God no, Theo. If you're still using Facebook, this may be hopeless." Seeing his dismayed confusion, Rachel laughed, "Kidding, but really, there's more. Before I got kicked out, I figured out that I had a problem. I could tell people my story, but I really didn't feel like I could teach women how to, what, access their bodies the way you taught me. And believe me, after my experience with Amber, I am so done with that part of things for now. I knew that I had to do something big, something so big that the message would get out to the whole world. I thought about it for a while, and then I realized it had to be you up front. I mean, I'm glad to help, but you know what you're doing, and really...."

"Thanks Rachel, that's very sweet of you, but you really should be...."

"You know, I really hope to never be told, ever again, never in my whole life, what I should be or do. Listen...to...me!"

In that moment, Theo became miserable with himself and wondered what was happening to him. To her. To his world.

Rachel smiled, "I know it's a lot. But I'm almost done, and I'm getting to the really good part, OK?" Seeing Theo's chastened nod, she continued, "Go. Fund. Me." Seeing his blank expression, Rachel laughed, "What did they teach you in school? OK, I did a crowdsourcing fundraiser. I told all of my followers about it, I promoted it everywhere and I asked for, wait for it, $10,000! You might wonder, 'Why $10,000?' Well, I just thought it was a good round number and...kidding, I found out how much it cost to book the university's indoor arena, you know, where they have the basketball games? My plan was to rent it and, since it holds 10,000 people, I'd invite 10,000 women to join us. The bad news is...I didn't raise $10,000."

This time Theo didn't rush to rescue her, and he kept his gaze on her as his eyes began to water.

"I didn't raise $10,000 dollars, Theo. Well, I did, but I blew past that number while I was sleeping that night. In one week, Theo, we raised $1,129,000 to host the First Annual #Polliwog Women's Conference. After I got kicked out, I just couch surfed with friends before getting the money and then going out and renting a house. I can sleep and work there while I'm organizing this. It's going to be great Theo, and I can't wait to see…"

"Whoa. Let me have a minute here." Theo paused and looked down. It was in that moment that he surrendered himself to the Mother once again, because She had provided his queen in his hour of need, one of the digital natives of this increasingly strange land. Looking up, his eyes shining with the tears that were streaming down his face, Theo said, "OK. Just tell me what you need me to do."

And so Rachel did for the next half hour, and then, before they parted, Theo shared about his concern for safety.

Rachel chirped, "Not to worry. We can afford the best security and…"

"That's not what I meant Rachel." And then Theo told her about the death threat and his conversation with Liz. He added, "You know, now that you've told me all this, I'm thinking that message could have been from your dad."

Rachel thought for a minute, "It really could be him." She paused for a moment to think and then said, "Theo, your safety is now very important to a lot of people. I have enough money to hire security for this office, I mean, so long as you plan on seeing people here. And no, before you ask, I don't mean some Rent-A-Cop, I mean licensed and bonded bodyguards. Just let me take care of that. I think you should have security 24/7 you know, at your home too, you know what I mean?"

"No, I can't do that. Jessa would absolutely freak out. My main concern is here at the office. I don't want anyone to get hurt," and then, remembering Liz's words, he added, "and that includes me."

"OK, Theo, but remember, we have enough money to do this right the very first time. Security will be tight, there'll be a news crew and a film crew and…."

"A film crew, why?"

"Two words, Theo: You. Tube. Dude, you need to get out more. Just let me handle it. I'll be in touch." And, with that, Rachel stood and strode confidently out of the office. Looking over her shoulder she added, "Expect a bodyguard here tomorrow," and then, without waiting for his answer, she left Theo standing alone. Stunned.

Deep within himself, in a place too deep for Theo to begin articulating what it was, lay a seed of apostasy. Theo never doubted his mission — there, his faith in what he was doing was absolute. In a similar way, once committed, he never doubted his faith in Christ.

But then there was his faith in his marriage with Jessa. He was so distracted by the cares of this world, the planning and execution of the war, the deep and wide gratitude he felt for the blessing of his son, that he failed to process these feelings. If he had done so, he would have known that this marriage was dead, dead, dead. It had been based on a lapse in judgment and had truly been dead on arrival.

Theo had no cultural or religious inhibitions to getting a divorce. What he had was something he had in common with all men: Hubris. His ego simply couldn't accept that he had tried to do something and had failed in the process. His thinking error was forgetting that it takes two to make a marriage work but only one to make it fail. His pride kept him from accepting his human capacity for mistake-making.

Chapter 20

The following week was a blur of frenetic activity for Theo. As advised, the morning after Rachel had left, on Tuesday, he saw a somewhat burly man, exuding an almost arrogant confidence, show up. The man's eyes shined with a level of awareness that Theo himself recognized as his own when he was "on the job." Before Theo could even ask who he was, the man introduced himself, his voice tinged with a slight accent, "Mr. Van Prooyen? I am Ari Stern, my firm, Executive Security Specialists, has been retained to ensure your safety and the security of this office. My other staff is currently out on assignment, and so I came in today. Usually I'm in the office, but when I heard about the nature of the threat, I made a point of coming in myself. I plan on being here every workday until someone can replace me. I may even stay longer if I develop a personal interest.

Theo raised an eyebrow at the notion of a bodyguard having "a personal interest" in his work, and Ari Stern's steady eyes didn't miss this.

"I can explain. My family is Sabra." He pronounced the word's beginning with a distinct "ts" at the beginning. "It means native. Native to Israel. Maybe you noticed my accent?" Ari smiled and said in a breezy manner, "We have a prickly pear in Israel. Like the pear, we are dangerous looking on the outside but sweet on the inside. In my work, I have found great success because of this sweetness in my character." He leaned in darkly to Theo.

Theo began laughing at the absurdity of this obviously dangerous man claiming that it was his sweetness that had paved the way to success in the security business. He asked, "And how does being a, how did you say it, a sabra, give you a personal interest in this job?"

Ari paused before answering, "How much time do we have before your clients start showing up?"

"About an hour. I got here early to get the office ready and do some charting. I'm way behind." Theo had never seen someone other than one of the tribe's warriors listen or think with such a sense of physicality as Ari. He seemed to Theo to take in the information, and then — somehow physically rather than mentally — decide to explain himself.

"My sister Raya served in the IDF, the Israeli Defense Force. Everyone does, even the women. Everyone gets drafted and has to serve," and here he deliberately paused before continuing in a bitter tone, "except the Haredim, the ultraorthodox. They can serve," he said bitterly, "but hardly any of them do. Everyone else must serve, just like me, just like my younger sister. I already knew the Haredim were useless, but I didn't know how bad they were until one day, when my sister got on a bus in Jerusalem, she was spit on by one of those momzers." He shook his head and pursed his lips in anger, "And, can you believe it, she was in uniform. That putz knew that she was risking her life every day she served to save his, and that momzer had the nerve to spit on her." And here he looked at Theo, his eyes ablaze with a cold intensity, "The fundamentalists are going to ruin this world if they are not stopped. I mean all of them. The Haredim and the Salafi Muslims. And here you have evangelicals. They're all the same. So that," he declared, "is my personal interest. I hate them all."

Theo nodded his head in understanding, and then remembering Elizabeth and his sudden revelation of her spirit guide, the hummingbird, took a moment to open his third eye and really *look* at Ari. Then he saw him for who he was in the spirit world: the bear. The spectacled bear of Theo's beloved cloud forest was generally somewhat avoidant of The People, but Theo had become the owl hiding himself against the foliage and had watched a large male bear hide himself at the approach of an adult mountain tapir twice the bear's size. The bear had fallen on the prey, twice his size, with a calm but utterly committed attack. The bear, the largest carnivore of the forest, mauled the tapir enough within moments that he began feeding on him while the tapir continued making its death rattle. It was all , thought the watching owl that was Theo. He realized he could count on Ari for a similarly efficient level of lethal force if it were needed. Aloud, Theo said, "My officemate may be uncomfortable with your feelings about evangelicals."

"I am a professional. There will be no problem," Ari's personal openness disappeared, as he once again became Ari Stern, IDF veteran and private security specialist.

Again, Theo nodded before adding, "All right, then, I'll be getting to it. Do you need anything?"

Ari Stern smiled, "I'll be here until you leave, and then I'll walk you to your car. You're sure that's all you need?

Theo smiled back, "I'm good for now."

****

By the time Thursday afternoon came and went, the office had settled into a routine that Theo found himself looking forward to. He was busier than he'd ever been, and he found that Ari's presence had made his life easier. He hadn't realized how much of his brain's bandwidth had been devoted to staying vigilant. Even the clients seemed to be more comfortable as Ari moved around, sometimes pretending to read, and then glancing up sharply as he heard footsteps in the hallway outside the office, letting his right hand float away from his magazine and up ever so slightly toward his chest, where, Theo presumed, Ari carried something very lethal. Ari always gave newcomers the once over, determined that the women were alone and obviously hesitant with anxiety over their situations, and then returned to blending back in with his surroundings. Elizabeth, once introduced, had welcomed the protection, and she frequently asked Ari if he'd like coffee or anything else she was helping herself to.

Friday morning, as Theo lay alone in his bed, he thought about how easily Ari and Elizabeth seemed to take to one another, "Those two seem to really be getting along." He smiled at the thought, and then throwing back the bed covers and hoisting his legs over the side of his bed, Theo gingerly put both feet on the floor. Easing his weight onto his clubfoot, Theo began shuffling through his early morning routine, and then made his way out to the kitchen to find Jessa sipping her coffee at the breakfast bar.

"Hey stranger, I haven't seen much of you around here lately," Theo offered.

Jessa seemed to not hear him as she stared down at her coffee cup and then said those foreboding words, "We should talk."

Theo had never seen anything good follow such an opening, and so after pouring himself a cup from the carafe, he wordlessly sat down and waited to hear what his wife had to say.

Jessa took another swallow of coffee, and then, "Pastor Rob and his wife know what you're up to Theo. I told them myself."

Theo looked at her, eyebrows raised in his familiar, "I have no idea what you're talking about," look.

"Oh, come on Theo. You know exactly what I'm talking about. You're counseling women, hypnotizing them, getting them abortions, and you don't even have the decency or...or the faith to be ashamed of yourself."

"We've talked about this. These women have privacy, and they have confidentiality, and I can't talk about why they see me. But, as I've said before, I don't provide women with abortions..."

Jessa interrupted, "I know, I know. You already said that Theo, and if you think it makes a difference whether you kill the babies yourself or you counsel them how to do it on their own, well, it doesn't make a difference Theo. Everyone at the women's Bible study knows what you do, and so does Pastor Rob."

"Well, I knew that he knew because all the clients he'd referred to me disappeared overnight. I guess I'm naïve in not figuring out that you were the one informing on me."

"Don't go so high and mighty on me Theo. You know our church's position on the Right to Life. I'm only guilty of upholding a standard that you were supposed to be upholding. Theo, you're supposed to be the leader of our household! Whatever happened to, "As for me and my house, we will serve the Lord?"

Theo looked down. He thought to himself how this woman was able to get under his skin like no other. He let out a sigh, "Really? Joshua 2:14? That's what you see here? So, if we're going to use dueling Bible verses, I guess it's my turn. I'll see you and raise you with Matthew 7:1, OK? What about, 'Judge not, lest ye be judged?'"

"I hate it when you talk like that, and I hate you. There really isn't any talking to you Theo. You're like a...a devil, all silver-tongued and I know you can out-argue me, so I'll just stop." And just like that, she did stop.

Theo reached his hand over to hers, taking it. "What was I supposed to do Jessa? Just give up? I have to make a living and support you and Christopher. And I like helping these women who are coming to the office. This is what I've dreamed of for years, and my dreams are coming true."

Although Theo tried to hold onto her hand, Jessa used her body weight to pull away from him. "Fine, Theo. Just do what you do. I hope you know you're ruining our family."

Just then, Christopher came out of his room, quiet but very obviously aware that his parents had been arguing. "What's the problem, you guys? I couldn't even concentrate on my geometry homework."

Jessa glanced at her son before quickly looking away from him, "Nothing Christopher. Just never mind. You always take your father's side anyway." In the awkward silence that followed, she rose to her feet and walked away, somehow conveying the familiar expression of feeling put-upon and rage.

Seeing Jessa walking away from him was disappointing to Theo, but he was more concerned about his son's immediate wellbeing. "Hi son. Sorry. Your mom and I aren't getting along so great."

"No kidding," Christopher said as he sank his weight onto the barstool that his mother had just vacated. "Ah, Dad, would you mind driving me to school again? I spent a lot of time going over my homework and...."

"Absolutely. Hey," Theo added, "Would you mind getting the car started while I get dressed? I left it in the driveway. I'll be quick," he added.

Christopher smiled. He knew his father always had his back. "It feels good, Dad, when Mom's so mad that I know I can count on you."

"You always can, Chris, you always can," Theo said, laying his hand on his son's shoulder. "Hey, here's my keys, I'll go get ready."

"I'll be waiting outside Dad. Thanks."

Theo limped back to his bedroom and had just enough time to pull on a pair of pants before he heard a sound he hadn't heard since leaving the forest. It was the same sound, the same world-ending sound, made by the miners who looked for gold near the rivers of his home. Without thinking, Theo ran outside on his misshapen foot as if he were an animal running for dear life.

There, in the driveway, were the twisted remains of Theo's car, burning every bit of fuel that had been left in the vehicle's gas tank. Theo screamed out an instinctive, guttural cry and ran toward the remains of the burning car. He was driven back by the flames, his hands, face and upper body roasted into blisters, as he again and again ran toward the car — and in it, his son, his Christopher. Theo's ears were filled with the roar of the flames and his own howls of anguish, now joined by those of his wife, as the two parents watched the cremation of their beautiful son, who was no more.

Theo pulled at Jessa as she began heading toward the vehicle. She fought him until her legs gave out from beneath her, and Theo somehow found the strength to carry her back, away from the end of their world. Backing up enough to escape the worst of the heat, the two collapsed onto the lawn, their voices still inhuman in the face of a catastrophe that was beyond words.

Someone had phoned the authorities, and a fire truck was the first emergency vehicle on the scene. Theo's mouth gaped open again and again in silent cries as he watched the team of firefighters go about their work extinguishing the blaze that, by this time, had spread to the garage door and the roof of the house. As the fire was subdued and only charred remains were left behind, Theo found himself unable to stand, unable to speak, unable to think. His wife was taken aside by a firefighter who wrapped her in a blanket, and the woman accepted that human gesture of caring the way an inconsolable baby accepts swaddling. Theo eventually noticed that he was being cared for by a paramedic only long after his care had begun. The medic, a woman, first put out his still smoldering clothing. The woman's voice kept speaking in an insistent but patient tone, "Sir, are you having any trouble breathing? Sir? Sir, I repeat, are you able to breathe?" Theo nodded his head. "Sir, I need you to tell me, can you breathe?" This time, Theo nodded and, black sputum leaking between his lips, croaked out, "Yeah. But my son..." and here the medic, much stronger than she appeared, restrained him as he tried to move again toward the car. "You need to hold still now; they're doing everything possible for your son. Now, please let me give you this oxygen." With that, she fitted him with an oxygen mask and reminded him in a firm, somehow loving tone, "Now breathe. Yes, that's right."

The paramedic spoke to the other EMT at the scene, "We need to get them both on board and to the hospital. She's in shock, and he's got a lot of second-degree burns and some third-degree with evidence of inhalation injury. He needs two large-bore IVs now. I'll do that. Let's go." Theo fought weakly as the two got him onto a stretcher. Then the door of the ambulance shut, and he lost consciousness under the glowering eyes of his wife.

Theo had seen much death and suffering in his young life. He had seen the brutality of men over women in marriage, of the hunter, both human and animal, over their prey. He had fought the destructive darts of evil sorcerers, betrayals, and the eco-terrorisms of warring prospectors, miners, and loggers.

He did not realize that he had never suffered as prey. He had not prepared for this.

No one can.

Chapter 21

Theo settled his weight at first gingerly, and then more heavily, into one of the overstuffed armchairs of his living room. His unfocused eyes gazed bleakly into nothingness, giving the lie to the pain he had to be feeling from his burns, especially his hands, still wrapped in sterile gauze. His burns were hardly registering on his mind.

"I am so sorry, Theo, I am so sorry," Rachel Carson spoke softly through her tearing eyes into the private space that the two of them seem to solely occupy, despite the quiet activity in and around the house. Ari Stern was quietly busy in the kitchen doing something that was of utter disinterest to Theo just now.

Theo gave one barely perceptible nod of his head before giving the wannest of smiles at no one in particular. He sighed heavily again, and yet again tears began pooling in his eyes before first breaching the dam of his lower lid — and then, streaming down his face.

Rachel attended Theo in his grief, despite the tears streaking her own cheeks. She swallowed hard and frequently as she blotted his cheeks with tissue after tissue. Ari walked into this scene with a quiet stride, the slightest clink of teacups on the small table before Theo were the only betrayal of Ari's physical presence into Theo's consciousness. This moment was far from the first time that the Israeli had attended those who were grieving, and he knew what to do and what to definitely not do. And so he asked small questions of Theo, requiring small answers, and he left the deeper, hurtful work of sympathy to Rachel. Ari knew that both were needed, but that, at this moment, the last thing Theo needed was to deal with too many heartfelt emotions. One truly caring person, and he recognized that as Rachel, was enough in this moment. And so he asked, "Theo, do you take sugar with your tea?" He paused again with the sugar and a teaspoon in his hand.

Theo was startled by the banal question spoken in the gentlest of ways, and coming up from the murky depths of his heart's loss, he shook his head in the negative before quietly adding, "No. No, thank you." Merely responding to his question allowed his consciousness to return to the point that his hands rose from his lap as if to take the offered teacup.

"No, let me help you...." Rachel's voice trailed off as she saw Ari making eye contact with her. She then became quiet as the two of them waited for Theo to come back from wherever he was.

Theo's eyes focused on the teacup, and the moment became somehow fuller — until the dainty teacup almost on its own became part of 'life goes on' reality. As he reached for the steaming cup, Theo's focus sharpened; when he took hold of it, he looked like a climber pulling himself up the face of the cliff outstretched far above where he had climbed so far. A moment passed with his cup and saucer resting on his lap. He breathed heavily, one time, from the exertion of coming back to this corporeal world. He took one sip of the hot brew and pulled back sharply before blowing over the cup, and then, taking another swallow.

Ari, sensing the time was now right to share the briefest of needed communications, got to the point in a quiet voice. "Theo," he started and waited for Theo's eyes to meet his, "You need to know that you are alone in the home. Your wife asked me to tell you that she was going to her family's house and that she'd prefer to not hear from you." He waited, giving Theo a moment to absorb the news, and if he could, to respond.

Theo's near catatonic expression relaxed a bit with the news, and he shook his head with acquiescence. He looked down into his cup and then gestured for more tea. He said gently, yet ruefully, "A man's enemies: the members of his own household." The familiarity of the simple, yet disturbing words formed another support for Theo's ascent from hell.

Ari nodded quickly. He wasn't familiar with Christian scripture, but he recognized the intoning of wisdom and the comfort such words gave those in shock from the cruelty of their world. He wasn't particularly religious, but he'd sat Shiva many, many times in his military career. As he watched Theo, Ari remembered the way mourners, even the nonbelievers, had made their way back into the healing of community through the recitation of ritualized prayer. He believed in that moment that Theo was making the same journey back. Ari did not consider himself a man of faith, but he had faith that Theo's painful journey back to this world was essential to their going on as a team.

Rachel recognized Theo's quote, old words from Matthew 10, but she'd never seen anyone apply them to modern times or modern hurts. She wondered quietly, thinking about her own faith for a moment.

Theo took another, slower, sip of his tea as he became incrementally more composed.

Ari continued, "Theo, it is all too clear that we underestimated the lethal danger your enemies presented, and because of that, I've placed teams of two men around the home for now. Eight-hour shifts. They are all good men. You and everyone else here will be safe, and they will stay here so that you can be free to...to attend to what you need to do." He said this last with the air of one who was used to authority and used to the respect for that authority from those around him.

Theo looked up briefly and after meeting Ari's steady gaze, smiled a bit and nodded his head in surrender. Then, looking at both of them, Theo said, "If I'd accepted your offer earlier, I suppose my son would still be alive." He smiled weakly as he looked down.

Whatever was going to be said next was lost, as just then there was a knock at the door. Ari looked toward the entrance of the home and said, "I'm going to check, that's the knock code my men use when we're working. They already know we don't want to be disturbed right now, so something is up." He walked down the hall toward the front door of the house. Looking out the window, Ari saw the police cars parked on the street, and then, going to the door, he opened it with his foot behind the door. He took a look outside, and then he opened the door wider, planting himself directly opposite the four officers with his own men behind them.

"Yes?" Ari's voice was friendly in tone but nevertheless firm. No one was getting in without his approval.

The officer in the lead spoke in a voice so low and soft it was hard to believe for a moment that he was there on official business, "This is the home of Theo Van Prooyen?"

"What's this about?"

Realizing that he'd started from a position of weakness, the officer started over, "Are you Mr. Van Prooyen?"

"What's this about?" Ari's face took on a stubborn look as he repeated himself in a way that let everyone else know what he knew: No one, no one was coming into the house without his approval. Each of the seven armed men at the door became aware that the air had suddenly become thicker. The four policemen in particular didn't like being surrounded by the three Israelis.

"I know this is a terrible time, and I told my sergeant not to force the issue today, but I have a warrant for Mr. Van Prooyen's arrest, and I need to know, is this his home and is he here?"

"You do know that his son was blown up last Friday, right in the driveway just steps from where you are right now? He was murdered by terrorists. You do know that he just got home from the weekend at the hospital? That his hands are still bandaged from trying to pull his boy from the fire. You *do* know all that?"

Caught between his duty to follow a lawful order and his own sense of the very wrongness of his actions, the officer at the door was visibly mortified. "Yes. Yes, I do know that, and Mr. Van Prooyen has my deepest sympathies."

"And *this* is how people in this country show their 'deepest sympathy?'"

Visibly in anguish, the officer could only repeat, in a near helpless voice, "I have a warrant."

"What is the charge?"

"There are two: Practicing medicine without a license and operating an unlicensed abortion clinic." The officer looked down at the paper he was holding but hadn't bothered to interpret the obviously political charges.

"*Momzerim*," Ari swore, looking at the four uniformed men.

"What?" the officer asked as he helplessly watched a very bad situation become more humiliating by the moment. This was unlike any arrest he'd ever made, and he was looking forward to some stiff drinks later to try to get the taste out of his mouth.

Ari glared, set his jaw for a moment before saying, "Stay here," in that commanding tone of his. He shut the door, locking it. *Momzerim*, he repeated to himself before drawing himself up and turning back down the hall. Reaching the living room, Ari looked at the two he was assigned to protect. His face reflecting how sick he felt to be relaying the message, he said, "Theo, there are four officers at the door with a warrant for your arrest on charges of operating an abortion clinic and practicing medicine, both without a license and both, of course, absolute dreck. I can keep them at the door for a while if you want, but I think we need to comply, as sick as this is."

Before Theo could pull himself or any words together, Rachel jumped in, her eyes alight with raw intelligence, "OK, Ari, Theo will surrender but before you go to the door, listen to me." She took a deep breath and continued, "Ari, I'll want you and your men to follow the police to the station. Phone me once you know that location. I don't want Theo to disappear somewhere like so many of this D.A.'s arrestees. I'm going to call an attorney I've already spoken with and let her know what's going on. I know Theo can get bail, and I'll want to know what his bail is right away. I'll be down to join you all with a check, make bail, and then return here. You good with that, Ari?"

Ari had served for years in the IDF, and he had already gotten a sense of this young woman: He knew a master tactician when he heard one, and so he simply smiled and said, "Of course. I'll let them know he's getting ready, and believe me, they'll wait. At the door, they'll wait. We'll all just wait. Together." He smiled grimly.

Rachel moved to gently touch Theo's upper arm, and then remembered that he was likely burned there — and so she held her hand for a moment in the air before returning it to her lap. "Theo. Theo, do you remember when you told me that you had a plan?"

That day Theo remembered as if it were so long ago. That day he had felt the universe come together and heard the voices of the ancestors whispering to him, "Now is the time." He could see it all on that day. Now he felt very small. Nearly worthless. He hesitated, "I know I said that Rachel, but...."

"Theo." And here Rachel smiled at him, "Theo, now I need you to believe me. Now I have a plan." Then the young woman leaned conspiratorially in toward him and whispered, "Say nothing to the police or anyone else until your attorney gets there. Remember, there is no one there who is your friend except Mr. Fifth Amendment. Just keep saying, 'I need to speak with my attorney.' Can you remember that?"

Theo shook his head 'yes.'

"Now I need you to say it," she said intently. She waited.

"I need to speak with my attorney."

"Again, only firmer."

"I need to speak with my attorney," Theo's voice picked up strength he didn't know he still had.

"OK, then get what you need to feel comfortable, and then I'll walk you to the door, OK? Do you need to go to the bathroom? Never mind, just go ahead. They can wait till you're done."

****

Kate Barrie entered the station house with the sort of professional intensity that she seldom felt outside a courtroom, given her normally calm and relaxed demeanor. The click of her heels punctuated the hum of the business-as-usual atmosphere around her and stood in counterpoint to the lithe athleticism of her muscular physique. All of the regulars gave the attorney more than a moment's glance — partly as a response to the predatory staccato beat of her pace, but mostly because it was Kate Barrie. It wasn't often that she came right down into the station house, but everyone knew right away that there was some high-dollar client waiting. Because Kate Barrie, Esq. believed strongly in what her mother, a strong and fiercely independent woman, had taught her as a child, saying, "Honey, rich people need love, too." For Kate, that meant they deserved the very best in criminal defense representation, and she'd fought too hard for everything in her life to believe that "the very best" meant anyone but her. Approaching the desk, she was distracted by the young woman coming her way. She noticed Ari Stern standing behind the girl, keeping his eyes on, well, everything. She nodded at him, and then, before Kate could say anything at all, the young woman walked up and said, "You're Kate Barrie. I'm Rachel Carson. Thank you for coming down, but I thought you'd be here more quickly."

Kate thought to herself, *This girl is much younger than I thought but, hey, the check cleared so....* She did as she always did with unsolicited criticism — real or imagined — but aloud, she said, "And our guy is where, exactly?"

He's in custody somewhere...in here," Rachel said, waving her right arm helplessly at the entire building."

"Stay here," the attorney said to Rachel. She then walked up to the sergeant at the desk, and, smiling, said, "Sergeant, I'm here to see my client, Theo Van Prooyen, and I'd appreciate any help you can give me in making that happen."

Sergeant Cobb looked up at Kate, nodded her head at what, for her, was another of far too many black women in her America and said dourly, "Oh yeah, the abortionist. It'll be a while. Have a seat," gesturing with her head over to the benches filled with hookers and addicts recently brought in.

Kate smiled. She'd seen plenty of low-level functionaries who'd fallen in love with the power to slow down the entire rest of the world until they were good and ready to consider doing their job. "No thanks, I think I'll just go see the chief," and with that, she turned on her heels and walked toward the Chief-of-Police's office across the wide hallway, ignoring the spluttering of the Sergeant who quickly sensed that she might have made a big mistake.

"Hi Marsha, Chief Rogers in?" Kate said to the Chief's secretary as she breezed through the room and put her hand to the doorknob.

"Ah, yeah, but he's in a meeting right now, and he can't be...."

"Oh, he won't mind a bit," Kate loved these sorts of understatements that felt closer to what others, including her mother, thought of as bald-faced lies. She opened the door and entered, taking in the small group of uniformed men looking up at her from their seats around the chief's desk. The Chief was focused on the documents on his desk and didn't look up to see who'd entered.

"Marsha! I told you that...ah, Counselor! Everyone knows Kate Barrie, and if you don't you soon will be, ah, truly sorry to have made her acquaintance." Despite his obvious teasing, his smile was genuine, and he and Kate shared a moment of professional respect and fondness as they both held eye contact, ignoring everyone else.

"I'm sorry, Chief Rogers, to interrupt your meeting, but I knew you needed this," she said, handing him an envelope.

"Thanks, ah, Kate. What is it?"

"Oh, just a writ of *habeas corpus* for one Theo Van Prooyen. You have him in your jail, and Judge Reingeld thought maybe the county ought not incarcerate a prominent citizen who'd just been the victim of a terrorist act and lost his only son in the process. A prominent, long time, stable member of the community, and a licensed mental health professional who's helped countless members of the same community, and, who, needless to say, is still in need of medical treatment following his heroic attempts to pull his only child from the fire, and...did I mention he has a clubfoot? Can't even run across the street. 'Pretty unlikely to abscond,' is what the judge said I believe."

The Chief paused a moment to take this all in before saying, "Judge Reingeld? Your former husband, Judge Robert Reingeld? That Judge Reingeld?" Chief Rogers grinned. He knew how the game was played.

Kate Barrie just smiled and said, "How long? I'm in a hurry."

"Excuse me gentlemen. Let's reschedule this meeting till tomorrow."

As the other men filed out, Kate glanced around her, waiting until they were gone. "Oh, and Leo?" she said familiarly.

Folding his arms and leaning back in his chair, Chief Leo Rogers said, "Yes, Kate?"

"Please do me the kindness of having him brought out by that nice sergeant at the front desk — she has been so very kind."

Leo Rogers didn't even bother to ask. He knew Kate, and he knew his sergeant, and he knew that there was a score to settle here — and he wanted to just get out of the way until it was. The fact was that he had grown insufferably weary of racism, petty or deeply considered, and he was glad to be able to do something, however small, to kick that old hatred in the teeth. "Sure, Kate. Anything else?" as he reached for the phone. Kate just beamed her lovely smile and shook her head. He dutifully proceeded, "Ah, Sergeant Cobb, this is the Chief, could you please make sure to bring Theo Van Prooyen out to the lobby. Yes, dressed and ready to go. Yes, and please escort him yourself." There was a pause, "Yes. Yourself. Yes, his attorney will be waiting for him. Thank you, Sergeant." Hanging up the desk phone, he smiled at Kate, who was thinking that her client, the paying one, would be nervously waiting for her. She wagged her hand from the wrist and mouthed a silent "bye-bye" to the chief as she left his office. Leo Rogers had been glad to see her but felt an irresistible sense of relief to see her go, "I never want to get on that woman's bad side," he said aloud to no one.

****

Sergeant Cobb expected the worst as she escorted the bandaged man with the clubfoot out of his booking cell, where he'd sat with the drunks who made up the flotsam of the community's weekend arrests. The smell of their vomit was like breaking an ammonia capsule under his nose, so Theo was at that moment very much present with the world.

"Oh, thank you Sergeant Cobb! Thank you so much!" Kate Barrie's enthusiastic tone lofted above the attorney's now complete disinterest in the petty woman — now that she had paid back the woman's pettiness, she didn't even bother to attempt eye contact. Her real attention was focused on the bent, nearly broken looking man in front of her. Wrenching her attention away from him, Kate addressed Rachel and Ari, "Why don't you get him home now. My office will be calling tomorrow to set up an appointment so we can talk. For now, let's get the f out of here." And, waving her hand in the 'after you' gesture, she slowly followed the three as they made their way to the street, confident in her knowledge of the law and the politics of the game. As she pondered just what exactly she had gotten herself into, Kate grinned at the sudden, welcome taste of a bit of blood in her mouth.

Theo didn't want to think of the words, but he couldn't help himself — they simply came into his mind, not so much uninvited as always resident. He feared them.

> *"If anyone wishes to come along after me, let him deny himself and take up his cross each day, and let him follow me. For whoever wishes to save his soul will lose it; but whoever loses his soul for my sake, this one will save it. For what profit is there for a man gaining the whole cosmos but losing — or being deprived of — himself?"*

Theo wasn't ready now, but he knew he must eventually bow his head to this certainty: He had lost himself in his marriage. This cross of suffering and loss and humiliation that he was now bearing over the loss of his son was a severe mercy. It was the only way he would have let go of Jessa, something he'd been avoiding for years.

Chapter 22

The next morning found Theo slowly pacing in the living room. Finally, he let his weight sink into an armchair. Despite Rachel's bustling about as she set to make him tea and the muffled conversations and movements of the two, no, three bodyguards outside the house, his home felt empty and hollow. "No," Theo thought, "I'm the one who's empty and hollow." Theo didn't want to spend even a moment of his life hating anyone, including the millions of thoughtless enemies who'd plagued his people and their forest, and indeed, all the earth. But at that moment, he felt a bit of hate starting to warm the emptiness, and it felt so much better than nothing.

Rachel brought in the tea and sat down to appraise Theo's readiness for the battle ahead. She saw the distraction in him, and she had little hope that a cup of tea was going to remedy that.

Just then Ari came in, "All right. Everything is taken care of. The security cameras are live, and the men, my best, are ready. Theo, you have the space of some hours before we leave for the lawyer's office to seek what it is you need." And with that, he looked at Theo until Theo's eyes focused and met his own. "I know you are not yourself right now Theo. No one could be after what you've gone through." Here he smiled at Theo, a surprisingly gentle smile for so dangerous a man. And then he held up his right index finger, "But. You must find whatever it is that you need. I know that I don't know what it is. Some of us need hate. Some of us need anger. And some need fear. Theo!" And here his eyes hardened, and they remained set on Theo until Theo wrenched his focus back into Ari's eyes. "Theo," he said sternly, "later there will be time for all of it, all the unfinished business, all of the feelings. Right now is not the time. Later is the time. You see that, don't you?" And here Ari gave Theo the smallest of the smiles in his repertoire. He waited.

A few seconds passed. After a few more, Rachel spoke up, and Ari held up his finger, the sound "Zzzt!" escaping his lips. He would brook no distractions. They needed Theo, and they needed him now. More long moments passed. Then a full minute. Then another. Theo coughed and then reached for his teacup. Taking a sip of the hot oolong, he savored the taste for a moment before saying, "Thank you Rachel, this is the best cup of tea I've ever had." He sat there, breathing a bit normally for a change and then, finally, said, "I'm OK. Let's talk if you need to."

Rachel looked at him more soberly now that she'd had a chance to observe Theo's last exchange with Ari. She looked down, gathering her thoughts before saying, "Theo. We don't need to talk. Maybe you do. Maybe you should talk to whoever it is that you talk to when you need to talk. What we do need is for you to take care of yourself. Are you OK?"

Theo allowed his eyes to float upward for a moment at that question before choking on his answer, "But I can't go swimming now." He looked at his bandages and added, "It's not just these, I can never swim with Christopher again." He wept openly for a moment before pulling himself together, "No, I am definitely not OK. Right now, I don't know if I will ever be OK again." Theo took a very long moment for himself before pulling himself together enough to say, "But I get what you mean, and I do know where I can go to talk to someone."

Startled at this thought, Rachel protested, "Theo, I really don't think we should go any...oh," she finished when she realized that neither she nor Ari would go or even could think of going to where Theo intended to go. She glanced at her phone, "We have a few hours before we're supposed to be at Kate's office. Will that be enough time?

"We'll see," shrugged Theo. He struggled to his feet while the other two looked on helplessly, unsure how to even physically help him without causing him more pain. Theo padded his way down the hall to his home office. He didn't bother trying to turn his head as he said, "I'll be out when I'm ready." The socks on his feet muffled the noise of his passage down the hall. The white bandages on his hands and arms became part of the shamanic shroud he would wear into the spirit realm.

****

Alone, Theo glanced around the room he'd spent so many hours in over the years. He glanced at the floor for a moment, thought about maybe getting a pillow, and then, giving in to his body's pain, he simply sat in his desk chair. He knew that what he contemplated was likely going to be painful, and the chair seemed like a reasonable crutch for, *what I am now*, he thought. He took a breath and remembered himself. He remembered his spirit name given to him by his father shaman, and he intoned, "I am Qohelet, the speaker to the house of our ancestors, the one who speaks to all the houses of all the ancestors." He took another breath and then, quickly, another, followed by many more. Theo knew some in this land had learned the breathwork needed to get to the spirit world, but for him, for anyone as experienced with the medicine, it was much, much easier. After all, the ayahuasca had shown him long ago where he needed to go, and having been there so many times, Theo had confidence that he knew the way without the medicine.

****

As Theo moved into a trance state, he smiled for what felt like the first smile since the beginning of time — so broad and full of joy. He so needed this awareness of the web of life, this intimate connection with all that existed. The Mother floated him into a shimmering pool of fractalized colors where he met another soul, not one of the ancestors, but someone who seemed so very familiar. Theo knew that this was Chris, that he always was and that he always would be, and the two swam together for endless days. When the Mother called him out of the pool, she showed him what he did not want to see, things he did not want to know. Chief among these was that Christopher's existence transcended his relationship with his father, and this humbled Theo. All that was left was love. Grief was replaced by a humble and loving acceptance of who Theo's son was and who he had always been: God's child, and only God's child. Theo had been but the biological instrument of Chistopher's existence on earth. Underlying this new thought was both a sense of personal insignificance and great relief that the web of existence, and Christopher's place in that eternal web, endured and thrived. Theo was left with the rueful knowledge that he'd allowed himself to become lost, when what was needed was for him to remain mindful of the spiritual warfare he'd been enlisted to wage on this spiritually empty nation. His family back home, his tribe, and the entire forest were counting on him. Indeed, the more he learned, the more he realized how this place, his home for the last decades of his life, was the source of a contagion that could kill this entire world.

Of his own pain, Theo felt a grateful sense of resolution. His son's death in no way limited his son's eternal existence. In fact, instead of his son's death being about his son, Theo felt comforted by the last words of the Mother, who, of course, was the feminine aspect of his God. The words, far from sounding as harsh or even as petty and jealous as they once had, were so logical and so comforting now: "Whoever cherishes son or daughter more than me is not worthy of me." Theo now knew that his son was a part of the infinity of all things, and that to love him more than the cosmos that he was but a part of was simply insane. Theo realized that in his thoughts he would now be able to place flowers on his son's grave, peacefully and with gratitude.

Returning, Theo took one last slow breath as he came out of his trance. He had been right to seek out the Mother, but, as always, she hadn't given him what he wanted so much as what he needed. "She is a loving mother," he thought for the thousandth time, "but she is not a gentle mother." Moving to his feet, Theo took a moment to become reoriented to this world, and then padded into the living room while reciting verses from the third chapter of Qohelet:

"Everything has a season, and a time for
every matter under the heavens.
A time to be born and a time to die.
A time to kill and a time to heal.
　A time to keep silent and a time to speak.
A time to love and a time to hate.
A time for war and a time for peace."

Full of a radiant inner peace, Theo knew that now was a time to speak and now was the time for war.

****

"That was only a little over two hours Theo, are you sure you've had enough...." Rachel's voice stilled as she saw the look in Theo's eyes. He's back! she thought to herself.

"Maybe Ari could help me get on some clothes?"

"Sure, I'll get him, he's outside," Rachel answered.

"Thank you, Rachel. Let's get going."

****

After settling in at Kate Barrie's office, Theo felt that he was exactly where he was supposed to be. He didn't know what was going to happen, but he knew that this was a divine appointment. After Ari had checked the security situation at the office and left one of his men in the waiting room, he was persuaded to join Theo and Rachel. They sat across from the attorney, who observed the Israeli's inability to slow down to a truly complete stop as his ears cocked to listen to the noises of the waiting room and his eyes returned to the windows as if expecting an airborne attack.

Kate cleared her throat briefly before making her presentation, "You all probably already know some of what I'm going to say, but I always think it's helpful to get the thoughts of a team before proceeding in these matters. First of all, you, Theo, are charged with two crimes," and here she glanced down at the paperwork in front of her, "one count of Practicing Medicine without a License and another count of Operating an Unlicensed Medical Facility, that is, an abortion clinic." Here she looked up at Theo, "The first charge is a felony in this state. Theo. It's a very serious crime, and if you are found guilty of it, then you are likely to be spending some years of your life in prison, starting at perhaps eight years at the least." She paused, glanced at her small audience, and saw that even the bodyguard had become still in the face of this threat. She continued, "The second is a civil offense, but it comes with serious sanctions including as much as a $5,000 fine for every day the facility was in operation. They're saying here," and just then she lifted up above her head the document she was holding before letting it fall to her glass desk and then, leaning forward to place her forearms on the desk, "that this dates back about three months. So we're talking a potential fine of nearly half a million dollars, Theo."

Looking around her, Kate saw the three quiet (*Good. I so do not need drama*, she thought.), but unafraid faces (*Definitely not normal.*). She plowed ahead. "So I have a few questions for everyone before I share any kind of legal opinion. First of all, Ari, how long have you been involved in protecting Theo?"

"My firm was retained only 13 days ago. I personally went to Theo's office after that, and I am taking responsibility for his security. I was there every workday. That was the total extent of my involvement up until the bombing."

"About that, I have some friends in the police who've given me copies of initial forensics reports. These were rushed due to the seriousness of the crime, and we're lucky to have them so early." Kate glanced quickly in Theo's direction, aware that her remarks could have sounded insensitive, "I...I'm sorry Theo. I've never shared my condolences on your loss. I can't even imagine what you're going through. I'm sorry." Kate was amazed at herself, as she'd never in her life uttered so sincere an apology – much less one that was longer than a simple, two-syllable "Sorry." She didn't like the feelings she was experiencing, so when Theo acknowledged her apology with a nod, she felt relieved as she continued, "The bomb was a relatively simple one. It went off as soon as the car was started because it was wired to the ignition. The explosive seems to have been dynamite, but they're still checking on that."

"I'm pretty sure it was dynamite. The smell and taste are acrid.

Once you've experienced it, you don't forget," Theo's eyes seemed focused on another time and place.

Kate wondered but didn't ask how a marriage counselor would know about dynamite, but she forced herself to conclude, somewhat uncomfortably (*What's wrong with me?*), "And that's about as much as the police know for now." Again, she looked at the three and was gratified by their attentiveness — but somewhat put off her game by their calm and her own uncharacteristic disquiet.

"OK, I have to ask," she burst out, "what's going on? We're talking about some serious business here, and no one seems particularly upset. I have to confess that in my practice of the law, I've done more than a little hand holding with my clients. You three look more like you could take care of me. WTF?"

The three visitors glanced at one another. First Ari spoke, "You know what I do for a living. I am a professional. I know what authority's all about, and here, in this office, so long as I keep everyone safe, I am doing what I am supposed to do. My clients have authority over me, and I have authority over my men, and here, well, here you are the authority. You will tell us what we need to know."

Kate nodded her head, and then, turning her gaze upon the two sitting right in front of her, "And you two? What about you?"

After glancing at Theo and seeing his nod, Rachel spoke first, "This whole thing is because of me, and I guess, you could say because of my big mouth. I went to Theo for counseling about three months back. I was pregnant and I didn't want to be. He explained to me that I didn't have to be — pregnant, I mean. I told him I knew all about adoption options, that I couldn't see ending all my plans for life by becoming a mom at 18 and raising a child by myself, and I told him that I could not and would not have an abortion."

Kate raised an eyebrow, "So...he talked you into one? I mean, I'm just asking, and just so you know, this isn't the last time someone's going to ask hard questions. It's my job to ask."

"No, I remember that he said he didn't think abortion was necessary or the best option or something like that. We talked a lot about what the Bible had to say, 'cause that was important to me." She paused before adding, "It still is," she added quietly. Gathering her thoughts, Rachel continued, "So, when I said that I was ready to hear about other options, Theo explained to me that my mind and my body had the ability to, how did you put it, Theo?" She glanced at him before remembering, "He said my body had the ability to let the fetus know that now was not a good time for me to be hosting company."

"Huh? What did he mean by that?

"Well, Theo taught me about hypnotic trance work and how it could raise or lower a pulse, your blood pressure, or even your temperature. I guess you might know that already?"

Kate was getting impatient, but she knew this was important. So she nodded before saying aloud, "Yes."

"So Theo taught me that I could control the flow of blood to my womb along with the level of the hormone that helps the fetus stay attached. It's called 'trypsin,' and I learned how to do that. Knowing what to do, you know, if I wanted to, well, it was amazing! I really had a choice, and best of all, it was a choice that I felt God had built into me. That night, at home, I entered the trance the way I'd been taught, and I said goodbye to the little polliwog, you know, a sort of 'Come back another day' goodbye. You see?"

Kate remained still as she had become lost in a flood of memories, remembering the panic she'd felt about being pregnant at 17. She had already been accepted to Howard University, and she did not want her life to be over because she'd gotten pregnant. She damn sure didn't want the father of any baby of hers to be the type of loser boyfriend she'd finally figured out was not so interesting as she had first thought. He wasn't all that interested in her either, as he remained loyal to his first love, cocaine. Kate did not want the life her mother had, and so she went to get an abortion at a local clinic. But first, before getting the care she wanted from the doctor, she had to pass a gauntlet of fundamentalist religious maniacs. Some of them shouted, "Murderer!" or "Baby killer!" She saw one of them get out of his car, which had a baby carriage on the roof of it with a Halloween-like mock-up of a baby's corpse stuffed inside it, and then, as she walked the gauntlet of crazies, he ran up and threw liquid on her, saying, "I cleanse you and your thoughts with this holy water!" Inside, once she'd checked in and settled down, she'd overheard another woman say that one of the protesters had spit on her. During her consultation with the doctor, she noticed his curt manner and how he shook his head in disapproval. Before her eyes, he morphed from someone who could help her into just another white man. He'd then said something unwelcome, something downright disapproving of her and her "lifestyle." Hearing another disapproving voice, another male voice, another white man all but "tsk, tsking" her to hell and back, Kate set her jaw and waited patiently for her procedure to be done.

Some months after her abortion, Kate had been approached on campus by students from Campus Crusade, people looking for another notch on their Bibles. She still took some satisfaction from the way she'd been able to dress them all down in such a loud and vulgar payback that the memory still felt empowering. She could still see them turning tail. Since that time, Kate had firmed up her own belief system: 1) She hated bullies, 2) she especially hated bullies who used the love of God as their justification for bullying, and 3) she would never suffer fools again, especially religious ones with a penchant for spiritual abuse.

"Ah, Ms. Barrie?"

Startled out of her reverie, Kate stammered, "Yes, yes. I see... mmm, so you had the choice, and you chose to exercise that choice?" She watched Rachel nod and added, "And there was no surgical setting, no surgical procedure, and Theo never touched you? Is that right?" Again, Rachel nodded. Kate sat back to absorb this news. It was hard to take in that this, this thing was even a thing. She'd never heard of it. She was pretty sure no one had. "So...you didn't even, ah, make the choice you did until later when you were alone at home?"

"Right."

"So, there must be more to the story. You, for sure, didn't drop a dime on Theo, right?"

"Huh?"

"You didn't file any kind of complaint, right, against Theo? With the authorities? Complain to your parents maybe?"

"No, absolutely not, none of that." Rachel sighed heavily, "What I did do was try to help a friend. My friend Amber, I mean, she's not my friend now, but whatever...she told me she was pregnant, the father was a married man — her coach, and like, a member of our church no less. She was only 16, and I just thought I could teach her what I'd learned and well, it wasn't that easy."

"No? Why not?"

"Because she's crazy, that's why! She got all hung up on her guilt, which I don't even think was real, and she confessed her 'sin' at a church meeting. I couldn't believe it when I saw it! Anyway, that's what happened, and that's how the pastor got involved, and that's how the law got involved."

"How's that?"

"You know the DA? Mike Juanarena? He goes to our church."

Kate sat back in her chair and blew out one big, long breath. She knew Juanarena, she'd even briefly served as an Assistant District Attorney with him before he became the DA. She shuddered at the thought of the man and the ruthless ambition that led him to prosecute as loud and as shamefully as possible cases that had called for nuance — where yes, a law had been violated, but the legal remedy sometimes caused more damage to the community than the crime ever had. He especially delighted at prosecuting any sort of sex crime because he knew there was never a downside. There was never a supportive group or an advocacy movement for sex offenders. For Juanarena, sex crimes or any crime with a sexual component wasn't so much a violation of law as it was a cancer needing to be cut from the body politic. Juanarena wasn't so much an attorney looking for the truth as a zealot, making a moral diagnosis and then wielding his scalpel as viciously and self-righteously as he could get away with. Turns out, he got away with it pretty far. There seemed no end to the satisfaction some in the community got from the freedom they felt to hate without reserve or self-consciousness.

Kate blew out a second long breath. "So, I think I see how Theo got on the DA's radar. He's been angling to run for higher office in the next election cycle, and this case must have seemed like a gift from the heavens." She explained, "This is his specialty, sex cases and saving the community from the sexual misdeeds of those around us." Seeing the questioning looks of the three in front of her, Kate explained, "Oh, you two didn't have sex with each other, but it's a case with lots of sex in it, babies being conceived out of wedlock, and now," and here she looked at Theo, "we've got us a sleeper agent who's poisoning the minds of our youth. Next thing you know, women will start thinking they deserve respect." She shook her head bitterly.

"I know I haven't been asked, but I just want you to know that hypnosis is a technique approved of for use in this state by my licensing board. So I haven't violated any ethical guidelines at all to my knowledge." Theo became still.

Kate looked at him and nodded her head in acknowledgement. She looked at Rachel and asked, "Rachel, how does an 18-year-old get the money to hire someone like me? I'm not exactly at the low end of the pay scale," she added, smiling.

"When my parents found out about my involvement and my support of Theo's ideas and his work...his ministry, really. At least, that's what I think it is," and here the younger woman smiled at the older, who, at that moment, felt the same way. "Well, when they found out, they kicked me out, and I had to find a place to live." Seeing Kate's eyes expand in shock, she said, "Yeah, right? My dad especially freaked, you know, since God always confided in him first. It must have been hard for him," she said slyly. "OK, well, it was all OK because I could go out and get whatever I needed, including a house with some office space. And how, you're wondering, did an 18-year-old do that? Well, I started a GoFundMe to help finance getting the message out, and about a jillion people gave me a jillion dollars and so we can afford bodyguards and offices and...lawyers. I wasn't planning on using the money for legal defense though. I mean, we will for sure, but it wasn't part of the plan."

"What was the plan, Rachel?" Kate asked quietly.

"It was a good plan. I planned on renting the university's indoor stadium, you know, the one that they use for basketball games? Yeah, so, we were going to rent that and then publicize the event."

"The event?"

"Oh. Sorry. We wanted to fill 10,000 seats with women who wanted to learn what Theo had to teach them. There would be news crews and a private camera crew making a documentary for YouTube, and you know, whatever. It was such an exciting idea," she added wistfully.

Kate Barrie sat for a while, she looked at them all, one by one, and then her gaze moved to the more expansive view offered through the window as if she needed more room for her next idea. Kate lifted her powerful jaw and pursed her full lips as she took in the image of an arena with 10,000 women. She smiled at the thought, "Maybe this is going to work," she mused.

"OK. I have a plan." Here she paused, as first Theo and then Rachel turned their eyes toward one another. After a moment's remembrance of how they'd each used the same phrase in their short history together, both laughed. Kate didn't know why she joined them, but her face broke into a grin, and she added, "Oh boy, do I have a plan."

She gestured for Ari to come over and join them in a closer conversation. Kate wasn't concerned about her office being bugged because, after all, although she'd been plenty hated and plenty successful financially, she'd never been particularly significant. "But this," she told herself, "is f-ing significant. This is going to turn the world upside down." She bent her head lower and said at a near whisper, "Rachel, go ahead and book that arena or stadium. Go ahead and have your rally. Can you get that done in the next 20 days?" Seeing Rachel nod her head quickly, she asked Theo, "Theo, can you really do this? Can you hypnotize a stadium full of women?"

Theo gave a weak nod and added, "Yes." He paused as if to gather himself before affirming, "Yes I can."

Kate smiled and said, "Oh, Theo, you have no idea how much defense attorneys love to play offense. Now, can you all lean in a bit more, please. You know, the walls have ears." It was hours before they all left, walking in wonder out into a world that was about to die.

In a manner unforeseen by any theologian, the Word became flesh in the dark days of Theo's grief and in his very body. In his final battle against the enemy, after losing everyone and everything that had ordered his life, he became focused on his mission, his reason for even being in this adopted country. He knew that in comparison with his enemies, he had always been outnumbered and had always been discounted as the bespectacled little man with the pronounced limp. It was time for his last move in the seemingly hopelessly lost chess game where the grandmaster, with so few pieces left, quietly makes one last move and, with that move, it is checkmate. And so now, when the words came, he was free to utterly embrace them for their true meaning as the spy and master saboteur he was:

"I send you forth as sheep into the midst of wolves; so be as wise as serpents and as guileless as doves."

Taking on his grief for his camouflage, like the forest owl that guided him, Theo so very much did not appear to be a threat. No one ever saw him as he became Death. But now Death, small and guileless as a dove, was on the wing. Already it was too late for his prey, the beliefs that so formed the ground beneath the feet of his enemy. The hatred of nature and especially human nature in human sexuality. Now Death was descending upon their perverse view of life. Silent. Sure. Doom was upon them, not any person but the powers and principalities of beliefs, of dogmas, of control that justified the perversion of millions of humanity's children.

Chapter 23

"Kate was really smart about this," Theo said as he looked over Rachel's shoulder at her computer monitor. There, as the two sat in her home office, he watched as the audience for Rachel's video on YouTube continued to grow. "Look, we just hit 9,000 views! It's hard to believe that it's only been up a few hours."

Rachel smiled with a look of grim satisfaction at her work. "Using #Polliwog across all platforms has really worked for us for sure." Then, swiveling her office chair around so she could look Theo in the face, she continued, "I already had the audience, and I already had their financial support, so even though everyone has to get a ticket, every one of those tickets is free of charge. First come, first served, right?" Seeing Theo nod at that, she added, "An even bigger gift here is that you're the one catching all the heat, and no one takes anyone my age seriously. I doubt very seriously that the DA has any idea that #Polliwog exists, much less what it is all about, and even less that at our Rally for Women I am not going to be the main speaker. So cool." Here she looked at Theo and smiled devilishly.

Theo laughed, and then more soberly, asked, "Do you think we'll be able to get a decent turnout?"

"Oh, So. Little. Faith! Theo. Look, it's a women-only event, and security and day care are provided — so, yeah, I think women of all ages are going to show up, and I think we are flat out going to be turning people away at the door. But no worries for them, because the film crew is going to rock that video and get an unedited version up on the net before we all get home. Even if we somehow got shut down and the video was pulled, in one hour there will be so many copies floating around that nothing can stop it. To tell you the truth, this is the easiest part for me to imagine, because it's already happening. Look!" and with that, Rachel clicked open another window displaying ticket distribution numbers. "9,000, no, make that 9,478 views and we've got 3,277 women already with tickets. Plus for sure there will be loads of live streaming before, during and after the event!"

"How do you know they're all women? I mean, won't some men try to crash the party?"

"I'm sure that some of these are men, I mean, if only out of sheer orneriness." Just then, her businesslike attitude disappeared, and out came a sarcastic teen feminist imitating imaginary male leaders, "We mustn't let the ladies meet without adequate supervision."

"So then what happens, I mean, if men show up, what happens then?"

"You're kidding, right? 'What happens then?' Theo, Ari happens, that's what happens. I mean, I hope it doesn't get violent, but Theo, there's going to be a news crew there. This is a BIG event, and our town has seen nothing like it. No one has, really. A women's rally to celebrate women's control over their bodies! I mean, I'm really young, but even I recognize this as a big event. So, any publicity over weird men trying to get into a women's rally just makes the event bigger."

"But the date is so soon."

Rachel put on her patient face that she busted out whenever older people just didn't get the power of the net. She nodded and made what she hoped looked like sympathetic eye contact before saying, "Theo, we've only needed ten days lead time to have an event because that's how communication goes now. A global village, remember? That date was open at the arena, and we had the money, and now our people have ten days to figure out how to clear their calendars and get there. We've got the parking, the security and the daycare. All, and I mean all of our service providers are licensed and bonded, so we are good to go. The question is: Will you be good to go?"

****

Theo sat in his dressing room as the arena filled. So far, any concerns he might have had were proving to be totally manageable. Theo sat with himself for a quiet moment and then began to pray. As he did, he remembered Jessa in his prayer, and the divorce papers he'd been served earlier that day. "There's no point in bringing that distraction to Rachel, Kate, or, for that matter," he laughed at himself, "to my own need for focus."

He wasn't nervous, but he was quite aware that, like Ari, he too knew what authority's all about. He too knew that he was both under authority and in authority. Moreover, he knew that this gathering was not really about him in the least. He smiled as he contemplated how tonight he was merely a vessel containing a message. Tonight was not about his ego. It was not about how clever he was. Tonight had nothing to do with him. If anyone, tonight was all about the women gathering outside. Theo thought of the women in his tribe and how much they had endured and how so many of them had understandably faltered in their endurance and had taken their own lives. Theo knew that killing his enemy was the only way to save the women he'd cared about as well as the women he didn't know, who were loved by their own men. Theo smiled at the grim prospect of defeating his enemy, and as he slipped into his own trance, he recited the words from Paul's letter to the church at Ephesus:

> "We are wrestling not against blood and flesh, but against the Archons, against the Powers, against the Cosmic Rulers of this darkness, against the spiritual forces of wickedness in the celestial places. Therefore, take up God's panoply, so that on the evil day you might be able to resist and, having accomplished all things, take your stand."

Theo felt happy as he came out of his trance, still savoring the battle ahead. Finally. And then he remembered how each day since he'd met Rachel — and especially every day that he was aware of her as their Queen — the sheer velocity his mission had taken on had become breathtaking. He was pondering these thoughts with awe when he heard a knock at the door and Kate Barrie burst in.

"Hi there, Theo. I don't want to upset you, but I do want to..."

"Kate! What are you doing here?"

"Wouldn't miss it for the world, Theo, not for the whole f-ing world." She favored him with a fierce smile and then said quietly, "Theo, I need you to shut up and listen because I have updates. First of all, the good news, everything tonight is a go. We're at max seating capacity with over 10,000 women in the crowd. We were a little surprised by it because we didn't expect it, but, well, the cops showed up."

"What? Why?"

"Well apparently some little snitch squealed on us, and the DA ordered the storm troopers out to see just what it was all about. Just as they got here, all ten of them were met by Ari's men, and I'm telling you, there were plenty of them. Security told the cops it was a private event, and Ari told them, "Your services are not required." I think that's how he said it. The cops did not like the sound of that, and for a minute, it looked like it was about to go sideways. But *then*," she paused dramatically, "a miracle happened. Out of the blue, I mean out of the blue comes this guy from the crowd charging in, demanding to be let in 'cause he has a ticket, I mean, you know, to a *women's* rally? Really. I watched this, Theo, I can't f-ing believe it. And then this guy panicked when he saw Ari's men, and then he pulled a gun. I mean, a gun! And Theo, one of the cops yelled, 'Gun!' and then everyone pulled guns out. And get this, the guy, the one who started it all, froze for a second, and that was all one of Ari's guys needed to grab his gun from his hand and then he punched him in the throat. Oh my God! The cops jumped him, cuffed him, and then, get this, they threw in with Ari and they asked how they could help 'secure the scene.' So now, guess what Theo?" She didn't wait for his answer before announcing, "Your event is now under official police protection." Then, standing with her clenched fists at her side, Kate growled, "I. Love. This. Case!"

Theo smiled and thought again of his meditation on Ephesians, which was interrupted by a knock on the door. The woman Theo had learned was the stage manager came in and told him, "You're on in five!" He knew that he was to make his way to the stage.

****

Rachel looked out at the crowd and smiled. Her body mic picked up the most subtle sounds, so she took her time as the whistles and yells grew for a time. She was in no hurry to end the festivities because this would all be getting serious enough soon. *This is a very happy group of women*, she thought to herself. Taking a few more moments to appraise them, she thought, *No, the word is triumphant. I've never seen such strong, triumphant women before*, and with that thought, her eyes filled with tears that she allowed to flow down her face for some minutes before speaking. "A few of you might recognize me from my videos and whatnot." And the crowd created a mushroom cloud of sound that, when it hit her, was more than Rachel could emotionally digest. She swallowed and then smiled, saying, "So, hi everyone, and welcome. Tonight, you're probably expecting me to talk about my experience, and I hope you're not going to be disappointed, but I was thinking you might want to have an experience of your own."

Now it was the assembly's turn to join in, and then one woman screamed, "Yes!" Soon, 10,000 voices joined together in affirmation. It started subtly with a few women, but then it grew until everyone was chanting the syllables, "Pol-li-wog, pol-li-wog!"

Rachel listened for a minute to the power she heard from them, then using her arms to calm the crowd gently by saying, "Let's bring it down a bit, sisters. Tonight, you could hear me talk about my experience with my therapist Theo, but I thought it was better to hear it from him yourselves. Sisters, Theo Van Prooyen!" and with that, Rachel threw out her arm and gestured stage right to welcome Theo into the warm circle of the gathered women.

Theo did his best to walk out as unencumbered looking as he could. But although he may have gotten used to his club foot and to his hands still swaddled in white gauze, this was his first public appearance. What the women saw before them was shocking for a moment, but then, as they hushed their applause, enthusiasm giving way to tenderness, the lame man made his labored, slow walk to center stage. There he stood and as his face panned the gathering. Theo raised his bandaged hands and stretching them out to his utmost, seemed to gather every soul to him. A dignified homage of applause grew louder and went on for a full minute, then another.

Waiting for the crowd to hush, Theo stood quietly for a moment before the gathered assembly and then spoke, "My name is Theo Van Prooyen. I know that not all of you share my faith in any way. I also know that some of you might. You all know my story: Two weeks ago, my 14-year-old son was killed by a bomb meant for me." And here he again raised his still bandaged hands to the crowd, "My hands were burned when I tried to save him from the burning wreckage," and he wept openly, crying into his bandages. Taking all the time he needed to compose himself, Theo allowed his hands to come to rest at his side before he continued, "My faith teaches me that 'Whoever cherishes father or mother more than me is not worthy of me; and whoever cherishes son or daughter more than me is not worthy of me." I have never understood those words before in the way that I do today. Today, I know why you are all gathered here, and I know what this gathering means to you. Today, I know that you are the reason I am still alive because you together, all of you, are the body of the God that I worship. I know that my son lives in you tonight." Here he paused as the crowd became even more still, and then he raised his hands again in a fresh embrace of each soul around him as he slowly turned in place. Then, planting his feet in place as if to root himself into the earth, his gaze swept the assembly and his eyes briefly met those of Ari, "You are my mother...and my brothers." His voice changed as he started anew, "Since I came to America, I have been called Theo." Here he smiled and said, "And I like that name. But my father and mother didn't name me Theo. They named me the longer form that inspired the name Theo. They named me Prometheus." And here Theo smiled as he considered his parents and their love for this world. I believe that my parents were saying something when they named me after a being so full of love for mankind that he was willing to lose everything if only to help humanity. My parents knew that our love of God must never take the place of our love for mankind. They knew that the love of God was in service to humanity precisely *because* He loved us. Today, I want to show you God's love as I understand it."

"From the beginning, humanity has always had the capacity for entering a trance state. In that altered state, we can learn how to set aside pain, to lower our blood pressure or pulse, and even learn to see deeply into the spirit world in visions. Our ability to enter the trance state is a part of our species, of who we are. It is a God given part of who we are or, if you prefer, a wonderful part of our evolutionary path." Here, Theo paused for a moment and then continued, saying, "I am willing to guide you into yourselves if you are willing. If you are willing now to enter your own trance and to learn what Rachel has learned, please get comfortable in your seat. Not to worry," he added, "for those of you who find this difficult right now, there will be follow-up training after tonight. No one will be left behind," and with that, he smiled. Theo waited a moment until the sound of rustling diminished. "Now I'd like you to put your hands on your knees, palms up, and begin with me to breathe, comfortably, just breathe in the same relaxed way that you've done since you were a baby." And as Theo's voice wove a spell of soothing enchantment, those who were ready for trance work, the great majority of the assembly, entered a new world.

Kate Barrie found herself beginning to settle into a trance and then shook it off, telling herself, "C'mon Katie, we're working here." So she instead watched the better part of 10,000 women learn to not only get into a trance, but also learn how to control the flow of blood and of the trypsin in the blood so that any woman might be able to release an embryo she was not ready to host. The whole induction into the trance took less than 30 minutes, and Kate realized that she had just watched, if not a miracle, then certainly the dawn of a new age for women and for all of humanity. The tough lawyer allowed herself a few moments of tears, unashamed at her response to it all.

"And, *three*, as you come out of your trance, you will remember each and every step that we have taken. *Two*, if you choose, you will be able to practice and perfect your trance work so that *one*, your bearing of a child will always be a matter of your volition.

Welcome back, everyone." Theo beamed at the gathered women for a moment and then concluded, "And now, Rachel has a few words for you about what you can expect to see in the future. I thank you so much for allowing me to be a part of your lives today." Theo's eyes glistened with tears of affection, "You are my heroes. You are the ones who will save this world. Thank you."

There was a quiet moment where the newly becalmed and empowered women sat with their freshly acquired strength. And then, they gave Theo the calm, respectful applause of equals as he limped from the stage.

Rachel returned to center stage and addressed the crowd, "Thank you all for making this possible tonight. As you make your way home, please remember those who needed to be here tonight but couldn't, oh maybe three and a half billion or so." She paused to allow for the scattered chuckling. "Tonight, most of you have learned how to take control over your own womb. Practicing your trance work can be done quietly and discreetly, and you will benefit from practice. There was a film crew here tonight, and the unedited video of tonight's event will be on the web in an hour or so. Please download it if you can because we're not sure what the world is going to do with us. You know, Big Pharma, self-appointed moral crusaders, of course, and the politicians who suck up to do their bidding. This was Theo's gift to us, but now it's ours, so let's use it wisely. Goodnight."

Kate stood there, lost in her thoughts and her satisfaction with where her legal strategy was taking them, when she felt someone draw near. It was Ari, who had drawn very close without making a sound until he bent down to whisper into Kate's ear, "You are not going to believe this."

Theo couldn't help how the Word flowed through him as if he were standing in the stream of God's own consciousness. He smiled grimly at the reaction others would have to the trick played on them. He knew that the humor would soon be replaced by his needed response to yet another attack, but still, it was funny. He smiled to think of the king's rage:

> "Then Herod, seeing that he had been made a fool by the Magians, was furious and, dispatching men, he destroyed all the male children in Bethlehem and all its environs, two years old and younger, in accord with the time he had so exactly ascertained from the Magians. Then was fulfilled what was spoken by the prophet Jeremiah when he said, "A voice was heard in Rama, a weeping and a great lamentation: Rachel weeping for her children; and she would not be comforted, because they are no more."

Theo thought quietly for a moment about how this verse had been used as a proof text against abortion, when actually it was about real children who were murdered. In recent days, he had become as much this Rachel as anyone had.

Chapter 24

Michael Juanarena suddenly exploded out of his chair in the conference room of the DA's office, "He did WHAT?" The young peccary before him struggled, one hind leg trapped under the weight of the old caiman, still in shock from the explosive suddenness of the attack.

Brad Collins swallowed and took a moment to try and understand what part of what he'd said was in any way hard to understand. He knew he was trapped and yet didn't understand why or even how. He finally made a decision to simply repeat what he'd just said, only this time more slowly, "Last night, I got a call from a parent I know in church. He had discovered that his daughter was going to attend a woman's rally of some kind here in town. The whole thing had something to do with Rachel Carson, also from church, although, let's face it, the kid's only what? Eighteen? So somebody must have put her up to this or.... Anyway, I called a lieutenant I know down at the police department, you know Mike, we met him at Promise Keepers last year? Well, I emphasized my concern, and he agreed to send some men over there and see what was going on. I think they ended up apprehending a guy waving a gun around. Anyway, so, it's a good thing I sent them down there. After the incident and the arrest, police provided assistance with security, and that's pretty much it."

The old caiman stared at the young peccary thinking, *Someday soon, little pig, I'll be rid of all of you,* as he added Brad Collins' name to a growing list of future feasts. Juanarena was calmer now that he'd had a moment to collect himself and note his menu ideas for the future. He thought to himself, Wait until after the next election. What he said aloud was, "Brad, you said that they had an unannounced speaker, name of Theo. Theo Van Prooyen. You do know, Brad," and here he pronounced the name 'Brad' with the most effortless disrespect in simply lengthening the name's vowel before continuing ponderously, "that Theo is currently under indictment by this office. I know that you know that because you were there when I told the entire staff that I was personally heading up his prosecution."

"Yeah. Sure, I know that. The abortionist, right? If he thinks a little PR is going to save his butt in court, then he doesn't know you very well, am I right?" Here, Brad Collins laughed. It was one of those unfortunate laughs where all the rest of the herd knows you're already dead meat and it's easier for them if they pretend not to hear your squeals. No one else in the room laughed, no one made eye contact with the meat's eyes — eyes that were still alive, but only in a mechanical sort of way, moving as they were from one side of their sockets to the other.

"So you know that he is my case, and you hear something about how he's going to speak at a gathering of, what did you say, women, and you didn't think to call me? Oh, Brad." Mike Juanarena rolled his eyes at the limp slab in front of him, hardly worthy of eating. "So, anyway, how many people did the police say were there, what was it, like a little church fireside room full of the Lutheran Ladies Guild? Brad?"

Brad Collins blanched, swallowed, and then he embraced his career death, "It was at the University arena. The police said it was sold out. About 10,000 people."

Mike Juanarena became still as death for a moment, and then he looked down. Finally, he looked up and said to the unfortunate man, "Brad, I want you to go to your office and make an appointment with Pastor Rob. I'm saying that out of professional courtesy because you're an officer of the court and a brother from church. Make the appointment, OK, Brad?"

Collins nodded.

"And then Brad? Once you've made that appointment for some pastoral counseling, I'd like you to get all of your things together and put them in a box." Then, addressing his attending secretary he said, "Judy, can you make sure Brad gets one of our best cardboard boxes?" Juanarena waited until Judy had nodded nervously, once. "And then Brad, I'd like you to gather your things in that box and pick them up and hold them in your arms, like you might hold one of your crying children at home later tonight when they find out daddy lost his job today. And then, Brad, with your box held tenderly in your arms, I want you to make your way to the secure elevator and go down to the ground floor. And then, Brad, when you step out onto the street, I'd like you to look up where we are at the top floor of this building one last time because you are never, ever going to work in this building again. Brad, you are never going to practice law in this town again. Do you understand me, Brad?"

Stunned by the slow cruelty of the animal world he lived in, Brad nodded and then disappeared from that world. Forever.

No one spoke for a moment. It seemed impolitic to interrupt the digestion of so large a carnivore so quickly after such a meal. Finally, the old caiman looked up, and the smaller crocodilians paid him rapt attention as he said, "So, I hope it's perfectly clear now that if someone hears anything about Theo Van Prooyen, that I want to know immediately. I don't care if you find out that he reads Jane Austin, or if he actually eats gluten, whatever it is, I want to know! Is that understood, hatchlings?"

Surrounding the table of the conference room, little crocodilian heads nodded.

Satisfied that order had been restored out of the chaos of a case careening out of control, Juanarena began giving orders to his staff, especially his investigator. He spoke to the inner circle of his team, "Tomorrow is the prelim. I want a final copy of a gag order on the judge's desk before noon today so that I can shut Theo Van Prooyen up for now until we can shut him down for good."

Conveniently for the court, counsel for the defense had also filed a motion just hours before the prosecutor's motion.

When Juanarena got his copy of her motion, he read it and laughed, "What a stupid woman." Then he made some notes and called in Judy, "Judy, tell your family you're working late tonight."

Judy did as she always did. She nodded. Nervously.

****

The following day in court, once the formalities had been observed, the world's most civilized knife fight began.

"Michael Juanarena for the State, Your Honor. Your Honor, I would like to object to defense counsel's use of a last minute and puerile motion for dismissal of the serious criminal charges in this case. The State has a vital need to see this case prosecuted and to put a dangerous criminal behind bars, and we will not stand by while defense counsel makes a mockery of these proceedings!" And so Juanarena began, his stentorian voice peeled through the courtroom in a manner calculated to impress and to intimidate. The judge actually winced initially, before sighing and setting his jaw grimly for the abuse his ears had to suffer. Toward the end of his initial remarks, Juanarena concluded, "And that Your Honor is why we request that you deny this motion to dismiss these charges, and after making our own case in this hearing, we hope you will grant our motion to impose a gag order on the defendant."

The judge smiled, not so much because he liked Juanarena or his arguments, but at last, the man had stopped talking. Addressing the defendant's attorney, the judge asked, "Ms. Barrie, do you have some remarks prepared?"

Kate Barrie smiled beatifically, "Yes, Your Honor, the defense does have a few small ideas to share with the court. We argue that the evidence, as disclosed in the Criminal Complaint, is simply irrelevant, and it does not support the State's allegations. In fact, your honor, we argue that the evidence, as the State presents it, is simply not evidence of any crime whatsoever. And we would beg the court's indulgence to introduce evidence of our own that is utterly and entirely exculpatory of the charges against Mr. Van Prooyen."

"What is the nature of the evidence you wish to present?" asked the judge.

"Photographic evidence, Your Honor," and with that, Kate Barrie lifted a large manila envelope from the documents she'd brought to court. "The defense wishes to present photographic evidence of a presentation made by Mr. Van Prooyen at a very large and public assembly in this very city in the last week."

"And this evidence from the last week is somehow exculpatory of a crime he's alleged to have committed some months ago in the past?"

"Yes, Your Honor."

"If the State has no objections?"

Michael Juanarena hadn't exactly been caught napping, but he had been thinking ahead about his presentation. He'd assumed that this case, like so many of his others, would effortlessly get out of the preliminary hearing with little more than a rubber stamp, and then he'd be in front of a real judge. Truth be told, he'd never seen a preliminary hearing ever go against the prosecution – at least, none of his prosecutions. The lower court judges just had too much to lose politically to not send a case further up the chain. He'd listened, well, sort of listened, to Kate Barrie, and he'd thought, "Photos? Like I give a crap." Aloud, he unctuously declared, "In the interest of justice, Your Honor, the State is open to a full judicial review of any evidence that might protect someone unjustly accused." And with that, he waved Kate and her manila envelope of, (*What? Polaroids? Ha!*) photos she might have to the bench.

The judge took her envelope and opened it. As he reached in, he snorted just enough to draw the D.A.'s eye forward warily.

"Ah! What's this? A thumb drive?"

"Yes, Your Honor, on it you'll find the complete video record of every utterance of Mr. Van Prooyen."

"Objection, Your Honor! Defense is up to her old tricks of bait and switch. This is not photographic evidence! There has been no proof of the authenticity of this bit of so-called evidence, and the People object to its inclusion in this proceeding, Your Honor."

Kate made as if to speak when the judge raised his hand to her to hold her comments. Turning to Juanarena, he said, "But

Counselor, aren't you the one who said that, what was it, 'in the interests of justice' the State would support a full hearing of 'any evidence' that might be exculpatory?"

"Yes, Your Honor, but...."

"The Court will allow it."

"But Your Honor..."

"Counselor? I took you at your word. The State had an opportunity to object, and with the State's typical generosity in the cause of justice, the State expressed openness to 'any evidence' of this nature. This is a preliminary hearing, Mr. Juanarena. We can afford a little leniency, can we not?" And with that, the judge smiled at Juanarena, having framed the matter in such a way that, for once, Juanarena knew he was boxed in.

"Yes, Your Honor."

"Well, good, now that we're all eager to see this evidence, let's get to it. Bailiff?" Once the evidence had been admitted and tagged, everyone in the courtroom watched as images of Rachel introducing Theo, and then Theo's own presentation played out on the large screen. Thirty-five minutes passed before Theo was finished and said goodbye to the assembled women. The courtroom was still, as if in recognition that they had all been witnesses of something bigger than expected. The earth had shifted under the feet of the prosecution.

"Ms. Barrie, are you willing and able to present witnesses to the effect that this video record is a true and accurate record of the events of that night?"

"Yes, Your Honor. If it pleases the court, we can call..."

The judge held up his hand to indicate that would not be necessary. "Mr. Juanarena, I have read the Criminal Complaint and your other filings in this case, but I want you to tell me right now, as an officer of the court," and here he looked very sternly at Juanarena, "do you have any reason to doubt that this is an authentic rendering of Mr. Van Prooyen's presentation that evening?"

Juanarena felt frozen in time. He finally shook his head, and after clearing his throat, at a near whisper said, "No, Your Honor."

The judge breathed deeply and closed his eyes momentarily in a spell of reflection and then again addressed the confused D.A.,

"And the behavior that we have seen in this video, is this not the behavior that is alleged in your filings with this court?"

There was a longer, much longer pause from those at the prosecution's table. Finally, Juanarena rose again and said, "Yes, Your Honor, but, if it pleases the court, the context of Mr. Van Prooyen's acts renders a different view that the State believes puts his behavior in a different light and..."

"Ms. Barrie, I assume this video has been uploaded to the 'net?"

"Yes, Your Honor. And downloaded, as of now, just over one million times."

"All right. Thank you, Ms. Barrie. The court is ready to render a decision at this time." The judge paused, shuffled some paperwork and said, "I find that there is no evidence that a crime has occurred. I find no evidence that Mr. Van Prooyen has violated any state statute. I dismiss all charges in this matter against him, *with prejudice*," and here the judge stared at Juanarena, and they were both thinking *due to prosecutorial misconduct*, with one tempted to say it and the other hoping to all gods crocodilian that he would not.

Juanarena again stood, "Your Honor, I obj..."

The judge leaned forward, "Don't say it, Mr. Juanarena. Don't say it. If you have any problems whatsoever with this court's judgment, then you may want to take a moment to reflect and to consider your role as an officer of the court and to consider your own mental health needs." He smiled before adding, "I hear that there are some good therapists in this town," and with that, he looked at Theo and again smiled. Then, looking out on the court, most of those present staring at the proceedings in a state of shock, he pronounced, "Court dismissed!" He struck his gavel, and the bailiff yelled, "All rise!" and the judge walked from the bench into his office thinking to himself, *And I thought my last month before retirement might be boring! Well, well.* Theo sat down in shocked and grateful relief.

Theo wasn't sure, even after hearing what was said, what had transpired. But then, his attorney stood and turned to the shocked Juanarena, extending her hand in a sportsmanlike manner saying, "All the best, Mike." Juanarena stared blankly at her for a moment before his eyes grew hard with hatred. He pointedly declined the offered handshake and strode off angrily. Seeing that they were alone, she sat down saying, "Give me a minute, would you Theo?" With that, she took out her briefcase, removed a compact to use the mirror and freshened her lipstick, grateful that she'd grabbed her favorite on the way to court. There was something so right about this particular blood red Smashbox shade. It was then that Theo saw the animal spirit he'd missed in Kate, the jaguar who had just snapped the vertebrae of an older, larger caiman and was simply grooming her bloodied fur after the kill.

"That's better," she beamed at Theo. "Let's go celebrate."

> "Everything has a season, and a time for
> every matter under the heavens. A time to weep
> and a time to laugh. A time to mourn and a time
> to dance."

Theo's heart became afraid in these days because he knew he would be comforted, and he was not sure he could stand it.

Chapter 25

The cork from the bottle of champagne popped loudly, and Kate squealed with unguarded joy, "I *love* this case!" With that, she filled four glasses with the effervescent bubbles, and after handing one to Theo and Ari, she handed one to the underage Rachel with a wink, raised hers and gave a toast, "To life!" before taking an impressive draw from her drink. Ari had no reservations and drank deeply after echoing his own toast in agreement, "L'Chaim!" Rachel joined in more tentatively, as this was her first experience drinking with adults — and she wanted to savor the spiritual significance of the moment.

Theo hesitated, and the longer he did so, each one of the other three took note and wondered what was going through his head. Seeing their looks, Theo smiled and explained, "I haven't told any of you about some of the more personal developments in my life." He smiled again, shyly, not yet truly used to feeling part of a team here in America. He had been alone in his mission for so long that it felt odd to trust again, even his what? Comrades-in-arms? *Yes,* he thought, *we are comrades-in-arms,* and with that he swallowed and smiled at the deliciousness of the bubbles in the expensive wine. After having joined them in the toast to celebrate, Theo's smile disappeared as he related how, the day before the assembly, he had been served with divorce papers.

Kate, as someone who knew all about this sort of suffering, spoke first, "Oh, Theo, I am so very, very sorry. There's no good time for this sort of thing, but that timing must have been terrible for you." Something about Kate's tone told Theo that she understood perfectly how he felt.

"Theo, I'm sorry. Please let me know if there's anything I can do," offered Ari, always the practical problem solver.

"I...I don't know what to say. I mean, I feel bad for you, but I never dreamed, I mean, you're my counselor, and I guess I just had no idea you had a life where something like that could happen. I mean, oh, I'm so sorry Theo. I really don't know what I'm saying."

Theo smiled as the contradiction grew between Rachel, their Queen, and Rachel, the teenager having her first drink. Looking around the room, Theo acknowledged their love and support, saying, "I know you are all there for me. I just didn't want to deal with it at the time, and I didn't think it would help any of us. I guess I thought it was just a distraction." Again, he smiled, "And frankly, I'm not the one who is usually sharing his burdens with others. Thank you all." He gazed warmly at each one, and after raising his drink again, took another sip. Everyone joined him in a quiet display of solidarity. "But," he added solemnly, "there's something more."

Kate, still enjoying the satisfaction of her most recent kill, was quick to respond, "Theo, have you ever heard the expression 'buzz kill' before? C'mon, give us a minute to savor the sweet success we've enjoyed here. There's no rush!"

"There might be a little bit of a rush," Theo murmured. Seeing Kate raise a questioning eyebrow, he clarified, "My board wants to strip me of my license. I got the notice of the hearing right after the assembly, but again, we were dealing with so many other unbelievably more serious matters that I just thought I could keep it to myself for the short haul. After all, if I was going to prison, losing my license was the least of my problems. But now...it's really just about all I have left."

Only Kate, a licensed professional herself, really understood what he was saying. Revocation of licensure meant loss of income, loss of professional identity, loss of purpose, and a pitiable melting away of years of work and emotional investment. The enormity of what Theo was facing after losing his son, and now his pending divorce, was daunting – even to the tough attorney.

The other two in the room didn't know what to say.

Theo laughed aloud as he added, "And I got a call last night informing me the church elders were meeting this week to disfellowship me. They said the process was 'an act of love' and was in response to their belief I was living in 'a state of sin' for which I was 'unrepentant.' If I want to be present for that, well, they're meeting this week, the day after the board meets."

Kate shook her head bitterly before saying, "Jeez, Theo, if it was me and they told me it was an act of love, I think I might want them to love me a little less." Then her eyes narrowed, "You know, I smell Mike Juanarena's cologne in all this stink." Theo saw the jaguar's eyes grow hungry.

"Disfellowship?" Ari questioned aloud.

"Something like Catholic excommunication,'" explained Rachel.

"Ah!" said the taciturn Israeli.

"Whew," Kate exclaimed, "Theo, this is a lot to take in. But, after everything, do you really even care? I mean, it's not like they've been there for you in all this?"

"To be honest," Theo smiled weakly, "I'm pretty numb right about now. I don't know what I feel or what to think."

Rachel stared at Kate as if to say, "*Do something!*"

Kate went on, "The one thing I know, Theo, is that retaining options is better than having them taken away. We should, I don't know, maybe make a *plan?*"

Everyone but Ari laughed at the word that each of them had used at critical beginnings in their past together. The normally reserved Israeli spoke thoughtfully, "What I have learned is that there are no great operations, not even the most successful, without some losses. Theo, yes, you may lose your license, and yes, you may be thrown out of your church. But Theo, consider our wins. You will not be convicted of a felony. You will not go to prison. And I know you would have been happy to pay both prices if that meant being able to teach women, to teach humanity, about our true power to control our bodies. There are women who will never have to fear pregnancy as a result of rape ever again. There are women in war zones and elsewhere around the world who will never have to be forced to bear a child against their will. There are women, and men too Theo, who will bless you forever for what you have done. And we're worried about a meshuggah church that doesn't want you? You should be so lucky! And a license? To do what, counsel meshuggah marriages? Don't you all realize how big this is? Theo, whatever you do for a living, it sure as hell won't be counseling."

Theo smiled at Ari's confidence. He didn't feel the same, but he knew that his mission had been accomplished. He knew that Ari was right about the size and scope of the mission, even if Ari didn't understand the fullness of Theo's motivations. Theo felt certain that the video of the assembly was a fatal blow against a host of evil entities, "the Cosmic Rulers of this darkness" Paul had warned of in Ephesians.

But still. The truth was that Theo had built a life in America, and he, the lame man with the owl-like face and the round glasses and his weathered cane, was a warrior. It was not in his nature to take abuse lying down. He would fight. Even in losing, if it came to that, Theo would leave a blow the enemy would never forget.

****

Theo watched as the elder member of the Board of Examiners clicked her pen nervously for maybe the 100th time, her steel-gray hair almost blue in color. Her cat-eye glasses would have appeared retro chic on a younger woman but on her, they simply looked as though she was using her frames from a very long ago 7th grade.

As Theo waited for the Board to get to him, he had nearly three long hours to consider the 14 board members present as they worked through their admin agenda. He had been a bit nervous at first, but as the opening agenda items droned on, the boring procedures had dulled his initial attentiveness. The meeting was called to order by, surprisingly, the county Undersheriff who seemed to have no real expertise on counseling but who, with his position on the Board, gave the rest of the members a comforting sense of authority. The minutes were read. Then approved. Theo's eye moved on to the single black member of the Board, a younger man than nearly all others present who stayed quiet for nearly the entire hearing. He noted that Rachel, sitting with Ari in attendance, was looking at him encouragingly. He smiled back at her.

The Board voted in a new member after she'd made a longish speech on her own behalf, circling back so many times to the most banal of self-congratulations that Theo smiled as he wondered, *When is she going to mention being the valedictorian in her kindergarten class?*

The Board then reviewed a series of administrative disciplinary cases involving counselors who'd been engaged in one sort of misconduct or another. All of the counselors "in trouble" made statements of contrition, testifying to how remorseful they felt about their past conduct, about their need of a second, third, or even fourth chance, or of how their new humility has helped to "inform their practice." It surprised Theo that all the older Board members seemed quite comfortable in their role of confessor. And they dispensed absolution generously, as religious leaders might with guilty sinners finally confessing their sin. Theo noted that the absolution dispensed was in direct proportion to the self-profession of guilt. One board member who, like the Undersheriff was not licensed, seemed to particularly relish her role in the inquisition of a licensed counselor. She then questioned another petitioner, "How can you do better self-care?" Her appearance was a remarkable study in the passage of geologic time: There was the early bad girl period with tattoo references to drugs and the counterculture of two generations gone, then there was the later good girl period where the tattoos seemed to reflect religious faith, followed by the upper strata of large gauges in her ear lobes reflective of a desire to present a more youthful statement. These gauges were shiny and new looking; the newer ink colors on her arms were sharper, bolder than the obviously older work. Theo found himself completely absorbed in her visual history as the board droned on.

"Can I have a motion from the Board?"

"I make a motion."

"I second that."

A vote was taken, and a career was salvaged from moral ruin.

It was now Theo's time in the box, and as he looked around, he realized that the tired board members were both drained and bothered at having to deal with him. The Undersheriff read the accusations against him, "Mr. Van Prooyen? It says here that you not only encouraged young girls to get abortions, but that you also taught them how to perform abortion on themselves by use of hypnosis." After reading this last piece, the man looked a bit confused, and he looked around the table at the assembled board members, "Is that right? I mean, what does that even mean?"

The board's legal counsel from the State A.G.'s office perked up. He ponderously lifted his head from his supporting hand. The skin of his face stuck briefly to the man's palm, the cheek's resting place. As the attorney unlimbered himself from his headrest, he read from his notes, "I believe this complaint has been filed by the local district attorney, Mr. Juanarena, who reports that he conducted a lengthy investigation into Mr. Van Prooyen's professional conduct, and he has supplied us with documentation containing the results of his investigation — including various witness statements."

The Undersheriff listened attentively and then asked, "So, has everyone had a chance to review the documents?" Heads nodded, enough of them anyway.

"So I understand that you have one or more witnesses, Mr. Van Prooyen?"

"I have one, a former client, Rachel Carson, right there," and then Theo used his chin to point in Rachel's direction.

At this point the A.G.-appointed legal counsel objected, saying, "I don't see how having students testify is appropriate, especially one who is alleged to have been the victim of Mr. Van Prooyen's... ah...questionable techniques. I think we could simply proceed by having Mr. Van Prooyen give us his side of things and then take it from there if we have any further questions."

The Undersheriff, as lead administrator, might have seemed like an authority figure to some on the Board, but he had correctly intuited that this was a complex legal matter in need of some real lawyering. Unfortunately, all he had to work with was the sleepy Assistant State Attorney. He had already calculated that the A.G.'s lawyer was likely well acquainted with Juanarena and that he was being very careful to avoid any potential political payback later. He smiled knowingly at this knowledge of the game and how it was played. He knew that the next time this lawyer was looking for a cushy public job, Juanarena would owe him a favor. This thought reminded him of his own exposure to Juanarena, because not only did they go to the same church, but that someday there would be an election for a new sheriff. So he said, "I rule that the young lady will not be a witness. Now I need a motion to close the evidentiary portion of our deliberations."

The lady with the cat-eye glasses spoke up, "I make a motion to close the evidentiary portion of the deliberations on Van Prooyen."

Theo looked around wildly, utterly at a loss, "Ah, wait a minute, I have a witness."

"I second," said another board member.

"A motion has been moved and seconded. All voting to close the evidentiary portion of this hearing, raise your hands. All those voting say 'nay' to the motion. The motion is carried, and the evidentiary portion is closed."

Over Theo's verbal protest at the rigged sense of the hearing, the Assistant State Attorney advising the board reminded everyone that once the Chair had made a ruling on excluding a witness, that witness was excluded. He said the motion to terminate the evidentiary portion of the hearing was duly made, seconded, and voted on, and so it too stood with the force of law.

"I have a few questions for Mr. Van Prooyen, if that's all right," said the blue-haired woman peering over her cat-eye glasses. Seeing the Chair acknowledge her with a nod, she smiled and continued, "Mr. Van Prooyen, I understand that a lot of this complaint has to do with hypnosis. I find that unusual, and in a case like this involving young people, it concerns me. Do you use hypnosis a great deal?"

"Yes, I do. I have been trained extensively in its use, and the use of hypnosis in psychotherapy has been known, accepted and even embraced by the profession for many decades."

"But not that many people in the profession use the technique, I mean, of those professionals supervised by this board, its use is, I think we could say, rare?"

Theo nodded his head, and then after prompting from the Chair, he said aloud, "Yes, I suppose."

"I find that suspicious in itself," she stated with no intent other than that of casting a shadow of suspicion over Theo's use of hypnosis and over Theo. She continued, "And I guess I don't understand why you would try to influence young people, young girls, to get an abortion — or should I say, to give themselves an abortion. Can I say that?" Just then she looked at the Chair for approval, and getting it, continued, "I mean I think I speak for a great many of us on the board who value the sanctity of life, and even the suggestion that you would talk this way, I mean, whether it resulted in a terminated pregnancy or not, just seems very wrong. In fact, I think this sort of, if we can even call it 'counseling,' rises to the level of corrupting our youth. What do you have to say for yourself?"

Theo thought for a moment, and then he accepted his fate, "I do help women, *adult women*, learn how to use their own bodies in a way that was not invented by me, but instead was created by the same powers that gave rise to the development of the eyes, the kidneys, and the brain. Women have always been capable of doing this. I'm being accused of showing them how to, yes, terminate a pregnancy that they do not want and that they do not give their consent to. It's not surgical, and no drugs are used —but if you want to call it an abortion, I can't stop you."

"So, you basically admit to the accusations leveled by Mr. Juanarena?" asked the lone black man on the board. "I mean, young girls, still teenagers, were caught up in this, Mr. Van Prooyen."

Theo smiled, "Well I admit that I did teach women how to use their bodies in a way that they could control. I believe that they have a right to this because it is their body after all. I also believe that, even if someone believes abortion is wrong, that forcing a woman to have a baby against her will is a greater wrong."

"Well, that's just murder," said the kindergarten valedictorian, the newest member of the board. "I mean, in this state we do have a fetal personhood law, and you would be in violation of that law, I do believe."

"No, I've already been through that side of things in court, and I'm not in violation of that particular miscarriage of justice. Perhaps that's because I simply teach women how to control their bodies, and then they can choose whether or not they are ready to host company."

"Is that your euphemism for abortion?" asked the Geological Wonder.

"Well, I think words matter, and again, since there is no surgery and no drug is involved, I think another term is to be preferred. The real problem here is that so few people seem to think women capable of making these sorts of decisions on their own. I mean, whether we use my language or yours, right?"

"We'll be asking the questions here, Mr. Van Prooyen," interrupted the Chair after being nudged by the attorney from the A.G. and whispered at for a moment.

Theo smiled. He already knew the lay of the administrative land, but something Kate Barrie had said was prompting him to continue speaking, "Create a record, Theo, just tell the truth and let them hang themselves. We'll get 'em on appeal."

Theo continued, "So, rather than a secret surgical procedure or getting some medicine in the mail off the internet, women can quietly decide for themselves how to manage their wombs. No one would even have to know she'd ever been pregnant, which, if you think about it, is a long overdue bit of privacy."

"I think even learning about this technique could be interpreted as 'Endangering a Child,' and that level of endangerment would be a felony," said the board's official investigator, a retired counselor who now served the Board as their private investigator. He had remained silent up until this moment but he seemed to take professional satisfaction in making this point.

Theo made eye contact with Rachel for a moment and smiled as he took the death blow in this, his last moments as a licensed professional, "'Endangering a Child?' Well, that's what is so entirely wrong about all of this. Only a child is a child. My client was legally an adult so she is not a child. Her pregnancy didn't involve a child because a fetus is not a child. An embryo is not a child. And a zygote is not a child. And none of these things, not one of them, are a child any more than a polliwog is a frog. Even children know this. Even children know that polliwogs are not frogs. This is so confusing to all of you only because of your need to control the women around you. You actually think that this is your business, but it's not. If you really think that fertilized eggs were people, then you would be demonstrating outside of fertility clinics that have freezers full of fertilized eggs! You don't really believe that those fertilized eggs are people, and I don't believe that polliwogs are frogs. This is all about control, and that's all it is. You should be ashamed of yourselves. And the only way you justify this is that you do all of this in the name of God, as if He were in an incompetency hearing and in need of your legal guardianship."

****

Moments later, the vote was taken, and Theo told Rachel he was really surprised that he'd gotten five out of fourteen board members to agree with him. Maybe Kate could do something after all.

Theo pondered his fate. His career seemed over with his licensure now gone. His Christian marriage was ending in divorce. He had dodged the label of "felon," but he hardly believed that was the last he'd hear of that slander. He had no home, no family, and now it appeared he was to be cast out from the church his parents had served with their very lives. He sighed and then unexpectedly laughed. "Father, forgive them, for they know not what they do."

Chapter 26

On the day of the church's proceedings against him, Theo found the church's parking lot much fuller than he'd anticipated. Ari, who was driving, raised an eyebrow in question. Theo simply shook his head, rolled his eyes, and shrugged his hands up into the air in his silent commentary with the man he now thought of as his friend. Theo realized that he had no idea what to expect. He had assumed that the church would have liked news of his impending disfellowship to be kept quiet.

As Theo got out of the car, he pulled himself up and out through the door, leaning heavily on his cane. As he began his usual pained limp toward the church's entry, Theo marveled at how his Israeli bodyguard was able to somehow blend his strong stride into Theo's own impaired gait. Just then they both caught sight of a familiar friendly face.

"Hi, guys," Rachel said in disarming good humor. The young woman surveyed the jammed parking lot before continuing, "I called around, and it seemed that no one knew about this little hearing of Pastor Barton's. Amazing what a little Twitter blast can do, isn't it?" she said in a made-for-comedy sunny voice. "I also heard someone gave a heads up to the local TV news, and they'll be here any minute." She leaned forward to both men and gave them a conspiratorial wink, "Three reporters are already in there embedded with the congregation."

Theo didn't know what to say, but his smile — stretching from one side of his round face to the other — spoke for him.

"Oh yeah, I almost forgot," she said with her own grin, "Our downloads are over two million. 127 countries, can you believe it?" She added hurriedly, "You two go on in. I'll be along once I've oriented the news crews to the set up." Now, looking Theo warmly in the eye, she smiled, grasped his free forearm with a strength that surprised him and said, "No matter what happens in there today, Theo, you are my brother forever."

Theo's eyes filled with tears as he looked down. It had been so many years for him, more than he'd realized, since he'd known a true sense of tribe in this godless land. This country was full of lonely, isolated people, and Theo realized that he'd become one of them. Rachel's words reminded him how long it had been since he'd felt understood and loved. He did nothing to stop the flow of tears down his face, and then after a settling breath, he said, "And I am honored to have you for my sister, O Queen of Tears."

Rachel seemed to understand, nodded her head briefly, and with a gentle smile, turned to face the incoming vans from the local news stations.

The two men made their way into the church, Ari glancing inside to make sure all was clear before holding the door so Theo could enter. As they walked down the foyer wondering where in the building they should go, Elizabeth came out of the sanctuary and hurried over to them. Her face, Theo noticed, was both welcoming and serious, "Theo! Ari! I am so glad to see you both, especially before the hearing."

"Liz, we're looking for the office where the hearing is being held. It's a little confusing with all the people here, and I don't know what's going...."

Elizabeth looked at Theo, her eyes broadening into saucers, "You on't know?" She sniffed in theatrical disapproval, "Well, Theo, you're good enough as a counselor I suppose," and here she looked up and rolled her eyes in friendly exasperation. "Theo. Everyone who is here is here because of the hearing. Some people want your head...OK, a lot of people want your head, but a lot of people are here in support of you. Both sides demanded, *demanded* an open hearing. So," she concluded, "we're all in the sanctuary. It's as full as a big Sunday service, and Pastor Rob does not look happy about it — although you know how he is," she nodded knowingly, "He always puts a brave face on, but this is different." She said, in a loud whisper, "People were quoting the Bible to him, can you imagine. Luke 12:2, no less," and here she quoted, "*There is nothing thoroughly veiled that will not be unveiled, or hidden that will not be known.*"

Theo nodded and stared at Liz as he added the next verse, "*Thus the things you said in darkness will be heard in the light, and what you whisper in private rooms will be proclaimed on the rooftops.*" Then he nodded, almost entirely to himself. "Well, then, I guess we should go in."

They opened the door into the large auditorium to find, just as Elizabeth had said, the sanctuary was quite full. Up toward the front on the raised platform sat the men on the Board of Elders. Pastor Rob presided over the group that was to decide his fate — at least as far as Pastor Rob's church was concerned.

Theo found himself feeling a sense of numb equanimity. He thought to himself, "It's OK if the church casts me out, it's OK if they don't." The numbness he felt he chalked up to the trauma of recent events in the last month: his son had been murdered, his wife was divorcing him, he'd been put on trial for felonies, and even though he'd won, his counseling practice was dead, and... and millions of women were learning The Way. Theo smiled to himself as he reflected on what he'd tell any of his patients in such a situation: "That's a lot to carry."

He and Ari began threading their way to the front of the church, as he assumed that there would be seating for him. The congregation quieted as they noticed the two men making their way down the aisle. They were a study in contrasts. Theo was lost in his thoughts, while Ari's senses were hyperaware of the facial expressions and comments he heard in passing. He was aware in a manner known only to those who have fought and seen death dealt. His body's deliberate movement served as a warning of his own familiarity with and willingness to inflict harm. The angry men who'd been gossiping freely about what they'd do to Theo if any of what they'd heard was true found themselves staring into Ari's stony gaze — and there, found something that made them ease off a notch or two.

Theo's eyes met those of Mike Juanarena, who had turned in his aisle seat to face Theo. The man was gloating at what he was assured would be Theo's painful comeuppance. Theo paused in the aisle and asked Ari, "A moment?" Then he limped closer to the powerfully built man in his seat, leaned over and looked him in the eye, "I saw Satan fall like lightning from heaven." And here Theo gave an owl-like quick blink of his eyes before adding, "It's over for you." The old caiman shuddered, closed his eyes, and retreated back into the dark water. Theo looked up, blinked at Ari and smiled, "Sorry, I had a little business to finish up."

Just then, Pastor Rob walked up, and after glancing nervously at Ari for a fleeting moment, greeted Theo as if this were any other day and not a day for an ecclesiastical lynching. He seemed upbeat, "Theo, we have a seat for you, and ah, your friend here in the front row. We'll call the meeting to order in a few minutes, and we'll call you up at the appropriate time. All right? Thanks, brother!" And with that bizarrely cheery note, he was off, the camouflage of the serpent's scales blending into the social background of the church that preferred in-house predators.

Theo and Ari didn't say a word until they found their seats, and then, turning to Theo, Ari whispered, "I might have to move now and then for tactical reasons. Don't think I'm leaving."

Pastor Rob slithered up to the microphone, trying very hard not to look nervous. He was never nervous, but no one had told his face that today. His eyes held fear in them for those discerning enough to see it, and his hands visibly trembled as he took the mic in hand.

After the invocation, Pastor Rob faced the congregation. He stood there for a moment, struggling with a last, pesky flicker of conscience about what he intended to do. Then he remembered that he hadn't spared his own son the rite of exorcism in order to save him from the demon of homosexuality, and this thought steeled his nerves. He said, "Our church is a loving church, but even in the most loving church, we must sometimes discipline one another with the goal of restoring those who are rebellious back to full fellowship. Today we are all gathered to determine whether or not our brother, Theo Van Prooyen, needs such loving intervention. Tragically nowadays, the exercise of such loving discipline, in the form of disfellowship, continues to be a neglected obligation. At least this is true in our modern times. It was not so in the church of Paul, and it was not so in the church of Peter. The apostles enjoined us to put away the wayward among us so that we might ultimately save his soul. That is why, on this day, we have gathered, all of us, to consider such radical discipline."

Theo found himself appreciating the man's native political cunning. He was presenting the entire affair as an expression of the will of God, and he swept everyone present into the mandate for discipline, as if his spirit guide, the boa, was hypnotizing a room full of spider monkeys — so intelligent, but no thumbs. His thoughts were interrupted by Barton's next words.

"Theo Van Prooyen. Please rise. You have been accused of promoting abortion, a vile practice eschewed by our church and in defiance of the Word. You have been charged with criminal acts related to helping women obtain abortion through means that are tainted with the demoniac influence of hypnosis. By finding legal loopholes, your lawyer may have been able to help you evade those criminal charges of the state, but we, the people of God, are held to a higher standard, and so too do we hold you to that standard. What have you to say in this matter?"

This was Theo's opening. Pastor Barton had simply meant he wanted to know if Theo would plead guilt or innocence in the matter. But when the lame man pulled himself up out of his chair and looked sadly at the gathered congregants before smiling a bit, the pastor felt as uncertain as anyone else about what to do. After all, he'd never even seen anyone in a disfellowship proceeding, much less officiated one himself. The crowd maintained silence as Theo shambled across the carpet leaning on his battered cane. His round face, set off by his glasses, accentuated his owl-like appearance. Theo looked like the cloud forest owl himself, all-seeing, wise, and yet somewhat comically befuddled by the bright overhead lights.

Watching this, Liz remembered how easy it was to underestimate this man. *No one can imagine, no one can know how dangerous he really is,* she reflected, smiling to herself as her thoughts hovered over the scene, her sharp bill always ready to defend her territory.

Pastor Rob started to speak some four different times as Theo made his way to the platform, but each time he found himself stopping with an inaudible hiss of frustration. He knew Theo, and he respected the man's strengths, but Pastor Rob knew how it would play out if he were anything but kind and considerate in his handling of someone perceived as being "handicapped," much less "crippled."

Finally, after Theo had made his slow ascent up the steps of the stage, he made his way to the microphone for his first and his last sermon.

"Please allow me a moment to express my thoughts. I promise I'll be brief." Theo smiled at the people who had been such a big part of his life since coming to America. "As many of you already know, I am the orphan son of Jayden and Jana Van Prooyen, a couple who were sent out from our church as missionaries to the forest people of Peru. As hardly any of you know, Theo is a nickname; my dad was a scholar of Greek, and my mother one of art, and together they named me Prometheus after the one who betrayed the command of the gods in order to help humanity." And here, he looked at the congregation for a moment, as he waited just the right amount of time to say, "It was a big name for a baby." Quiet laughter filled the room. Theo smiled again before continuing, "My parents died in the jungles of Peru trying to share what Mark's gospel calls "the good tidings of God." Instead of sharing with the natives, they died, and those same natives shared with me their own spirituality. Because of my beautiful foot, I was adopted by the shaman of the tribe, and I was educated in all the ways of the spirit world. As an educated person of the forest, over time it became clear to me that western culture's invasion of the Awajún's territory was a clear violation of all that was right. Eco-pirates were destroying the forest for wood and gold, and along with killing the forest, they were killing all the life depending on it. Missionaries of all kinds were the cultural part of this material invasion, and neither of them had respect for the thousands of years of spiritual journeying the Awajún, the People, had made or for all they had learned. This invasion, your invasion, was destroying everything sacred, everything beautiful, everything that was perfect in our lives. Our women were so distressed by this assault that they began committing suicide in ever increasing numbers. We had a life!

And so, we had to do something to protect it. We had meetings to talk about the war the West was waging on us, and we consulted with the spirit world and our ancestors through our medicine *ayahuasca*. Finally, after much seeking, the People decided to send you help so that this sick, sick world of yours...of ours, could be healed. They sent me. I was 15 years old." Here Theo paused to allow his listeners, Rachel, Liz, and Ari among them, a moment to absorb his strange tale.

"I came as an army of one. I know you all saw a boy and a crippled one at that. But! But, I had been in training for years, taking the sacred medicine and learning The Way. I became a warrior shaman in this world with the help of my spirit guide in the spirit world, and I was ready to do battle with the dark forces of this place." At this point the crowd stirred audibly in their discomfort.

"And then a miracle happened. I came to America where I met Jesus, the Anointed One, and I found him to be beautiful. I knew then that there was hope for this world, and in my journeys into the spirit world, I communed with the Anointed One, and I learned his ways. And his ways became my ways as I searched for how I was to fulfill my mission and save my people." The crowd seemed to relax even as Theo shared his Christian beliefs.

"And then, one day, the moment of battle arrived when I met one of the great spirits of this place. She was truly great, but she needed help that day so that her spirit could survive and become strong. This great spirit, whom I know as the Queen of Tears, was pregnant and did not want to be so. Her boyfriend was a pastor's son. For his part, he was trying so hard not to be gay that he had sex with her in an effort to escape himself. Then, as she fantasized about marrying him and having a life together, he let her know that he was leaving this area with his boyfriend to have a life elsewhere." At this last, Pastor Rob's blood drained from his face, and even if he'd wanted to, he could not have brought himself to speak.

Theo continued, "So I helped her. I explained that God had made her body in such a way that, if she wanted, she and she alone could decide that now was not the right time for her. I explained to her that she did not have to be hosting company within that secret and sacred space within her. I explained to her how she could access this sacred space that God had made her. I taught her how to engage her God-given gift, or not, as *she* desired." Here Theo paused again, his audience rapt with fascination over these disclosures, and then, as Theo continued, he raised his voice to a commanding volume and tone that no one in the church had ever heard from him. "And *that, that* is why I am before you today. I helped a woman understand God's ways inside her body and how she could use that gift to save herself as she desired. I helped a woman understand that she, and she alone, was responsible for her choice to keep or to discard her pregnancy!" Theo looked around a moment and then raised his voice to take command of the hubbub about him. "And before you ask, let me answer the question some of you are thinking, 'But Theo, are you saying that killing an innocent human baby is right or acceptable in any way?' The room stilled as if everyone was holding their breath as one.

Then Theo spoke with authority, "There was no baby. An embryo is no more a child than a polliwog is a frog. And because of my training in the forests of Peru and my faith in Jesus, I believe that all life is never ending, and that we all live together in a consciousness that is all-knowing and forever. I believe that we are all a part of the body of Christ, we are all part of God, we are all one with the father. I am on trial today for believing in the omnipresence of God — how many of us believe God is everywhere and in all things."

The auditorium erupted into pandemonium. Pastor Rob looked in horror at the chaos about him. The elders of the church all seemed to want to shrink back, trying to retreat from words and thoughts that they'd never signed up to hear. Some people were so repulsed by what Theo said that they seemed to be on the verge of violence, but they were instead engaged in fierce argument by those who thought that if God Himself lived in women and that He had made women capable of deciding for themselves, then the church should honor that at the risk of blaspheming God's name.

Just then a voice rose above them all, "You kill babies, and you've taken my daughter away from God, and you deserve to die." It took Theo a moment to locate the source of the outcry, and when he did, he saw that it was Larry Carson, Rachel's father, coming through the crowd quickly. In his hand was a gun. Theo glanced at the right side of the auditorium and saw Ari, gun drawn, hurtling bearlike through the crowd to intersect the man's path. But clearly, Ari wasn't going to get there fast enough, and he couldn't get a clear shot because of the crowd.

Carson stopped, extended his right arm, aimed and squeezed the trigger just as Rachel shouted, "No!" throwing herself between her father and Theo. The loud crack of the pistol stilled the crowd, and then Larry Carson looked down, first stunned and then horrified at what he'd done. His bullet had caught his daughter just so, and suddenly, nothing else mattered. He dropped his gun just as Ari was upon him. The bodyguard snatched up the firearm and secreted it somewhere on his body while the father, crazed with horror, clutched his daughter to his breast. "No, no, no," he moaned.

People were trying to get away, but some in the church were medical professionals. Among them were those who stepped forward to render first aid, attempting to staunch the flow of blood from her wound. They found their way, impeded by the grief-stricken father who refused to release his daughter, until Ari, without wasting a word, struck the man across the back of his head with the butt of his Glock. Once unconscious, the father was unceremoniously pulled aside, and those present began to care for Rachel, whose eyes looked up the ceiling, empty in shock.

"Let me in! Let me in!" Theo didn't walk like a crippled man unless the camouflage suited him, and now he was fully in his avatar, an owl of the cloud forest, effortlessly gliding past the people in his way as he made it to Rachel. Theo could see that the bullet had gone through her upper chest, close to the shoulder, and he spoke his heart, oblivious to the onlookers as he urged powerful spirits to intervene. "Queen of Tears, Queen of Tears! You knew I needed you and you came to me! My queen, my queen!"

Rachel was still breathing when the ambulance came and snatched her up for the ride to the hospital. The police arrived at the same time and took Larry into custody, perversely stopping first at the same hospital that would try to save his daughter's life in order to attend to his now throbbing head wound.

Theo and Ari raced to the hospital without words. They paced the waiting room for hours as they waited for news to come out of the OR. They were joined by Elizabeth and her 13-year-old daughter as they all waited to hear what the surgeons would have to say.

Alma Rodriguez, working the desk at the gate at the Dallas/Fort Worth International Airport, looked up, but not too far up, at the short man with a face as round as an owl's. He even looked owlish as he peered at the monitors with the flight information. He smiled after he became aware she'd noticed him, "Is this the right gate for the 10:15 flight to Lima?" She smiled, nodding, and added, "You can do all of your check-in on your phone if you like."

He smiled even more broadly, "I don't have a phone," as if he were a patient who'd found out he didn't have cancer.

After taking care of checking in, he saw that he had some time and headed for the bookseller's stall. There, he perused the headlines of the world's daily news: various iterations of stories like "Women in Control of Own Bodies" and "Church Upheaval!" made up most of them. He looked at the business news and saw that Big Pharma stocks were taking a hit from an unexpected decline of contraceptives and a fear that this new tech would utterly disrupt the industry. Perhaps the biggest change was in the world of politics, where suddenly, the label "pro-life" was no longer relevant in terms of voting. Things were changing fast. Far faster than those who wanted to resist change could cope with. They had no idea how to keep the control they needed to survive or how to keep the money flowing as it always had.

Satisfied with his survey of the news, Theo settled into one of the cushioned chairs near his gate and removed the already well-worn note from his pocket, the hospital letterhead at the top of each notepad-sized page. He read Rachel's words again and smiled. *The Queen of Tears has said there is so much more to do, so much more to fight for. And yes, we also have a need for rest and a need to heal,* he thought as he folded the note away, carefully storing it in his pocket. His heart at ease, he slipped into a nap and rested until he was abruptly awakened by the call for his flight.

****

Nearly 12 hours later, the dusty bus was wending its way into the San Martin region in northern Peru. Traversing the Alto Maya River basin, the bus dropped off the last passengers at the end of the line in the city of Tarapoto. Among the stragglers, one particularly tired man got off at the very last bus stop. He was traveling light compared to the other gringo tourists and had only a daypack, like the ones students use to carry books. As he shambled away from the bus, the driver noticed that the man seemed unexpectedly confident as he headed off without asking for directions. The driver, a kind man, watched him, his limp now obvious as he took off away from the town's small hotel district. He watched, wonderingly, as the little man stepped off the road at the trailhead that led to the territory of the Awajún. He almost shouted in warning, but the man was already gone, moving more swiftly than expected of a cripple. Swearing softly, the driver put the bus in gear and headed home to his family and a cerveza. He prayed for the funny looking little man.

* * * * * * * *

The green fronds of familiar plant friends caressed Theo's face and arms and neck as he hiked into the forest. He passed a village and asked a young man for a drink of water only to be met with a sullen response in the Awajún language. Theo answered back in the same tongue to the man's surprise. The young man ran off telling everyone to come see the gringo who speaks the language of The People. A celebrity's welcome included, finally, the water he needed.

Theo pressed on for hours more, occasionally sipping at the plastic bottle of water he'd been given. Then through the foliage, he saw a house that he knew better than he knew his own back in America. There was a middle-aged woman bent over in her garden. Considering the season, she was near harvest time. As Theo approached, he deliberately hummed a tune from an anen he'd learned to use when trying to find one's way after getting lost. Finally, the woman looked up, surprised. She stared a moment, leaning into the direction of the stranger. She stumbled forward, choked on her words, and then ran forward, nearly knocking Theo off his feet. "My Etsa. My Etsa. You have returned." The two simply held each other for minutes as the tears flowed down their cheeks. Ankuash came just then. His father looked at him intently, holding him at arm's length until he was satisfied with what he saw. "Come, you must eat, and then we will hold ceremony for you. You have been too long without the medicine. Then you can tell us all just how well the war went for you. The spirits have already told us that you have done great things, but we want to hear from you, my son. My beloved son."

And so, Theo, or as his people know him, Etsa, made his way home, escaped to civilization, living to tell the tale of a people who'd forgotten themselves and their God, but who were beginning to find themselves again.

Maybe the world had a chance now.

Acknowledgments

Writing *Polliwog* was stepping way outside my lane as a licensed Marriage and Family Therapist. It was humbling to take an inventory of all the voices and minds who contributed to making me into someone who could write anything, much less a novel like *Polliwog*. But the initial empowerment to even consider writing like this came from the many hundreds of clients I've worked with over the years who have all struggled with the consequences of failing to manage their sexuality intelligently. Pretty much no one does this, but my clients have had the courage to talk about their failures. I owe them the deepest thanks for helping me to grow and to start seeing human sexuality for the powerful and wonderful force of nature that it is and which we are all a part of.

Thank you first to the many university teachers and mental health professionals who have helped me to learn not only the techniques of counseling and hypnosis, but also the ethics of respecting individual choice. They quietly labor, planting intellectual seeds and never knowing where and how they might spring up. To educators everywhere, my debt is beyond ever repaying. From those who taught me in elementary school to my high school anthropology teacher to my counseling program in graduate school, it seemed to me that mine was only one of many voices creating the pages and characters of *Polliwog*.

I have had many early readers who all helped with their feedback, both the enthusiastic kind and the angry "how could you do that" kind. Thank you especially Rose Todaro, Erin Amistoy-Mariano, Ursula Guerrero, Diane Holland, Deena O'Daniel, Bonnie Aquilino, Steve Cooper, Richard Tucker, Dr. Jennifer Janiga, Renee Hinojosa MSM, APRN, McKenzie Oakland, Alison Cirvelli, Brianna Profera, John Whittaker, and Sasha Mereu. All of these plus my loving and very helpful editor Mikalee Byerman.

I am profoundly grateful for the many texts and authors who have influenced me and who are (mostly) listed in the bibliography. All of them are worth taking a look at, but a few stand out. If you haven't yet read *Educated* by Tara Westover and *Pure* by Linda Kay Klein, then you owe it to yourself to take a look at these two for some insight into how religion can impact not only women but all of us. Lastly, a film, 1985's *The Emerald Forest*, inspired the idea of a boy growing up in the Amazon to return to the home of his father, and Heinlein's *Stranger in a Strange Land* contributed the idea of the boy born away returning to help a damaged world where our beliefs had poisoned so many.

I know I already said "lastly," but give a brother a break here. With the internet age, I have two really important articles for you to review. The first is a one-page bit by Rachael Rettner called, "Fate of a Fertilized Egg: Why some Embryos Don't Implant."

https://www.livescience.com/43157-embryo-implant-signals-pregnancy.html

The second is from the New York Times, and as I was conceiving Polliwog, there came this article by Carl Zimmer on metamorphosis that you are really going to love.

https://www.nytimes.com/2019/03/25/science/metamorphosis-evolution-animals.html

An important trip to Peru was inspired and facilitated by one of the best friends ever, Sensei Vince Salvatore, who just happens to run the finest Aikido dojo in the West. Haven't been to Peru? Go. Please pay your guides more than they ask.

For my own experiences in journeying into the astral plane, I have to acknowledge the most helpful of guides, Tory and Justin. You two brought a world to life for me, and that world was, unbelievably, in me.

I have nothing but love for my friend Rafael, an artist collected all over the world who not only designed the background for the cover art but who was also my companion on most of my journeys into the astral plane.

I have found few more important than some of the truly awful people who have auditioned for the role of leading villain in my life. None of you know how really destructive and abhorrent you are, and I have to believe that you've made your families truly miserable. But, truth be told, you have been both an inspiration for my figuring out a number of relationship problems, and some of you appear in a suitably fictionalized way in this book. If you do not see yourself here, it's no big deal because the rest of us can, especially those who love to control "in the name of the Lord."

Lastly, Sharon Ann Burnside (aka Sharon Ing, my wife), you have left your love and support in every page of this book. From our first conversation about abortion where you mentioned that "little polliwog" growing in a woman's womb so many years ago to all the loving hours you've humored my yammering over ideas since, well, to you I dedicate not only this book, but all my life's work. Thank you, baby.

Partial Bibliography
of Works Informing "Polliwog"

As I pondered and wrote, the following works provided inspiration and important background. Anyone who cares to make the journey with Theo might consider these authors and their works, all of them lovely in their way. Some of the books and authors who influenced me and helped create Theo were not read for this specific task but were read long ago (and many times) in my younger years and simply stayed with me. I shall not list Edgar Rice Burroughs whose "Tarzan" series helped inspire the notion of a baby, very out of place, coming of age in a jungle. This is a longish list but nevertheless is regretfully missing so many authors who influenced me along the way.

2019, "The Hebrew Bible," (see "Qohelet) translated by Robert Alter, published by W. W. Norton & Company.

1954, "The Desert Music and Other Poems," by William Carlos Williams, published by Random House.

1961, "Stranger in a Strange Land," by Robert Heinlein, published by Ace/Putnam, whose inspiration also contributed to Theo's character as a wonderful and wonderfully fish out of water character who brings healing from afar to his people and helps redefine what spirituality can do to help.

2017, "The New Testament" translated by David Bentley Hart and published by Yale University Press helped me to see the Bible in a new and fresh light.

2002, "Cutting Through Spiritual Materialism," by Chögyam Trungpa, published by Shambhala Classics was inspirational for his subversive view of true spirituality.

2017, "The Islamic Jesus," by Mustafa Akyol, published by St. Martin's

Press, reveals to us with an utterly different and truly kind prophet, simultaneously throwing the Christian Nationalist's monstrous divinity (of the last several years) into the shadow of irrelevancy.

1988, "Developing Ericksonian Therapy: State of the Art," published by Brunner/Mazel for a loving description of a man and a scientist of human nature most likely to be an alien from another world.

2014, "The Induction of Hypnosis, An Ericksonian Elicitation Approach," by Jeffrey K. Zeig, Milton Erickson Foundation Press.

1972, "A General Theory of Magic," by Marcel Mauss and translated by Robert Brain, published by Routledge.

1999, "Ayahuasca Visions," by Luis Luna and Pablo Amaringo, published by North Atlantic Books.

2017, "Cultural Discontinuity, The New Social Face of the Awajún," by Glend Seitz, published by Amakella Publishing.

1986, "Tsewa's Gift, Magic and Meaning in an Amazonian Society," by Michael F. Brown, published by the University of Alabama Press.

1987, "Swidden-Fallow Agroforestry in the Peruvian Amazon," Editors W. Denevan and Chistine Padoch, published by the New York Botanical Garden.

1972, "The Jívaro, People of the Sacred Waterfalls," by Michael J. Harner, published by Doubleday/Natural History Press for the American Museum of Natural History.

2018, "Educated," by Tara Westover, published by Random House.

2018, "Pure," by Linda Kay Klein, published by Touchstone.

Polliwog Reader's Guide

by Steven Ing

Helping reading groups is a journey fraught with artistic peril. How much to share? How much is too much? And, let's face it, since Polliwog is an obvious argument for bodily autonomy and against religious fundamentalism's penchant for controlling others, how much can we all safely talk about without getting into a culture war over religion? The following questions are offered with the intent of facilitating deeper, more personal conversation. I'll leave the staking out of political territory to you readers!

1. How comfortable are you with talking (and listening!) in groups about sexuality and politics?

2. Joining a religion is, for most of us, an elective experience. We join up to enhance the quality of our lives. Polliwog questions this assumption, but how fairly do you think it does so?

3. All religions seem to have a lot to say about sex, including Rachel's. Do you find any religious thinking about sex helpful? If so, can you share this?

4. How do you think the world, especially the world of politics and religion, would change if women had control over their bodies as described in Polliwog? How would it be better? Could it possibly be worse than our current situation? Could we, should we trust women, after all?

5. Considering a world where women could decide whether or not they bore children, who would stand to lose the most in terms of power? Who would gain?

6. Trance work (hypnosis) can facilitate control over variables like pulse, blood pressure, temperature, and pain management.

What do you think of the science behind Polliwog? Are you personally ready for this kind of control over your body?

7. Polliwog is part science fiction, part magical realism, and part crime thriller. How did you feel about the mash-up of genres? How did it work (or fail to work) for you? How would you describe it to others?

8. If the author could teach your daughters how to control the level of trypsin in their wombs, would you want them to know how and why? If not, why not? Do you wish someone would teach you how to do this sort of self-hypnosis trance work?

9. Throughout Polliwog, character names carry powerful meaning. Choose a few names from the many characters, and describe how those names convey meaning beyond that which is communicated on the page.

10. In your opinion, what is the central conflict presented in this novel? Is this conflict interpersonal, intrapersonal, political, societal, or a combination of all of these?

11. Appropriately, Polliwog uses abundant symbolism in the form of animals. Discuss a few of the pervasive animal symbols, and describe how those symbols add extra layers of meaning and understanding.

12. The author calls the italicized portions between chapters "intermezzos," a term that translates to "a light dramatic, musical, or other performance inserted between the acts of a play." What is the purpose of the intermezzos in Polliwog? What do you notice about them as the characters in the intermezzos and those in the book begin to meld more concretely?

13. In your opinion, what happens after the events in Polliwog for Etsa? For Rachel? For society at large? Consider both political and social ramifications.

14. Theo is on a quest to get revenge for the people and he ends up giving a gift to all humanity. How does the Queen of Tears factor into that?

14. Theo's journey to America is initially motivated by wanting revenge for The People. He ends up giving a gift to all of humanity. How does the Queen of Tears and her being a vessel of compassion factor into the outcome?

About the Author

Steven Ing is a licensed Marriage & Family Therapist whose unusual practice consists primarily of forensic work with those convicted of crimes involving sex and violence. He has written several editions of a humane treatment manual for his forensic clients, a textbook used at the college level on the topic of sexual needs, and numerous articles on human sexuality. In his idle hours, he dreams of playing the viola and of writing an updated theory of human psychosexual development that is only 125 years overdue. The 2022 murder attempt on his life has accelerated the pace of his work. He and his family live on the outskirts of Reno, Nevada, just under the highlands of the Toiyabe National Forest. This is his first novel.

STEVEN ING

"The integration of our sexuality with human spirituality remains our greatest obstacle."

– Steven Ing

CPSIA information can be obtained
at www.ICGtesting.com
Printed in the USA
JSHW010807180723
44874JS00002B/128